"Since we're *not* friends, may I ask you a rather rude question?"

Beatrice blinked. "Excuse me?"

Charles's green eyes sparkled devilishly. "Why aren't you married?"

"A great many people aren't married," she retorted defensively. "I could be asking you the same question."

"Yes, but I don't want to be married. The fact that you're in London for the season implies that you don't share my sentiments. What's stopping you? You're intelligent and amusing, not to mention," he added quietly, his eyes darkening, "the most beautiful woman in town. Are you sure you're really looking for a husband?"

Beatrice colored again. "Are you proposing?" She knew that she shouldn't have asked him this question—there was no telling what sort of outrageous answer he'd give— yet the question had slipped out all the same.

Charles leaned in closer yet again, this time to whisper in her ear. "Not *marriage*."

* * *

Reforming the Rake
Harlequin Historical #774—October 2005

Reforming the Rake

Sarah Elliott

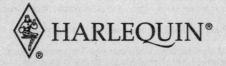

TORONTO • NEW YORK • LONDON
AMSTERDAM • PARIS • SYDNEY • HAMBURG
STOCKHOLM • ATHENS • TOKYO • MILAN • MADRID
PRAGUE • WARSAW • BUDAPEST • AUCKLAND

ISBN 0-373-29374-7

REFORMING THE RAKE

Copyright © 2005 by Sarah Lindsey

This edition published by arrangement with Harlequin Books S.A.

® and TM are trademarks of the publisher. Trademarks indicated with
® are registered in the United States Patent and Trademark Office, the
Canadian Trade Marks Office and in other countries.

www.eHarlequin.com

Printed in U.S.A.

Available from Harlequin Historical and
SARAH ELLIOTT

Reforming the Rake #774

This book is dedicated to Laura Langlie
for her patience and tenacity
and to Elizabeth Sudol
for giving much-needed encouragement.

Chapter One

May 12, 1816

Charles Summerson, ninth marquess of Pelham, hadn't *meant* to spy. No, he actually felt rather embarrassed for not closing his window right away—after all, he'd merely stuck his head out to check the temperature, and, having decided that he would not require a heavy coat for his ride in the park, had no reason to linger.

Nonetheless, he lingered.

It wasn't even Charles's *own* window, for that matter; that is, it was his *former* window. He was temporarily staying in his boyhood room at his mother's Park Lane home while his own town house underwent repairs. Still, he had grown up in that very room, and in all those years he had never appreciated how prime a vantage point his window was for observing the goings-on in his neighbor's garden. Not that he'd ever been particularly interested in her goings-on before, and frankly, he wasn't interested in them now. Lady Louisa Sinclair had lived next door to the Summersons for as long as Charles could remember. She was one of those society matrons who was perpetually just shy of sixty years old…preserved, he assumed, by the vinegar that ran through her veins.

Today, however, was different, for today Lady Sinclair was not in her garden. Quite the contrary. Instead, there appeared to be an entirely different variety of female in his neighbor's garden: definitely younger, and far gentler on the eyes.

Charles quietly observed the unfamiliar girl for several minutes without moving. He hadn't the faintest idea who she was, and from his position he could make out few details. She was sprawled out in the middle of Lady Sinclair's pristine lawn, facing away from him. and propped up by her elbows in order to jot something hurriedly into a small book. Charles wished he could see her face. All he could really see was the back of her blond head, bent so avidly over her writing.

He let his gaze travel down her body, or what he could see of it, anyway. She wore a pale yellow dress, the same color as Lady Sinclair's daffodils, and Charles noted that it was appropriately, albeit disappointingly, modest. He had to rely on his imagination to fill in the details that the dress concealed: a tall, slim frame, gently rounded hips, small waist…ample breasts. He silently willed her to roll over and satisfy his curiosity.

Her legs lay flat behind her, and Charles let his gaze roam down even farther. He noticed that her slippers had abandoned her feet and now lay haphazardly on the ground at her side. He could see nothing of her calves—as was proper—but he could see her feet quite clearly. Periodically, she wiggled her toes in the grass.

He knew he really ought to turn away, and surely would have if it weren't for those damned feet. But seeing a woman's stockinged feet only made him all the more curious to see the rest of her, and as she was so focused on…well, whatever it was she was doing, there was really no chance of being discovered, was there?

After a minute, the girl paused in writing to leaf through the pages of her book. Charles would have given just about anything at that moment to read along with her—rather salaciously, he hoped that it was her diary, where she recorded her deepest secrets, hidden desires….

He forgot about the contents of her book entirely, however, when—seeming to forget for the moment that she was a young lady—the girl bent her leg back, letting it sway carelessly back and forth; her skirts slipped down to pool around her knee, and he was treated to a clear view of her trim ankle and shapely calf.

He raised an eyebrow in appreciation. Charles supposed he ought to feel rather depraved for observing her unawares, but niggling morals aside, he just couldn't avert his eyes. He even contemplated heading down the hall to knock on his sister's bedroom door to ask if he could borrow her opera glasses.

However, his nefarious thoughts were interrupted before he could make that decision. The sound of a shrill voice rang out from next door—probably that termagant Louisa Sinclair. "Bea! Come inside now! We have to get ready."

"Coming…." The girl responded slowly, without closing her book or making any sign to rise.

After a minute, the voice came again, more insistent this time. "Bea! We'll be late as it is."

With great reluctance, the girl closed her book, but she didn't get up right away. First, she rolled onto her back, stretching like a cat and crossing her arms behind her head. She looked up at the sky, a faraway expression on her face and the faint trace of a smile about her lips.

Charles *really* should have looked away then. She could have turned her gaze up toward his window at any moment, and he'd feel like ten times a randy schoolboy, which wouldn't do at all. But the problems that discovery posed were the furthest thing from his mind. For a moment, in fact, he forgot to breathe.

God, she was beautiful. He'd been admiring her body before, but her face… Perfect, tiny nose and generous lips… Charles swallowed hard. With her lying on her back as she now was, his prior imaginings were confirmed. She was indeed slim, but definitely curved in all the right places. He still couldn't see all that he would like—the color of her eyes, the slant of her brows—but the general picture of beauty was undeniable.

Charles wondered at her age. She was definitely young, he decided, but not too young…twenty, perhaps? Twenty-one? He tended to avoid innocents, for the simple fact that they were usually looking for husbands, and he definitely did *not* fit that category.

Holding her book close to her chest, the girl rose and began walking toward the door. She paused, however, just before entering, tilting her radiant face up to the sky to enjoy her last few seconds of sun. Then, with a look of disappointment, she headed indoors and broke the spell.

Charles waited to see if she'd reemerge from the house. After several minutes had passed with nary a sign of her, a more profitable course of action came to his mind.

Charles rose from his position at the window and left his room, heading down the long hall to knock on his sister's door. He ignored the portrait of his great-great-grandfather, who glared at him disapprovingly from beneath his abundant eyebrows.

"Lucy? You in there?" he called through the panel. At eighteen, Lucy was having her first season. Despite the twelve years age difference, they had always been very close, although Charles was still trying to get used to the fact that she was no longer a child.

Lucy opened her door and grinned at him. She was a pretty, petite girl and shared her brother's raven-black hair and green eyes. Indeed, except for the fact that Charles stood well over six feet tall, the resemblance between them was uncanny. "Did you miss me, Charles?" she asked cheekily.

He snorted. "Don't flatter yourself, Lu. Came to see what you were doing tonight."

She arched a single brow. "Could it be that you're interested in accompanying me? That would be a first."

"I went along for your debut two weeks ago," he protested.

"That doesn't count, and you know it. You *had* to come. Besides, you told me that would be the first and last time."

He had said that—he could remember his words distinctly. "Perhaps I've changed my mind. What are the entertainments for the evening?"

"Just one that I know of—the annual Teasdale ball. That's where I'm going."

Charles nodded, as if debating whether to attend, but he'd already made up his mind. There was little he'd rather do less than attend Lady Teasdale's blasted ball, but he wanted to know more about the girl in the yellow dress. Lady Sinclair had ushered her inside to get ready for something, probably this particular function. "Perhaps I'll come along."

"But you can't stand Lady Teasdale!" Lucy exclaimed.

Charles realized this conversation wouldn't be as brief as he'd hoped. He entered Lucy's room and sank into her large armchair, trying to come up with a plausible excuse. "I realize that I've been lax in my duties, Lu. I shouldn't leave you to face the vultures alone."

"Charles, Mother always comes with me. It's not as if I'm without a chaperone."

"Ah, but you forget, Lucy, that Mother doesn't know the men out there as I do. I should hate to see you wasting your time with the wrong sort."

She gaped in disbelief. "How can *you* be so suspicious? You're the worst of the lot, Charles. And did it ever occur to you that maybe I don't *want* your blasted company?"

He pretended to look shocked. "Can these be the words of my own dear sister?"

Lucy wasn't about to give up. She loved her brother dearly, but he could be a tad overprotective at times. She tried to put him off one last time. "Well, whether I want you there doesn't matter. Besides, you'll make Mother very happy. Just this morning she was telling me that it was high time you wed." She batted her eyelashes innocently.

"Mother says as much every day."

"Well, Charles…" Lucy was really warming up to the subject now. "I haven't told you this before, but Mother has *really* been thinking about finding you a match recently. Seems she's getting worried that you'll never wed."

"This is new?" he asked with a yawn.

She ignored his rudeness. "Well, no, not that in particular. But she has taken up an alarming new practice of carrying a notebook containing the names and parentage of every eligible girl she meets. Truly, Charles, she is never without it."

He just stared for a moment, his mouth slightly agape. "She's taking notes? What does this notebook look like, Lucy?"

She debated whether to tell him or not—what if he went looking for the book and stole it? Her mother would never forgive her, not to mention that Lucy would no longer be able to hold it over his head. But she knew he'd get the information out of her sooner or later. She tried to describe the book as vaguely as possible. "Well, I can't say that I've seen the outside of the notebook too often…it's always open when I see her with it. But I do believe it's leather. Oh, and small, so she can fit it in her pocket."

Charles had spent several years after university working for the War Office and easily recognized evasion. But his sister was as formidable as any French spy he had ever encountered, and he decided to drop the questioning for the moment. He'd find and destroy the book later.

"You're very helpful, Lu. I can't thank you enough…and I *shall* see you later this evening." And with a roguish grin, he rose from the chair and headed back to his room, deciding that his ride in the park could wait.

Chapter Two

Beatrice Sinclair sat very still, holding a slender pen poised over a blank page in her well-worn journal. She wrote three words, but crossed them out almost immediately. She waited for more words, better words, to spill forth. They didn't.

Frowning, she laid her notebook on her lap, realizing she was too distracted to give her writing the thought that it deserved. How could she concentrate on fiction when reality—her personal reality—was in such a shambles?

She looked around her bedroom for literary inspiration. The walls of her great-aunt Louisa's house were papered, variously, with pastoral scenes or with complicated floral motifs. Beatrice's bedroom was a pastoral room. Shepherds and milkmaids cavorted about the walls, and had the added bonus of having trompe l'oeil clouds painted on the ceiling. Personally, she would have preferred to be outside, but Louisa had just called her back indoors; she disapproved of young ladies getting too much sun. A single freckle could spoil a girl's chances completely, or so she claimed.

Beatrice turned her attention back to her journal and sighed. She'd kept it since her first season, five years earlier. Initially, it had been a diary in the true sense of the word, a place where she'd related each day's events—Beatrice had quickly realized that if she didn't occupy her mind in *some* useful fashion, she'd risk becoming as empty-headed as the rest of the ton. However, as the season drew to a close and she read over her diary, she'd realized bleakly how dull her life had become: party after dinner after ball, all with the sole purpose of snagging some unsuspecting male. It wouldn't have been so bad if she'd been even slightly interested in any of the gentlemen she met at these endless social events, but she had a difficult time dredging up the faintest enthusiasm for most of them.

By the end of that first season, Beatrice had resigned herself to one thing: in looking for a husband, reality and fantasy would never agree, and the less imagination one had, the better. Where were broad shoulders in the real world? Razor-sharp wit? Tall, dark and handsome? Clearly, these things didn't exist, and if one could accept that, one would never be disappointed by reality.

Unfortunately, this revelation came too late. By the end of her first season she'd earned the moniker "Cold Fish Beatrice" for her repeated refusals. By her second and third seasons, the many proposals she'd once received had all but dried up.

So she'd spent two years at home in the country and now—older, wiser and much reformed—she was ready to embark on yet another season. This time, though, she had a plan. Wisdom helped her realize that she needed an outlet for her imagination, so, at the sage age of twenty-three, Beatrice had stopped keeping a diary and had turned to fiction. This way, she hoped, she could invent whatever romantic hero she pleased, and resign herself to the stooped shoulders of reality.

So far, her plan wasn't working out as she had expected, but the season was only a few weeks old.

"Beatrice, this is not acceptable."

Louisa was glaring at her with extreme annoyance. Even when pleased, her great-aunt was a sight to behold, with her steel-gray hair, her steel-gray eyes, her long nose and her tall, thin body. When Louisa was irritated, however, *intimidating* took on a whole new meaning. She could incite fear in the stoutest of hearts with a simple curl of her lip, and all that saved Beatrice from quaking in her seat now was the knowledge that, deep down—very deep, perhaps—her aunt was generous, caring and devoted to her family.

Beatrice was afraid she knew what "this" meant, although she asked all the same, biding for time. "I'm sorry, Louisa—*what* precisely is not acceptable?"

Louisa snorted indelicately. "Your sister informs me that you don't plan to attend Lady Teasdale's ball this evening. Why did you not discuss this with me?"

Beatrice began guiltily, "Well…Eleanor mentioned something about there being a new production of *King Lear* at Drury Lane, *and* that she had no one to attend with her—"

"Beatrice, you already promised that you'd go to Lady Teasdale's. Besides, Eleanor is only sixteen! She hardly needs to be going to the theater. I should never have told your father that she could come visit you, even if it was for only a few weeks. *King Lear.* Humph," Louisa sniffed. "There's a man with three daughters for you…and look what happened to him. It'll only give Eleanor ideas. I'm just glad Helen isn't here to see it."

"I think you're being a little dramatic, Auntie. You couldn't find three daughters more devoted to their father than Eleanor, Helen and me, and I can assure you that Eleanor's motives are innocent. She just loves the theater."

Louisa rolled her eyes. "Back to the subject at hand, Beatrice. Truth is, Eleanor knows that you don't want to go to the Teasdales', and as she's too young to go herself, she figures there's no harm in you missing the ball."

"Is there?" Beatrice asked hopefully.

Louisa assumed mock disbelief. "Have you gone off and gotten married without telling me, Beatrice Sinclair? Of course there's harm in missing the ball—you're a desperate case."

Beatrice was used to these comments and knew that Louisa didn't really mean them…not entirely, anyway. She put on her most innocent face, which was sure to irritate her aunt. "I can't believe you would accuse me of avoiding Lady Teasdale's."

Louisa snorted again. "Do I look like a fool? You've been telling me that you didn't want to go since arriving here last month. Yes, Lady Teasdale is tiresome, but her balls are always well attended, especially by eligible young men." She sighed. "You're not even giving it a chance, Bea. The season has been in full swing for two weeks, and I made your father a promise."

"I know, Louisa…. I only thought that, as I have already been to Lady Teasdale's annual ball three times in the past—without, I should remind you, much success—"

"Who needs reminding? Clearly, you are not married."

Beatrice counted to five, praying she wouldn't lose her temper. "Clearly."

"And how old are you?"

She almost didn't answer. Louisa managed to mention her age at least twice a day, and Beatrice had little doubt that she knew precisely how old she was. "I am twenty-three, Louisa, a fact we have already established. I will inform you when this state of affairs changes."

Louisa clucked. "Impertinent chit. That's what you get for being long in the tooth."

"What?"

"With age comes a sharp tongue."

That's what I get from spending the past month with you, Beatrice thought, but said nothing.

"At any rate," Louisa continued brusquely, "I have discussed matters with your sister. She is determined to go to the theater, and I have decided to allow it—*if,* mind you, you can get your brother to join you." Beatrice groaned, and Louisa cackled with glee. "Yes, dear, I know *that* won't be easy. Ben'll be as excited about chaperoning his younger sisters to the theater as I am

about the two of you going. I don't think it's right for two unmarried girls to be traipsing off to the theater together. I don't
know what the world is coming to."

Beatrice sank back onto the settee. Louisa was right. Ben
would have no desire to escort them to the theater, and he probably already had other plans. Still, if she started begging now,
by curtain call he'd be so annoyed he'd take them just to make
her be quiet. Beatrice wanted to crow with joy, but wisely
schooled her features. "Thank you, Louisa. I know how much
this means to Eleanor. I'd hate to disappoint her."

Louisa smiled smugly. "Yes, well, I checked, and the play be-
gins at seven. You should still be able to make it to Lady Teasdale's at a decent hour once it's over. And see if you can't get
your brother to come with you."

And with that, Beatrice's hopes sank into the carpet, and
Louisa sailed from the room with all the dignity of the royal
barge. Beatrice collapsed even deeper into the settee, and closed
her eyes. It didn't help; she could still see the triumphant smirk
on her aunt's face. She opened her eyes and looked at the frol-
icking milkmaids on the walls. Even they looked smug.

Oh, she was dreading the evening to come. It was true—
Beatrice had been to Lady Teasdale's wretched affair three times
already. It was considered de rigueur for unmarried young ladies
to attend this annual event, and avoiding the thing in the future
was one of her few incentives for marrying. Lady Teasdale had
five daughters to still marry off and was a cutthroat competitor
who made a point of being rude to any ladies of marriageable
age *not* related to her by blood. Lady Teasdale's eldest daughter, Sarah, had come out the same year as Beatrice. Lady Teasdale liked to remind Beatrice of the fact that Sarah had been
married by the sixth week of the season—and to a viscount, no
less. In truth, Beatrice felt sorry for the girl—she couldn't imagine anything worse than being auctioned off to the highest bid-
der at the age of seventeen. But that didn't change the fact that

Lady Teasdale considered it her job to rub that detail in everyone else's face.

Of course, Beatrice had to admit that three seasons without managing to find a husband was rather pathetic. And if one counted her two years of restorative hibernation at her family's home in Hampshire, well…that did make five years of indisputable failure.

Not that she considered it to be her sole purpose in life to get married. She had no problem with remaining single…as long as she wasn't *trying* to wed; it was at that point that spinsterhood became failure. The secret to success, she'd decided, was to pursue spinsterhood the way most women pursued marriage. In fact, she'd become quite comfortable with the idea of remaining a perennial spinster, and hadn't even planned on going to London for the season at all. No, that was her father's idea.

"You know I love you, Bea," he'd said, trying to be delicate, "but for heaven's sake, do you think someday you'll get married?"

Beatrice had only grinned, not realizing that *this time he meant it.* "But however would you survive without me?"

He had sighed resignedly. "I should miss you, Bea, but as for surviving…don't take this the wrong way, but I dream of the day when all of my children find families and houses of their own, and I, God willing, can enjoy peace and quiet once more."

Beatrice had begun to get a bit nervous, but attempted to cajole him out of this new mind-set. "You'd take that back, Father dearest, after a week. Who would help you organize your library? Who would help you with your correspondence?"

"Who has ever helped me with these things?" he'd asked in confusion.

Beatrice had ignored that remark. "And what about entertainment? How about my harpsichord playing?"

"That, my dear, I would miss least of all. In fact, I hope you take the instrument with you. No—" he'd held up his hand as

Beatrice started to protest "—both you and your brother are of marriageable age. Eventually, I would like some grandchildren."

"But you just said you wanted peace and quiet."

"Beatrice," he'd warned.

She'd sighed. "All right. I understand…but yet, Father, I don't understand *exactly.* What are you proposing? It's not as if I've been avoiding marriage."

"It's not as if you've been actively seeking it, either. You've had two years respite, Beatrice. If your mother were alive I hardly think she would have allowed it. I've been too indulgent, and it's time you returned to London to give it another go. I've discussed this with Louisa, and she agrees. She's even offered to sponsor you for the season. You can stay with her in town."

Beatrice had already started to panic. "Aunt Louisa? Oh, no. Why can't I stay at our town house?"

"Because I won't be accompanying you, and your brother is there, indulging in God knows what sort of debauchery."

"I'll be a good influence on him."

He'd smiled. "More likely he'll be a bad influence on you. Louisa will keep you company—and make sure you at least try. I know you too well, Beazie. Left alone you'd just sit about and read novels. And don't," he'd added, looking at her firmly, "turn those sad eyes on me. I won't go with you. I went to town during your first three seasons, and I've already promised Eleanor that I'll be in town when she has her coming out in two years. And then Helen in just a few more years—"

The clock struck four, drawing Beatrice from her reverie. She'd been in London for nearly a month, and that had been a month of hard campaigning, at least on her aunt's part. No, her unmarried status was not from lack of trying, nor was it from lack of interest—her reputation as "Cold Fish Beatrice" seemed to have faded, and she'd gained a few brave suitors. Try as she might, she was plagued with the same problem of old. Beatrice knew that it was silly and unreasonable, but she kind of, just a little bit, *did* believe in love at first sight. There was someone out there for her. She just hadn't met him yet.

But there was no sense in dwelling on it now. She had to start getting ready for the theater. Her father was right: she did read too many novels, and she'd be better off if she pushed all romantic thoughts from her mind.

Chapter Three

Charles sorely regretted his decision to attend the ball. In general, he steered clear of that sort of thing, particularly if it were captained by Honoria Teasdale. He had been reminded of why he hated these events from the moment he'd walked through the door, when he'd felt precisely as if he'd been thrown to the sharks. Every woman in the room, be they mother or daughter, young or old, fat or thin, immediately began sizing him up, wondering if perhaps this was the year he'd be caught. Having no interest in marriage himself, he wouldn't have attended the ball at all if it weren't for that elusive girl in the yellow dress. And she, ironically, hadn't appeared. Charles was beginning to think he'd imagined her.

"Charles, dear, you look a little bit forbidding," his mother, Emma Summerson, chided as she approached. She was fair where Charles was dark, and petite where he was tall and athletic. When they smiled, however, their equally lopsided and charming grins immediately pegged them as being closely related.

Charles wasn't smiling now. He practically scowled at the glass of lemonade she handed him.

"Take that frown off your face, Charles, or all of these young ladies will be frightened."

"That is my fondest wish, Mother," he replied. He'd long ago learned that his dangerous dark looks were what drew women toward him. Nonetheless, he was being sincere. Most of his friends didn't relish the idea of marriage, but most of them also accepted that fate as inevitable, at least if they had a title to pass on. Charles, on the other hand, had vowed never to marry, his title be damned. Marriage, especially if it involved love, was far too dangerous. Charles had already lost two people he'd loved very much and refused to put himself at risk again.

His mother sighed resignedly. "Oh, I do wish you'd behave. Why'd you come tonight, anyway? You don't enjoy this sort of affair. You're not really worried about Lucy, are you?"

"I'm not worried so much, Mother…. I just think it's a good idea to make my presence known—sporadically, mind you—to keep these young bucks on their toes."

She sniffed. "Sporadically. I see. Very well thought out of you—after all, you do have a reputation to maintain. Wouldn't do for you to appear in polite society *too* frequently, would it?"

"You know, Mother, I rather thought that with Lucy out now you'd concentrate on her love life, rather than dwelling on mine."

"Although—" she said with a smile "—you could use the help."

"But," Charles countered, "I don't need you keeping a notebook with the fortune, ancestry and physical features of every unmarried girl you meet, in that order."

"Lucy told you?"

"'Course she did. She's quite fond of me, you know. Tells me everything."

His mother looked highly doubtful. "Well, she got it a bit wrong. My criteria are actually in the opposite order, dear. And I'm certain character and intelligence are in there somewhere, as well, although you sometimes seem to view those things as liabilities in a woman."

Charles began to grow alarmed. "What are you talking about, Mother?"

She put her hand to her chin in thought. "Yes…the order is character, intelligence, attractiveness, family, then fortune. We have enough money to put fortune last."

Charles raked an agitated hand through his hair, feeling for once that his own mother was one of the sharks he had to look out for. It was definitely time for him to leave. "This can't be happening, Mother. I have to go. I will walk home—it's just a few blocks."

She smiled smoothly, feigning surprise. "So soon? But I see Lady Abermarle heading your way—I imagine her daughter is behind her somewhere, not that you can see anything around that majestic form."

He shivered. "Then I will run home."

"One word of advice, Charles, before you go."

"Yes, Mother?" he said, glancing nervously over his shoulder as the large Abermarle shadow began to loom closer. Now it was *imperative* that he leave.

She leaned forward to whisper in his ear. "Always judge a girl by her mother, because in ten years, she *will be* her mother."

Charles nodded curtly and walked briskly to the door, hoping to God that none of Lucy's suitors ever met their mother.

His mother watched him fondly as he beat his retreat. Lucy walked up behind her grinning.

"I see you got rid of him, Mother," she remarked with definite satisfaction.

"Easily. You should never doubt me," her mother replied. She began to chuckle. "You should have seen the look on his face, dear, when I informed him about The Book…. He was looking at me as if I'd gone quite mad."

"As if?"

She ignored her daughter's sarcasm. "If Charles is going to be so ornery about finding a match for himself, I hardly see why he should come here and ruin your chances by glowering at all your beaus." She turned toward her youngest child. She'd been blessed with three children, but only Charles and Lucy had survived. Mark, Charles's junior by two years, had died in a carriage accident when he was thirteen. The memory still hurt, and she cherished her remaining children. They both made her so proud. They infuriated her, too, but for the most part her heart swelled with joy whenever she looked at them.

Her eyes began to mist up.

"Are you all right, Mother?" Lucy asked, resting her hand on her arm in concern.

"I'm fine, Lucy. I was just thinking about how much you and Charles resemble your father…Charles especially, the devil. Your father was quite the handful before we wed."

Lucy raised her eyebrows. "He couldn't have been as wicked as Charles. I can't see you putting up with that."

Her mother smiled and slipped her arm around her. "I never had to put up with it. From the moment we met he became a paragon—with, of course, the occasional reminder." She turned to look at her daughter. "I hope your marriage, when it comes, is every bit as special. Charles's, too."

"I shouldn't get my hopes up too much about Charles," Lucy warned. "He's in no hurry to marry at all. I suppose he will eventually, of course—he has the title to think about. But I wouldn't expect a love match."

Her mother merely shrugged. "He might surprise us yet. At any rate, he's gone now, and you can enjoy yourself. Lord Dudley is by the French doors, and I sense from his penetrating gaze that he's desperate to attract your attention."

Lucy rolled her eyes. "I noticed him, too, although I was trying to pretend I hadn't. I suppose I should go dance with him or else seem terribly rude."

"Yes, dear, I think you'd better."

As Lucy headed off toward Lord Dudley, her mother smiled benignly, pleased that she'd been able to send off her other child so easily. Children could be such nuisances sometimes, and she needed time alone to think…or rather, to scheme.

Wearing the same harmless smile, she let her gaze wander around the room. There had to be a better reason for Charles to attend the ball that evening than concern for Lucy. She was sure of it. It was only a matter of finding out *who* that better reason was and whether or not she was eligible.

It was nearly ten by the time Beatrice, Eleanor and Ben returned from the theater, and with every minute, Beatrice grew more alarmed. Louisa would be a veritable volcano by the time she reached the ball.

As their carriage rolled to a stop in front of their aunt's town house, Eleanor stretched, a contented smile on her face. All of the Sinclair children resembled each other very closely, save Eleanor. Whereas the rest of the clan tended to be tall and blond, Eleanor was petite, brunette and blue-eyed. "Time for bed," she said over a yawn, opening the door and sliding from the carriage. She looked back at Beatrice. "I *suppose* you could thank Louisa for letting me come out tonight when you see her. If you must."

Beatrice just smiled. "'Night, Ellie." But as Eleanor headed into the house, Beatrice nudged her brother. "Ben?"

"Hmm?" he mumbled, half-asleep.

"Do you think Louisa will be terribly peeved because we're late? It'll be eleven by the time we arrive."

He grunted. "Tell Louisa to go to the devil. I'm not going."

"Ben! I can't tell her that!"

"You can. What's the worst she can do?"

"Kill the messenger."

He turned to his sister, his head lolled back against the seat, grinning unrepentantly. "It's a bloody boring affair, Beatrice, and I've already done you one favor for the evening. No one should be forced to be in the same room as that Teasdale gorgon. You wouldn't go yourself, if you weren't scared of Louisa." He winked at her.

"I am not scared of her, Ben! You don't have to stay with her all season—imagine sharing a house with that woman when she's angry. Besides…" Beatrice paused for a moment, grasping for words. "It's just that, well…I really *should* go. I have a certain responsibility."

He shook his head in disgust. "I'm glad I'm not a girl."

"Why's that?" Beatrice snorted. "There's actually more pressure on you, you know—you're the one who has to produce an heir."

Ben shuddered in distaste. "Let's not discuss this subject now. I have plans for later and have to get going. Mind if John brings me home in the carriage? It'll be back by the time you're ready to go."

Beatrice shrugged. "Have a pleasant evening, Ben." I *won't,* she miserably added to herself as she climbed from the carriage.

Her feet trailed reluctantly for the first few steps, but the prospect of Louisa's temper prodded her into action. By the time she reached the front door, she had broken into a full-fledged run. Humphries, Louisa's butler, held the door open, waiting for her with a smile.

"Good evening, Miss Sinclair."

"Good evening, Humphries!" she called back, racing past him and flying up the stairs. He didn't blink an eye. He was used to her last-minute mad dashes.

Once in her room, Beatrice rang for her lady's maid, Meg, but wasted no time in removing her clothes on her own, a feat much easier said than done. By the time Meg arrived, Beatrice's gown was halfway over her head and she was stuck inside of it; she couldn't undo the buttons on her own and had decided to see if she could simply wiggle it off over her head.

She could not.

"Do you need help, Miss Beatrice?" Meg asked from the doorway.

"Obviously I need help. Pull!" Beatrice ordered in a muffled voice, one arm pinned behind her back, one held uncomfortably above her head.

Meg took a second to assess the situation. Beatrice was writhing about like a caught fish. "Stand still for a moment, dear. Let's try this in the conventional fashion." And with that, Meg yanked the gown back down, smiled at Beatrice's flushed face and proceeded to unbutton.

"Meg, you've saved my life. I don't know what I would do without you. Louisa will have been expecting me for nearly an hour already, and you know how annoyed she gets whenever she is…"

"Annoyed?" Meg murmured helpfully. Few people would dare to mock Louisa, but Meg had been in the family long enough to dare most things. She'd begun as Beatrice's governess, but had become her lady's maid and companion once Beatrice had outgrown the schoolroom.

Beatrice just grinned. "That's it exactly, Meg, although I suppose I can't blame her this time. If I'd known I would still have to go to the Teasdales', I would never have promised Eleanor that I'd go to the theater. I'll look perfectly exhausted by the time I reach the ball. Is that my new gown on the bed? I do hope it came out all right. Perhaps I'll wear it tonight."

Meg smiled. Beatrice had not yet seen the completed ball gown, as it had been a rush order from her modiste. "It came out beautifully, Miss Beatrice. The fabric matches your eyes perfectly."

"You mean brown?" Beatrice asked doubtfully.

"Not just brown, goose," Meg replied, lifting the gown from the bed with a flourish.

Beatrice's mouth dropped open in surprise. The gown wasn't brown at all. It was closer to gold, or even amber. The neck was square-cut, and the high Empire waist would accentuate her tall, slender form.

She turned to her maid. "Meg, it's the most beautiful dress I've ever owned—do you think it's all right for me to wear such a dark shade, though?"

Meg snorted. "It doesn't matter at this point. You wore enough pastels your first three seasons, and besides, light colors wash you out."

Beatrice looked slightly crestfallen. "Do you suppose that's why I never managed to get married? Was I not looking my best?"

"You're being too hard on yourself, Miss Beatrice," Meg replied. Beatrice was beyond beautiful, but had never managed to realize that fact. "If I recall, it wasn't that no one asked you to marry them, but rather that you refused all who asked."

"Only in my first season, Meg. I really *did* want to get married after that."

"Of course you did," she replied, not believing a word of it. She pulled the gown over Beatrice's head and began buttoning it up the back. "But I can't remember you ever mentioning being in love."

"Well…" Beatrice began guiltily, "I tried to be."

Meg clucked. "You did the right thing, dear. You shouldn't marry just because it's what you're supposed to do. More girls should follow your example."

"Meg," Beatrice countered, "that would mean the end of the human race."

"Pessimist."

"How do I look?"

Meg frankly assessed her for a moment. "Stunning—just a slight adjustment to the hair…there. You look beautiful. Here are your gloves."

"Meg, you are a queen."

"And you, Miss Beatrice, are late as usual. Stop chatting and move."

Beatrice ran out the door with a wave. She barely missed crashing into Humphries as she dashed down the steps to the door, causing him to spin around in surprise.

"So sorry, Humphries…I'm in a dreadful rush."

"Think nothing of it, Miss Sinclair. Your aunt is not one to be kept waiting. Please, continue rushing. John will be along shortly with the carriage."

Beatrice peeked out the doorway. "I think I see him coming now. Thank you, Humphries. I'll just step outside. Good night." She didn't even wait for him to close the door for her, but hurried out into the night, slamming it in her wake as the clock began to strike eleven.

Beatrice dashed down the front steps, trying to pull on her gloves as she went. John was just one house away, and he was already beginning to slow the carriage. Unfortunately, Beatrice was paying more attention to reaching the street quickly than descending the stairs carefully. At the final step she tripped. Her gloves went flying and Beatrice herself hurtled straight at an innocent passerby.

Chapter Four

Charles had walked briskly home from the ball, debating how to spend the rest of his evening. Typically, he would have met with friends at his club, perhaps later wandering out to a party—although not the sort hosted by the likes of Lady Teasdale. Tonight, however, he hadn't quite known what to do with himself. He'd felt too restless simply to end the night at his mother's house, but at the same time the thought of spending yet another evening at White's hadn't satisfied him, either.

Charles had still been pondering his plans for the evening as he approached his home, head down and hands buried in his pockets. That's why he hadn't seen her coming.

The girl in the yellow dress—which, by the way, was no longer yellow—had come tearing down his neighbor's front steps, and with no ceremony other than a startled squeal, had crashed into him full on, sending both of them flying to the pavement.

For a moment Charles just lay there, stunned. He didn't move. He was flat on his back and the girl was stretched across him, equally still. The wind had been knocked out of him, but that wasn't why he stayed motionless. No, for just a moment, he appreciated the novelty of the situation and pondered whether his luck had suddenly changed for the better.

The girl began to sit up. "Oh, I am so sorry," she murmured. "This is entirely my fault. I am terribly clumsy, you see, and if only I weren't so late…. Here, let me help you up."

She was quite a bit smaller than Charles, and he wasn't sure how she proposed to help him. When she tried to rise, she sent her elbow into his chest. Despite himself, he grunted in pain.

She held herself very still once more. "Oh, I *am* sorry."

He placed his hands on her arms. "You've already said so. Let's see if we can't rectify this situation." With that, he gently rolled her to one side and sat up. He held out a hand and helped her into a sitting position, as well.

For a moment, she stared at him in surprise.

Charles gazed back, and in the silence that ensued, he looked his fill. Up close, he could see the fine details that had been denied him earlier that afternoon: the pale golden streaks in her blond hair, the veins of amber in her velvety brown eyes and the faint hint of freckles running across the bridge of her nose. Other than those freckles, her skin was fair and smooth as cream, and where that skin faded into the rich gold fabric of her gown, just above her breasts… Charles's mouth went dry.

Young debutantes almost always wore white, and he found himself unconsciously calculating her age and situation once more. She still looked hardly much older than twenty, but she could be married at that age. And yet…she looked so innocent, her slender brows arched in surprise over those gorgeous brown eyes. Charles knew that she was looking at him with an interest to match his own, and his gaze was drawn to her mouth—her beautiful mouth—parted slightly in shock. Her lips were wide, full and delicately pink, and he knew in that instant that he would kiss them.

Not at that very moment, of course, but soon.

"Do you need any assistance, Miss Sinclair?" her coachman called as he stopped in front of the house.

The spell was broken. She looked up at her driver and smiled weakly. "I'm fine, John…just rushing a bit too much yet again."

"Yes, my lady," he said, biting his tongue to hold back his laughter.

Beatrice turned around to face Charles, wondering who he was. He'd hardly uttered a word, but the way he was looking at her immediately put her on her guard. Oh, he was clearly a gentleman, dressed impeccably in a snug fitting velvet coat and snowy cravat, but as for being a *gentleman*…he was far too heart-stoppingly handsome for that. His intense green-eyed gaze wandered over her body without reserve, and every one of his wicked thoughts was written in the appreciative curve of his lips.

Beatrice cleared her throat, trying to regain her composure. "I know I've already said as much, but I *am* terribly sorry. I'm in such a rush to get somewhere that I wasn't looking where I was going. It's just that I'm supposed to meet my aunt, and she can be a bit…unpleasant…when peeved."

His wicked eyes met hers with curiosity. "Who is your aunt, if you don't mind my asking?"

"Lady Louisa Sinclair—"

He began to cough.

Beatrice just grinned and continued. "Truly, she's not that bad, despite what you may have heard."

"It's not a matter of hearsay, Miss…Sinclair, was it?"

"Oh! I beg your pardon—I haven't introduced myself. I am Beatrice Sinclair."

Charles smiled and rose, extending his hand to help her rise. He should really introduce himself, as well, but he preferred to keep the upper hand for the moment. "Pleasure to meet you, Miss Sinclair—we shouldn't sit on the pavement for too long, I suppose. And by the way, I grew up next door to your aunt, and I know for certain that she deserves every bit of her reputation. If we lost a ball over her fence when we were little, we never got it back."

"Really?"

"Yes. I think she ate them."

Beatrice giggled, relaxing. "She's not so fond of children, is all. I wish she had some of her own because maybe then she'd give me some peace." Charles raised a questioning eyebrow, and she went on to explain, "You see, my aunt's taken me under her wing, of sorts, for the season."

"This is your first season?"

"Hardly. I hate to admit it, but this is my fourth season." Beatrice blushed, immediately wishing she hadn't revealed the exact number of years. "I'm sorry," she said, "I don't mean to bore you with the details. I always talk too much—that's why I'm always late. Anyway, I really should get going. I'm supposed to be at a ball with my aunt—I'm actually the only reason that she went at all, so it goes to show that I really ought to be there, hadn't I?" She knew she was babbling, but couldn't stop herself. The way he was looking at her—part curious and part something else—flustered her completely.

"Is it Lady Teasdale's ball you're missing?" Charles asked.

"Yes—have you been? Was it dreadful?"

An approving smile spread across his face. "Indeed, and I must say that you're not missing much."

She smiled back regretfully. "I didn't reckon that I was, but I really have no choice."

He was silent for a moment. His eyes slowly traveled down the length of her body. Every inch of her skin felt hot and tight under his gaze, and her stomach almost dropped to her knees at his next words.

"Perhaps we can think up a better alternative?"

For an instant, Beatrice was completely lost in his green eyes, unable to speak or move or even breathe. She was swimming.

Charles moved closer, his eyes fixing once more on her mouth. "Have you any ideas?" he asked, his voice dropping to a husky whisper.

She took one step back and mentally shook herself. "Only that I have to go, sir. I am late as it is."

He smiled. "Pity."

Beatrice nodded, and then blushed as she realized that nodding was probably the wrong response entirely. "Good evening, then," she said, forcing a businesslike tone.

"Good evening," Charles replied, then lightly grasped her hand, raising it to brush a soft kiss across her knuckles. She sucked in her breath, watching his dark head bend over her hand. She hadn't had a chance to put on her gloves before she'd crashed into him, and they had landed on the pavement along with everything else.

"My gloves," she said stupidly.

Charles let go of her hand and stooped down to retrieve them. As he handed them to her, his eyes never left her face.

Beatrice grabbed the gloves from his hand without saying thank-you or goodbye, and raced to the safety of her carriage.

Beatrice couldn't remember ever feeling so thoroughly embarrassed, or having her composure so completely rattled. It didn't help that her mind kept wandering down the forbidden path of broad shoulders and rakish good looks…broad shoulders and rakish good looks that hadn't even bothered with a proper introduction, she noted with irritation.

She looked down at her gloves, lying in a mangled heap on her lap. She'd spent the entire ride to Lady Teasdale's wringing them in worry, and now, as the carriage pulled to a stop in front of the Teasdale mansion, she was a mess of nerves. The small spot where his lips had touched her hand still tingled, and Beatrice felt like a fool. She'd just met the most devastatingly handsome man of her experience, and in the course of five minutes she'd knocked him to the ground, rattled on to him about her great-aunt and then dashed off like a ninny.

As she entered the house and wandered into the ballroom, she silently scoffed, *And people wonder why I've never wed.*

"Beatrice."

Beatrice turned around. Louisa's voice swiftly brought her back to reality. "Yes, Auntie?"

"I won't ask what took you so long, but take heed—I noticed. Where is your brother?"

"He, um, couldn't make it, Louisa."

"What excuse did he make?"

Beatrice thought about her brother's words and in a rash moment decided that she had nothing to lose at this point. "No excuse. He said to tell you to go to the devil. He wasn't coming."

Louisa looked hard at Beatrice for a moment, trying to keep the corners of her mouth from turning up. She failed; all women, even grouchy old women like Louisa, had a soft spot for Beatrice's roguish older brother. "He said that, eh? I don't know where he gets the nerve to say things like that to me, but it must be where you get the nerve to repeat it. Tonight's the last time I'll insist on him taking you anywhere. He makes you bold."

Beatrice didn't bother to refute her, looking around the room for any acquaintances so she could make a tactful escape. Instead, she noticed a handsome, middle-aged blond woman smiling at them and heading their way.

Louisa noticed, as well. "Oh! There's Emma Summerson. She's a good friend of mine. She has a daughter just a few years younger than you, and a most eligible son…if one could get past his reputation and reform him. He's a marquess."

"I couldn't care less about her blasted son," Beatrice mumbled.

"I heard you, Beatrice Ann Sinclair, and I don't like your tone."

Beatrice pasted a smile onto her face as the woman reached their side.

"Hello, Louisa!" she said, smiling broadly before turning her attention to Beatrice. "This must be the niece you were telling me about."

Beatrice smiled back sweetly. "*Great*-niece. And how do you do?"

Louisa glared at her, muttering, "Just when you were getting back in my good graces…. Beatrice, this is my good friend, Lady Emma Summerson. Emma, please meet my soon-to-be-disowned niece."

Lady Summerson smiled sympathetically at Beatrice. "Have you just arrived, dear? I have, unfortunately, been here for several hours and I don't think I've seen you before."

"I went to see *King Lear* on Drury Lane with my brother and sister." Mischievously, she turned to Louisa. "I told Eleanor what you said about getting ideas…. She thinks she will write her own version and call it *Aunt Lear.* She wants to perform it the next time the whole family is together."

Louisa mumbled something under her breath about ungrateful relations before turning to Lady Summerson with a resigned shake of her head. "Emma, if you don't mind the imposition, would you please escort my niece to the lemonade table before I really disown her."

Lady Summerson grinned, and Beatrice could tell that she was trying hard not to laugh. "Certainly, Louisa…she seems quite refreshing, and I could always use someone interesting to speak to."

Beatrice gave Louisa a hearty peck on the cheek. "I do love you."

As she and Lady Summerson set off, the older woman turned to her to remark, "Louisa is quite the curmudgeon, but she's told me so much about you. Much as she protests, I think she really enjoys having young people about."

Beatrice smiled, feeling guilty for being so impertinent in front of Louisa's friend. "I adore my aunt…I'm not usually so snappy. I've just had a rather trying evening."

"Well, you've come to the wrong place to improve it, my dear." She patted Beatrice on the arm. "I've always appreciated a sense of humor. Don't feel that you have to guard your tongue around me. And please, call me Emma. May I call you Beatrice?"

"Of course," Beatrice said, liking her immensely already.

Lady Summerson looped her arm through Beatrice's. "I can understand Louisa's sentiments, though. My daughter, Lucy, is just a few years younger than you, and she's been driving me to distraction all evening."

"Is this her first season?" Beatrice asked politely.

"It is, and I never realized how much work it would be. Other than Lucy I have only my son, Charles, and sons are so much easier."

Beatrice thought of her brother's words earlier that evening. "I can imagine."

"This isn't your first season, is it?" Lady Summerson asked.

"No. But it shall be my last."

Lady Summerson burst into laughter. "Well said, Beatrice. Have you already found your match? Or are you giving up so soon?"

They'd reached their destination, and as Beatrice was handed a glass of weak lemonade, she said with reluctance, "I'm sorry to admit it, but it's not as soon as you might suppose."

Lady Summerson tilted her head, curious for more details, but Beatrice looked uncomfortably around the room, not wanting to meet her gaze. She would *not* voluntarily admit to being on her fourth season twice in one evening.

Lady Summerson let her unspoken question drop for the moment. "Well, I think you should meet my daughter. Although she's only on her first season, she's as exhausted with the process as you seem to be. Let's see…" She paused putting her finger against her chin as her gaze roamed over the ballroom. "I'd introduce you to her now, but I believe she's dancing with Lord Dudley. Perhaps you would do me the honor of coming to my house for dinner? I'll be having a small gathering before Lady Parberry's ball, two Saturdays from now. You and my daughter will get on splendidly, and perhaps you can give her some advice, since you are so…experienced in these matters."

Beatrice laughed. "Thank you…I think. I should love to come, although your daughter can certainly use no advice from me."

"Nonsense. You can meet my son, as well. He's been staying with me while his house undergoes some repairs…actually, my house is really his house. He inherited it along with his title. But he has chosen to keep accommodations of his own, at least until he marries."

Beatrice sighed. "He's lucky, then. No offense to Louisa, but she doesn't know the meaning of the word *privacy*. You must enjoy having him home for a spell, though."

Lady Summerson shrugged. "True…although I must admit that at times I rather wish Charles would leave. I could use some privacy myself."

"You sound exactly as my father did when he tossed me out!"

"It's a universal sentiment among parents, Beatrice. We all want our children to leave and not come back until they have children of their own." Lady Summerson smiled. "I have to leave you now…I believe I just saw Lord Dudley follow Lucy onto the terrace, and I imagine she'd appreciate being extracted from that situation."

Beatrice shuddered slightly, thinking of Lord Dudley. She remembered him from her first season, when he'd asked her to marry him—twice. Apparently, he was still up to his old tricks. "I imagine you're right about that. I'll see you for dinner, then. Louisa can direct me to your house."

Lady Summerson looked momentarily surprised, then laughed. "I'm sorry. I assumed you knew that I live right next door to your aunt. That's how I know her so well—we've been neighbors for years. So please, feel free to stop over for a visit even before my party, dear." And with a wave, she was off.

Beatrice just stood there for a moment, stunned.

Next door? *Son?*

The room suddenly felt very hot to her. What bloody rotten

luck. Her terrible evening had just gotten far worse. How on earth could she get herself out of this predicament?

Beatrice wandered off, worrying her lower lip. Louisa had two different sets of neighbors, didn't she? One on each side? Perhaps Lady Summerson lived on one side, and the dark stranger—surely no relation—lived on the other. Indeed, Lady Summerson's son was probably small and fair like his mother. Beatrice clung to that thought as her only salvation.

Unfortunately, it didn't take long before her hopes were completely dashed. She scanned the room, searching out Lady Summerson to confirm that she looked nothing like the stranger. She was just in time to see her step from the terrace, her grateful-looking daughter following in her wake…her grateful-looking, black-haired and green-eyed daughter.

Damn.

Beatrice promptly turned around and headed for the ladies' retiring room. She needed to find a way to get out of this dilemma, although nothing immediately came to mind. She'd told Lady Summerson she'd go, and it would be rude to break her promise.

Lucky thing Beatrice left the room so quickly. If she hadn't, she would have viewed the peculiar sight of Lady Summerson ducking behind a potted fern hastily to scribble something into a small, leather book.

As they drove home later on that evening, Lady Summerson turned to her daughter and asked, "Do you know of Miss Sinclair?"

"I know of her, but I don't know her personally."

"Louisa only introduced me to her tonight, but I liked her very much and…well, I thought perhaps your brother might like her, too, so I invited her to our upcoming party."

Lucy snorted. "If Charles gets wind of this, he's guaranteed *not* to appear."

"Well, don't tell him. But tell *me*, Lucy, do you know anything of Miss Sinclair's reputation?"

Lucy thought for a moment, then shook her head. "I know very little, as I said. I believe she's generally well liked, although Dudley did say something about having proposed to her at one time or another. She apparently refused him—"

"Sensible girl."

"—yes, but he went on to say that refusing is something of a pattern with her. This is her fourth season."

Her mother's eyes widened. "Fourth season? My goodness." She clucked, thinking of Beatrice's evasive answer to her question on that subject.

"Dudley also mentioned that he was not the only one to propose to her. He said that she's notorious for turning men down."

"Oh, dear. Perhaps she won't do at all. You will keep your ears open, won't you? See if you can't find anything out."

Lucy sighed. This wasn't the first time her mother had set her to such a task. "As if I have any choice."

Chapter Five

"What do you think about this color, Bea?" Eleanor asked, holding up a deep green silk gown. She was to return to Hampshire later on in the day, and the two sisters were spending their last morning shopping. They'd been at the shop for only ten minutes, but already it was littered with the results of Eleanor's indecision. Gowns, hats and slippers were piled on a velvet ottoman, and that pile was steadily growing.

Beatrice sat amongst the pile, slouched with unladylike exhaustion. "Well," she drawled, turning to her sister, "I think it's beautiful, but perhaps just a tad dark for you. Where on earth would you wear something like that, anyway?"

Eleanor sighed. "You needn't rub it in." She was impatiently awaiting her debut in two years, not so much because she was in a hurry to wed, but rather because she, more than any of the Sinclair children, loved city life—especially the theater.

Beatrice smiled at her. "Just two more years, goose, and you can have all the ball gowns you please."

"I know…I'm just thankful Father let me come down to visit you at all. And I know that when it's my time, I'll appreciate it far more than you."

Beatrice sighed. She didn't mean to. It just sort of slipped out.

"Bea? What's wrong?"

"I don't know, Ellie…I'm afraid you might be right. I'd hoped this year would be different, but I'm getting worried that I'm not going to find the right person in time."

Eleanor hugged her reassuringly. "I know I don't have any experience in these matters, but I'm sure everything will work out. Truly, Bea, I can't even understand how you've managed to make it this far without being wed."

"Am I too picky?"

Eleanor smiled. "Not in most areas of your life."

"But as far as finding a husband goes—"

Eleanor gave in. "Well, yes, you *are* particular, but I don't think that's a bad thing. You shouldn't marry unless you find love. I'd hate to see you unhappy."

Beatrice sighed once more. "I know…that's what everyone says, unless you count Louisa, who thinks happiness should *always* defer to duty. But wait till you come out, and you'll see…. I'm not sure I even believe in love anymore."

Eleanor weighed that thought. "Perhaps. I'm sure that Father loved Mother, though."

Beatrice nodded slowly. "He did…but I don't think it's realistic for me to expect love like that. It might be possible, but it's definitely not probable."

Eleanor just shrugged, knowing better than to argue with her sister on this subject. "Do you have anyone in mind yet? I know the season has just begun, but…?"

Beatrice thought for a moment. "Well…I rather like Randolph Asher, although I'm not sure I could ever feel anything but friendly toward him. And Douglas Heathrow has been paying me a lot of attention."

"That's a start. In time, perhaps you'll have a few more names."

"Perhaps. But truly, Ellie, but I don't feel too optimistic. I think the ton perceives me as a spinster, and there's nothing sorrier than that. Louisa disagrees with me, though—she thinks I intimidate people."

Eleanor scoffed. "Shows how much she knows. You're quite amiable."

"I suppose," Beatrice murmured. "But I suppose she does have a bit of a point…as you may know, I did earn something of a reputation."

Eleanor smiled. "I've heard, but it's been two years. Can it still be that bad?"

"No…it's not bad. But if I were a man, I'd hardly flock to me. I mean, if you wanted to get married, would you ask someone who was almost guaranteed to refuse you? I think I'd rather court a girl who was more of a—a sure thing."

Eleanor looked slightly appalled. "A sure thing? You sound as if you're talking about betting on a horse at the races."

"No, truly, Ellie, it's not that different. Every year I've been out, I've received fewer and fewer proposals…six my first year, three my second, one my third and none so far this year."

"Well," Eleanor said practically, "you didn't want to marry any of them, anyway."

Eleanor shopped in silence for a few minutes, and Beatrice's mind wandered back to the handsome stranger she'd met the night before. Clearly her reputation hadn't intimidated *him*. Some devil inside of her made her say, "Actually, Ellie, I have received a proposal of sorts this year."

Eleanor clapped her hands together and took a seat next to her sister. "Bea! Why didn't you tell me? Who was it?"

Beatrice's eyes sparkled. "I said a proposal *of sorts,* Ellie. It was indecent."

Eleanor opened her mouth, scandalized. "Oh. That kind of proposal. Well, who was it?" She was leaning forward avidly now, for an indecent proposal was more interesting that a decent one any day.

"I don't know him, although I am rather curious. He's not the sort that I'm likely to meet at the social events I attend."

Eleanor looked worried. "He is of the ton, isn't he?"

"Yes," Beatrice answered slowly. "He reminds me of Ben, though…a gentleman by birth but not inclination."

"In other words, a rake?" Eleanor stated bluntly.

Beatrice nodded. "That about sums it up. He's a marquess… Charles Summerson. He lives next door to Louisa, or at least his family does."

Eleanor's mouth dropped open and then closed quickly. "I say, Bea, is he terribly good-looking?"

Beatrice cast an amused look at her sister. "You could say that…. I take it you've seen him about?"

Eleanor intently studied a bonnet, not meeting Beatrice's gaze. "I might have noticed him entering his house once or twice…."

Giggling, Beatrice picked up a pair of gloves from the ottoman and threw them at her sister.

Eleanor ducked nimbly. "Well, he was hard to miss. How did you meet him?"

"I…um, bumped into him on my way to Lady Teasdale's. I actually rather liked him—he wasn't stuffy and boring like all the other gentlemen I meet."

"But?"

"But he's definitely dangerous to my composure. It'd be best to avoid him completely, but it'll be difficult since he's living next door."

"Well," Eleanor said, "I wish you showed this much interest in suitable gentlemen. Are you sure that—"

Beatrice cut her off. "Yes, I'm positive. He is definitely *not* suitable. But my problem gets even worse."

"Does it?" Truthfully, Eleanor didn't think that having someone who looked like Charles Summerson interested in you was so terrible, but Beatrice had particular notions about these things.

Beatrice nodded gravely. "Yes—I met his mother at Lady Teasdale's, only I didn't know that was who she was. Anyway, she invited me to have dinner at her house in two weeks…so, in her words, she can introduce me to her son and daughter. What do I do?"

"Well, Bea, I hate to say this, but you have to go. It would be terribly impolite to turn down her invitation at this point."

Beatrice dropped her head into her hands forlornly. "I know. Perhaps he won't be in…. Lady Summerson mentioned that he has been staying with her only while work was being done on his own house, and I'm sure that by that time—"

"That doesn't mean that he won't come by for dinner, especially if he has designs on you."

"Yes, well, I'm sure he has designs on many women. Perhaps he'll have forgotten about me by then."

Eleanor looked at her beautiful sister and silently didn't think that was possible.

After a moment, Beatrice said suddenly, "It's not fair."

"What do you mean by that?" Eleanor inquired.

"He's obviously a thorough rake and totally unsuitable. That's what's unfair."

"You're not telling me that you wish he *were* suitable, are you? Do you fancy him?"

"Well," Beatrice began rather defensively, "I found him rather exciting. In all my experience being on the marriage market—" she cringed at the very phrase "—I have never found *anyone* exciting." She paused to look at her sister forlornly. "Why does he have to be the only one?"

Eleanor began to look worried. "Perhaps you should call off that dinner, after all…you can easily feign a headache, Bea. Lady Summerson will never know."

"I thought I *had* to go."

"I've changed my mind. I think you like Lord Summerson too much." Eleanor lowered her voice as two other women entered the shop. "Perhaps we could continue this conversation over an ice? What do you think?"

Beatrice smiled. "Let's *not* continue this conversation, but I do think that an ice sounds delicious."

They left the shop and headed down the street toward Gunther's.

On the way, Beatrice couldn't help but ask, "Do you think I'm being silly, Ellie?"

"Truthfully? Yes and no. If you're interested in him, I don't think you should give up altogether. It's what you've been waiting for, isn't it? Summerson is exceedingly handsome, wealthy and, so you tell me anyway, as charming as the devil. *But,* as you pointed out, that's why so many women feel the same way you do."

Beatrice sighed. "Point taken." Charles Summerson was *exactly* what she had been waiting for all along, but she had already determined that her previous aspirations were unrealistic. No, the wisest course of action would be to forget him entirely and settle on some nice, staid gentleman who never set her heart to racing—that sort was abundant during the London season.

Charles slept uncharacteristically late the morning following Lady Teasdale's ball. Although he tended to keep late-night hours, he usually still managed to rise early enough to exercise his horse in the park before it became too crowded. Last night, sleep had eluded him until the wee hours of the morning, and when he finally did drift off, his dreams had been visited by a golden-haired angel.

He stretched contentedly in bed and sighed, contemplating recent events. He'd been growing bored of late. Beatrice Sinclair was just the entertainment he needed.

Then he frowned slightly and sighed again. He really did have to move back to his own house soon. For one, his mother seemed bent on driving him to distraction with her endless matchmaking. More importantly, however, Charles had decided that he was definitely attracted to Beatrice Sinclair—too attracted to her. Just the thought of her sprawled out in the garden right next door, or even worse, sprawled out in bed, separated from him by little more than a few thin walls and the short space of his yard…it was precisely that image that had kept him up all night, and he wasn't sure if he'd be able to sleep soundly again until he moved back to his own residence.

He wasn't quite sure why he found her so intriguing…whether it was those faint freckles, or her slender feet. Maybe she interested him because she was rather clumsy and talked too much—a relief, when most young ladies pranced about like china dolls and conversed solely on the weather and the latest fashions.

But he did know that he wanted to learn more about her. It was her fourth season, and he found it peculiar that he'd never even heard her name before. Although he had spent some time on the Continent a few years back when he was working for the War Office, he'd quit that business nearly three years ago and had been in London for most of the last two seasons. Where had Beatrice Sinclair been then? She wasn't exactly the sort of girl one just missed.

And, he had to admit, he still wondered how old she was and why she wasn't married yet. When he'd first seen her on the street, he'd been struck by how innocent she had appeared—it had sent his blood racing, but it had also urged him to be cautious. Charles certainly wasn't renowned for his scruples, at least where romantic affairs were concerned, but he didn't make a practice of seducing innocents. It could lead to a lot more trouble than it was worth.

However, perhaps, Beatrice's appearances were deceiving. He hoped so. It wasn't possible to be so beautiful and make it through so many seasons untouched, unless the girl was quite a prude. From what he had observed, she certainly didn't seem to fit into that category. She didn't seem to be shy, either. Surely she couldn't be *completely* innocent.

Charles eased out of bed and rang for his valet, Smythe.

Several minutes later, he watched the elaborate process of his cravat being tied, while his thoughts drifted back to Beatrice Sinclair. Lucy would probably know something about her. His sister had always possessed an uncanny knack for knowing the affairs of everyone in society.

Charles's eyes narrowed on Smythe. Servants knew everything, as well. "Have you heard anything about the young lady who's staying next door, Smythe?"

The man looked up briefly. "I am acquainted with her maid, my lord. A rather forceful woman," he answered before turning back to his task.

"I see," Charles said, still looking into the mirror. Smythe was just making the final adjustments on his cravat, tugging here and there, but not before Charles caught a glimpse of the jagged scar that cut across the base of his throat. It was a gruesome reminder of his days with the War Office that he usually chose to ignore.

But then it was covered, and Smythe stepped away, admiring his handiwork.

"Will that be all my lord?"

Charles nodded and waved Smythe off. He hadn't been at all informative.

Ten minutes later, Charles wandered downstairs to the sunny breakfast room. He was relieved to see that Lucy was there, blessedly alone.

"Where is Mother?" he asked as he piled his plate with eggs at the serving table.

She looked up from the paper she was reading. "Off running errands for her dinner party."

Smiling knowingly, Charles took a seat across from her at the table. "Ah...will all the suitors be coming over, Lu?"

She smiled back sweetly. If only he knew *whose* suitors. "You could say as much, Charles."

"Suppose I'll have to be there, then."

Lucy nodded and folded her paper casually in her lap. Still smiling, she replied, "Yes, you'd better. Protection, right?"

Charles ignored her. He was in too good a humor to let her

gibes get to him. "Say, Lucy, you seem rather smug this day. Something happen to put you in such spirits? What have you been up to?"

Lucy had spent the morning tending to her mother's errands, as well. She'd already sent her maid over to Lady Sinclair's, hoping to get some information about Beatrice from her servants. "I had a few errands of my own…I had to go glean some information for Mother, actually. You know how meddlesome she can get."

Charles knew. He wasn't even going to ask Lucy what it was that their mother wanted her to ferret out. But the mention of gleaning information…

"Say, do you know Beatrice Sinclair at all, Lu?" he asked, hoping that he didn't introduce the subject too abruptly.

Startled, she choked on her tea.

"Lucy? I wasn't aware that that was a strange question."

Lucy wiped her chin and tried to appear nonchalant. "I'm sorry—it wasn't. Do *you* know Beatrice Sinclair?"

He thought carefully of how to proceed. He'd been hoping that Lucy would answer him with a simple yes or no, but clearly she wanted to pry. He didn't like to reveal too much of his private life to his sister, but he was also curious. "I don't really know her…but I should *like* to know her. I met her last night when I returned from the ball. She's Lady Sinclair's niece."

"Great-niece, actually," Lucy explained. "She hasn't been to town for the last few seasons, which would explain why you haven't met her before. Last time she was here, you would have been on the Continent."

Charles nodded. Lucy was being a veritable fount of information. "Is that all you know?"

"Her father's Viscount Carlisle. Her brother you might know from your club—Lord Benjamin Sinclair."

"We're acquainted. He was a couple of years behind me in school." Charles's eyes narrowed suspiciously. "You don't know Sinclair, do you?"

She smiled with forced patience. "I know *of* him. His reputation is as black as yours. I'm just very observant. That's how I know so much about everyone."

Charles snorted. "Well, if you know so much, Lucy, then why isn't she married?"

She shook her head. "That's what I'm trying to figure out."

"Why on earth would you be trying to figure that out?"

Lucy looked momentarily stricken, but recovered quickly. "I didn't mean literally, Charles…I'm not *actively* trying to figure that out. It just makes one wonder, though, when a girl as pretty as she is doesn't marry early on. She's also quite wealthy, by the way."

"I never realized you were *this* much of a gossip, Lucy," he said, shaking his head in bemusement.

"I'm not. You're the one asking all the questions, Charles."

"I certainly didn't expect answers as thorough as these. How do you to know all this?"

"I like to keep well informed. And, by the way, since you're curious, she apparently can be found at Larrimor's Bookshop on Tuesdays at two, almost without fail." Lucy paused, her brother's bewildered expression telling her that such precise information would require further explanation. "One of Lady Sinclair's servants mentioned it to my maid…apparently this is when Mr. Larrimor gets his new shipments each week. My maid passed this information on to me because I'd told her that I intended to visit the shop myself. She thought, perhaps, that Miss Sinclair and I might make a small party of it."

Charles mulled this bit of information over slowly, then asked guardedly, "Almost without fail, you say?"

"Yes…" Lucy drawled. He was taking the bait beautifully.

"Perhaps I need a new book myself."

She grinned. "I thought you might say something like that."

Chapter Six

At two o'clock sharp on Tuesday afternoon, Beatrice was in the back room at Larrimor's Bookshop, surrounded by several teetering piles of books. Mr. Larrimor had set aside these piles especially for her, having become familiar with her wide-ranging tastes.

A single, small window let light into the dusty room, and Beatrice had to bend over and look quite closely at the volumes in order to read their titles. He'd provided her with an assortment of novels, memoirs, even gardening treatises…. She picked up one book for a closer look. It was titled *The Life of William Kidd: A Sordid Tale, as Told by His Cabin Boy, Reginald Dawson*. She smiled. She didn't normally read books about pirates—that was a recent habit, one she'd begun only in relation to her writing. Pirates made excellent romantic heroes, and it stood to reason that she ought to know a thing or two about life at sea to write about the subject convincingly.

Beatrice had just begun thumbing through the pages of the dusty tome when she heard muffled voices coming from the front of the store. She stepped closer to the hallway in order to hear better.

She quickly wished she hadn't.

"Ah, hello, Lord Summerson. Can I help you with anything?" she heard Mr. Larrimor ask. Summerson. Could there be another Lord Summerson?

"I'm just looking around, Mr. Larrimor," a familiar voice responded. "I heard that you received your new shipments on Tuesdays and wondered if you had that book I ordered."

"I do. I'll put it on the counter for you, but please, have a look through the back room to see if anything else catches your eye—I haven't had time to bring everything out front yet."

In the back room, meanwhile, Beatrice had stopped breathing and gone into panic mode. She clutched her book tightly to her chest and pressed her spine against the shelf-lined wall. Thoughts of escape began racing through her head, but without any immediate solution. She was pretty much cornered in the book-strewn room, and she hadn't a chance of getting out undetected.

Unless…

Beatrice looked wistfully at the window. It wasn't so high up, really, and she was thin enough to fit through it. But she shook her head with regret. If it would have solved her problem, she could have just pulled over a chair, shinned up the wall, popped out the window like a cork and been on her way. Unfortunately, she knew it wouldn't solve a thing. The window would deposit her directly into the middle of Bond Street. And Mr. Larrimor would surely be most concerned when he discovered she'd vanished. In his worry, he'd probably say something about it to Lord Summerson, who would know exactly where she went and why….

She heard a creak of floorboards, followed by the soft sound of footsteps. There was no escape.

"Hello."

"Hello," she responded, turning back to the piles of books and trying to look unaffected by his presence.

Charles disregarded her attempts to ignore him. He ambled

forward until he stood next to her, then stopped. "You know," he began, an apologetic note to his voice, "I think I neglected to introduce myself the other night."

She bit her lip, but turned to face him. "Perhaps."

He bowed slightly. "Charles Summerson."

Beatrice nodded again, not knowing what else to do. Charles said nothing. Just continued to look at her.

She shifted uncomfortably, until she realized the reason he was looking at her was because it *was* her turn to speak. Still she said nothing.

"I see you've gotten to the new shipment first," he added with a smile designed to melt any obdurate female heart. "Find any good books?" Even as he asked this question he leaned in closer, trying to peer at the book she clutched in her hand.

Beatrice only gripped it tighter to her chest. "No. I haven't been here long."

"Oh. Well, then what are you holding?"

"A book." She wanted to slap herself as she uttered these idiotic words.

He smiled patiently. "May I see it?"

She shook her head. "No. I mean, that's to say, you wouldn't be very interested in it."

"I beg to differ. I am extremely interested," Charles replied. He could have added that the more she declined, the more his interest grew.

Beatrice didn't know how she could avoid showing him her book. She supposed there was nothing wrong with it….

She tentatively held it out for his perusal.

He raised his eyebrows. "Now I *really* must beg to differ. That looks very interesting indeed…it actually looks rather improper. Do you like that sort of thing?"

Beatrice blushed and shrugged. "A bit…. I was only looking." She wouldn't have told him the truth if her life depended on it.

Charles smiled. He knew she wasn't being entirely forth-coming. "Fascinating subject, isn't it?"

Beatrice just nodded weakly.

"Are you sure it's quite the thing for you to be reading?"

She held the book close to her chest once again. "Oh, no. I think it will be fine. Mr. Larrimor recommended it."

Charles chuckled. "Never fear. I was only jesting." He walked around the perimeter of the room, looking at the shelves. "Have you any suggestions, Miss Sinclair?"

She put her book down on a table and bit her lip again. She was a voracious reader and would normally have had dozens of suggestions. For the moment, however, her mind was blank. "Hmm...do you like novels?"

"I do, I must admit. I just finished reading *Sense and Sensibility*. My sister highly recommended it, and I must say I was rather skeptical, but..." Charles paused. "Have you read it?"

She shook her head, bemused at the thought of this dashing and dangerous man reading romantic novels. "No. I haven't."

"Perhaps I will lend it to you. That would be neighborly, wouldn't it?"

Beatrice gulped. "I suppose. I wouldn't want you to go to any trouble, though."

"Nonsense. It would be no trouble at all," he assured her, wondering why he even offered. He didn't usually bother with such niceties in his seductions. No, when Charles wanted to bed a woman he didn't typically find himself visiting her at her aunt's house to loan her a novel first. However, this was different. He didn't know why, but it was.

"I will drop it by later today, if that is all right."

She nodded her head slightly. "That would be fine...oh, but wait—I may not be in later. I'm having dinner with my brother this evening and have a few errands to run beforehand—I actually should get going now. I'm late again. But you could leave the book with our butler." Beatrice hoped there was no way for her to get caught in her lie. She *was* going out to dinner with Ben, but she certainly wouldn't be leaving her house for several hours; she simply didn't think she could handle two encounters with Charles in one day. She started to edge out of the room, hoping to hint at the fact that she had to leave.

He merely followed her. "I'll walk you to your carriage," he offered, placing his hand on the small of her back and guiding her down the dark hallway.

Beatrice would have protested if she'd had the words, but all she could do was follow his lead. Every inch of her body was aware of him—his smell, his heat, the light pressure of his hand burning a hole through the thin fabric of her gown.

When they approached the main section of the dimly lit store, Charles stopped, causing her to stop, as well, and look up at him in question.

But looking at him was a mistake. The dimness of the hall did nothing to obscure the heat of his gaze. If anything, the shadows made him seem even more handsome, more wicked. Without taking his eyes from hers, he leaned closer, and for one heart-stopping moment, she thought he was going to kiss her. Lips parted breathlessly, she waited.

He didn't kiss her, though. He merely reached out his hand and gently brushed something from her cheek.

"A smudge of dust," he explained gruffly.

"Oh." Heat rushed to her face, but she didn't know whether it was from embarrassment or from his proximity. It didn't matter…the soft pad of his thumb still rested on her cheekbone, and with what seemed like excruciating slowness, he let his hand trail along the line of her jaw, over her shoulder and down her spine, until it settled again at the small of her back.

With his small nudge, they were moving once more. She found herself waving distractedly to Mr. Larrimor as she passed him on the way out. Charles guided her across the street, stopping in front of her carriage to open the door. As he turned to help her inside, she had the sensation that he was about to kiss her once more. He wanted to. She could see it in his eyes, in the nearly imperceptible way his head tilted toward hers.

But he didn't. As if he'd just remembered where they were, he drew back slightly, his expression suddenly impassive. He merely nodded goodbye, closed her carriage door, and Beatrice was off, head swimming and heart racing.

Charles watched her carriage wind slowly through the afternoon traffic for a moment before he crossed the street to reenter the store. He knew he looked cool and collected, but inwardly the blood pounded through his veins.

God, he wanted her. It was ridiculous, really, for a man of his experience to be feeling this way. All he'd done was rub a bloody spot of dust from her face, and it had taken every ounce of his control not to throw her on the floor and make love to her.... If he did something like that again, he'd scare her off for good.

Charles was not surprised when, several hours later, Louisa Sinclair's butler informed him that Beatrice was out. He was almost certain that it was a lie, but no matter. He left the novel for Beatrice and turned to leave.

He was surprised, however, to see Louisa walking up the path just as the door closed behind him. She carried her parasol like a lance, and when her eyes lit on Charles he noticed her lip curl ever so slightly, making her resemble an aggressive terrier.

She looked him dead in the eye. "Good day to you, Pelham."

"Good day, Lady Sinclair. I hope you are well," he greeted her mildly.

She sniffed. "As well as can be expected. Have you business at my house?"

He silently cursed her lack of tact before saying, "Of sorts...I encountered your niece at Larrimor's Bookshop and just came over to lend her a book."

Her eyes narrowed skeptically. "Humph. That sounds remarkably out of character. Did your mother send you over here?"

Charles hadn't blushed since he was thirteen, but Louisa had a way of making him feel like he *was* about thirteen. "My mother?"

She nearly cackled. "Ah, you thought it was only your sister who had to be cautious around your matchmaking mama, didn't you, boy? Well, I have a pretty good idea why you were sent here."

Charles finally understood her meaning. If she wanted to make him feel like a callow lad, he could at least have fun with her, as well. "Madam, are you implying what I think you are?"

"Of course, my boy. Open your eyes."

"But Lady Sinclair—you're nearly twice my age! Think of the scandal! Of course," he added with a lecherous grin, "scandal has never stopped me before."

Louisa just sputtered, opening and closing her mouth several times in rapid succession. It was one of the few times in her life that she had been rendered speechless, and if Charles hadn't feared what would happen when she finally did regain speech, he would have remained to watch. Instead, he just doffed his hat and sauntered down her steps, wisely retreating before she could recover.

When Louisa did recover—it took all of ten seconds—she marched directly inside her house and up the stairs to her niece's room, swiping the offending book from the hall table along the way.

"Beatrice Sinclair," she demanded as she entered without knocking, "what has been going on here in my absence?"

Beatrice looked up from her dressing table in surprise. She was readying herself for dinner, although truth be told she'd been pretty much caught up in thoughts of green eyes and black hair and how to avoid them in the future. She hadn't the faintest idea what her aunt was talking about. "What do you mean, Louisa?"

Her great-aunt waved the novel under her nose. "I didn't even know that you two were acquainted. I do not condone it."

Beatrice blushed. "I simply ran into him in the book-store—"

"He informed me."

"Yes, well, he offered to lend me a book, being neighbors."

Louisa said nothing. She slammed the novel down on Beatrice's table, her nostrils flaring.

"Oh, Lousia, you're overreac—"

"Beatrice, I have been Summerson's neighbor since he was born, and not once has he lent me a book. I just can't believe he would have the audacity…in front of my very eyes…"

"Louisa! It's just a book."

"Don't be a fool, Beatrice. He is a rake."

"Oh, for goodness' sake, Louisa, that hardly means he doesn't read."

"That's not what I meant, Beatrice, and you know it. Summerson's just trying to lull you into trusting him."

She sighed in frustration. "I know his reputation, Aunt. I didn't mean to encounter him, and I'm not about to be 'lulled' into trusting anyone. Should I have been rude to him?"

"Perhaps," Louisa muttered. "That's preferable to running the risk of anyone seeing you with him. Look, Bea, to be perfectly frank with you, I'm quite fond of the lad—always have been. But he's notorious where women are concerned. Just stay away from him. He's too charming by half, and I don't want to see you make any mistakes."

Beatrice nodded, miserably wishing she were back home in Hampshire where life was simpler.

Evenly, she vowed, "I haven't made any mistakes, Louisa. I didn't *ask* for him to come here, and rest assured, I don't plan to seek him out."

Chapter Seven

Nearly a week had passed without Beatrice seeing Charles. Of course, this wasn't to say that she hadn't been thinking about him; no, she'd been doing that to excess. She could even admit to some mutinous feelings of disappointment because he hadn't sought her out—she'd flattered herself, she supposed, in thinking that he meant to pursue her. If that had ever been his intention, he'd clearly settled his attentions on some other hapless girl. By the time of his mother's party, he'd have quite forgotten her. *She* certainly had nothing to worry about.

If it hadn't been impolite, Beatrice would have whistled. It was a warm and glorious Saturday morning. The ground was still damp from the recent bad weather, but she didn't care. Louisa wasn't out of bed yet to tell her to stay indoors, so she put on sturdy boots, clipped a lead onto Louisa's English setter, Edward, and headed for Hyde Park.

The park was located right across the street and Beatrice set off briskly. These early morning walks were her only opportunity for exercise in the day; they were also one of the only times she had to herself.

As they entered a quiet, canopied path, Edward began pulling on the lead, eager to inspect the bushes.

"What is it, Eddie? Do you see something?" Beatrice gave Edward his head and he buried his nose in the bushes, snorting excitedly till he pulled out a ball. Edward dropped it on the ground watching her expectantly.

"Do you want me to throw it for you?" Beatrice glanced over her shoulder to make sure she was alone, then crouched down to pick up the ball. She unclipped Edward's lead. "Okay. I'll throw it, but you must bring it back, all right? Here goes." She threw the ball with all her might. He promptly retrieved the saliva-coated ball and deposited it at her feet.

Beatrice looked at the object in distaste. Edward looked at it with adoration. She sighed. "All right, then, I suppose I have no choice."

She stooped down to pick up the ball, pinching it gingerly between her thumb and forefinger, then threw it again, this time with more spectacular results. With a splash, the ball landed in a puddle, where it promptly disappeared.

Beatrice sighed. Edward stood at the edge of the puddle, whining and looking confused.

"You're supposed to go after it, Edward," she pleaded. He merely looked back at her with a long face. "Fetch, Eddie!"

He didn't budge, and she walked toward the puddle, contemplating the best way to save the ball without ruining her gown.

Beatrice was crouched down, gauging the depth of the puddle, when she heard the quiet clearing of a masculine throat behind her. She rose quickly and turned around.

"Might I be of assistance?"

She stared for a moment before answering, "Hello."

Charles walked forward nonchalantly. "Hello yourself."

Beatrice didn't know what further to say. She nodded and turned around once more. Then, a suspicious thought flashing into her mind, she asked, "You didn't follow me, did you?" She immediately blushed.

Charles looked offended. "I've walked my dogs along this

path since I was a boy—I only even noticed you because of the ghastly way you threw that ball."

She ignored his comment, only then noticing that he wasn't alone. Attached to a lead was perhaps the smallest, fluffiest dog she'd ever seen. It was entirely white, and its long hair obscured its eyes. All Beatrice could see of its face was a shiny black nose and the tip of its pink tongue.

"That's your dog?" she asked doubtfully. It certainly was an odd pairing.

Charles looked down at the dog, as well, somewhat disconcerted. "Er, no. This is actually my sister's dog, Egremont."

"Egremont?"

"Yes. It is a family name. Eggy for short."

Beatrice nodded, not knowing what else to do. She looked around. "Well, Edward and I ought to get going…."

"You're not going to get that ball for him? After being the one to put it there?"

She looked doubtfully at the puddle. "Well, it seems to be very deep."

"It does, although Edward looks disappointed. Perhaps I can help you?" Charles was feeling particularly gallant that morning, and was thankful for it. He'd practiced a great deal of patience that week by not seeking her out, and he didn't want to send her running in the opposite direction.

Beatrice weighed his offer. She didn't want to risk spending any more time in his company than necessary, but it was a kind offer. She nodded reluctantly. "I suppose…. How do you propose to do it?"

"It'll be easy," Charles said, placing Egremont's lead into her palm. "That's why gentlemen carry canes, you know. For helping damsels in distress." He fished around in the puddle for a moment with his cane, and rolled Edward's ball out.

The dog barked in appreciation, and Beatrice couldn't help but applaud briefly. "Bravo," she said, laughing.

He grinned roguishly and bowed with exaggerated chivalry. "May I demonstrate a proper throw, my lady?"

She smiled back and curtsied. "Indeed, my lord."

"All right, Miss Sinclair. Observe," Charles said confidently, before sending the ball flying off in a smooth arc. Beatrice watched as Edward galloped after it, swooping low to the ground to retrieve it. They waited in silence a moment for him to come trotting back.

He did not. With ball in mouth, Edward kept on running and disappeared into the park.

After about ten seconds of silence, Beatrice began to grow concerned. "Oh, dear. He's always come back before."

Charles smiled reassuringly, although the thought of having lost Louisa's beloved Edward chilled his heart to the core. "I'm sure he will…. Perhaps we had best follow him a bit, though. Just in case."

Beatrice nodded. "I think so."

She, Charles and Egremont started off, the former two keeping apace and the latter one lagging slightly behind on his little legs.

Beatrice looked back at Egremont with a sigh.

Charles noticed. "In Eggy's defense, my dear Miss Sinclair, *he* would have retrieved that ball himself."

She knew when to be quiet. Instead she turned around to pick him up and carry him.

"Here, let me," Charles offered gruffly, reaching out to take the dog from her arms.

He immediately wished he hadn't. It brought him too close to her. He could smell her hair, and the way his arm brushed against hers was enough to awaken his less honorable feelings. Charles suppressed them hard. For the moment, he wanted to enjoy the simple pleasure of her company.

She felt it, too. He could tell by the way her lips parted slightly in shock, her eyes widened and she instantly picked up her pace and began calling the dog's name.

"Edward!"

Charles followed suit.

As they neared Rotten Row, Beatrice began to worry even more. On a brilliant morning like this one, there were always many people about. Being seen with Charles could be disastrous. She halted.

"Problem?" he asked.

She blushed. "No...I just prefer to avoid this part of the park days. I only hope Edward hasn't gotten into too much trouble."

Suddenly, she saw him. She should have been relieved, but she was not. He had paused for breath at the foot of a park bench and had laid his head lovingly in the nearest empty lap. That lap belonged to Lady Barbara Markham. Although a luxurious mink pelisse enveloped her from waist to mouth, and a frothy hat obscured everything north of her eyebrows, Beatrice would have recognized her anywhere. Babs Markham was one of her aunt's best friends; she was also a notorious gossip and as bad-tempered as an adder.

Lady Markham's beady eyes peered out from between her hat and her fur, glancing disparagingly down her nose at Edward. Sensing new company, however, she aimed her gaze straight at Beatrice and Charles. Her target fixed in her sights, she lifted her hand to shield her narrowed eyes from the sun so she could peruse them better.

"I say," Charles said, "isn't that him over there?"

"Yes," Beatrice answered weakly.

"You don't sound pleased."

She began shaking her head. "Don't you see who Edward is with?"

He looked again and groaned.

Lady Markham, called across the lawn, "I say, Beatrice, isn't this your aunt's mongrel?"

Beatrice gulped. "It is, Lady Markham. He escaped from his lead...I do hope he hasn't been bothering you."

Lady Markham sniffed loudly in response. "Come closer, girl. I can hardly hear you. Who is that you're with?"

"Damn." Beatrice swore under her breath and took a step forward.

Charles raised an amused eyebrow at her language.

"I don't know what you think is so amusing. You're coming with me."

"Must I?"

She stared at him in disbelief. "You heard what she said. Lady Markham didn't leave you any choice. All she wants, anyway, is to find out who you are so she can gossip about this. She probably can't see you from this distance, and she wouldn't be able to stand not knowing your identity. Besides, you're the one who threw the ball."

Charles couldn't argue with that logic, and began walking, as well.

When they reached Lady Markham, she held up her quizzing glass. "Eh? Is that Summerson?"

"Good day to you, Lady Markham," he said smoothly, bowing.

She ignored him. "Beatrice, what are you doing with that lot?"

Beatrice felt ill. "Lord Summerson was merely helping me find Edward."

Lady Markham looked at Charles doubtfully. "Is that the case, Summerson?"

His composure didn't even crack. "Yes, Lady Markham. But afterward I plan to follow her into the bushes and make violent love to her."

Beatrice kicked him in the shins. Hard.

"Eh? I didn't hear you, Summerson. Repeat yourself."

"He said," Beatrice answered before Charles could make things worse, "that he would follow me to the street and make his goodbyes. That is all, Lady Markham."

She looked skeptical. "Humph. Not what I heard."

Beatrice maintained stony silence, vowing to strangle Charles at the first opportunity.

"Well," Lady Markham continued, "come take your dog, Beatrice, and tell your aunt I plan to visit her soon."

"I will, Lady Markham. Good day," Beatrice replied, hoping she sounded more lighthearted than she felt as she reattached Edward's lead.

The only reason Lady Markham wanted to come for a visit was to relay the news that she had seen Beatrice in the park with Charles. And Bea would be lucky if she were allowed out of the house alone ever again.

"Everything all right?" Charles asked after a few steps.

Without meeting his gaze directly, she said, "Oh, it's nothing. But I think it'd be a good idea for me to head home now. Lady Markham is such a gossip, and I really shouldn't be here with you unchaperoned."

Charles didn't want her to leave just yet. "It's not unheard of for a lady to walk in the park with a man, you know."

"Not with you, *you know.*"

"You have me there, I suppose. Can I at least accompany you home?"

Beatrice deliberated. Spending more time with Charles would be dangerous to her reputation and her state of mind. Yet he'd be walking in the same direction, and it'd be awkward for her to refuse his offer. "Well, I suppose, if you're going that direction anyway. Do you mind if we follow the path back?"

He shook his head. There would be less people that way, and he'd be able to be alone with her a little longer. He returned Egremont to the ground, and they set off.

For several minutes, they walked without speaking. Beatrice gave her undivided attention to the trees, the birds, the grass; she paid attention to anything that wasn't him. It wasn't an *entirely* unpleasant silence, although it was far from being comfortable.

Charles began to whistle.

She glanced at him sideways. His hands were in his pockets, and he looked so handsome that her stomach turned a somersault.

She quickly looked away, but after another moment of silence, she remarked, "You seem in good spirits."

He gazed at her. "I am, I suppose."

She didn't want to know why—she didn't want to know more about Charles than was absolutely necessary—but her natural inquisitiveness got the better of her. "Is there any particular reason?"

He pondered her question for a moment. It had been a very long time since he'd strolled in the park with a lady who wasn't his sister or his mother, and he had been wondering why. He was having a bloody good time. "No reason," he said. "Just enjoying the day."

They walked along in silence again. Charles remarked, "My mother mentioned that she's invited you to her dinner party." He hoped it sounded like mere small talk, but he was very interested in her answer. He'd spent several more sleepless nights thinking of all the tantalizing possibilities presented by having her in his home: the library…the terrace…the garden. Of course, there'd be even more possibilities if it weren't also his mother's home, but he was nothing if not creative.

Beatrice blushed. "Yes…she has." She was wishing once again that she had a way of getting out of the party, but she liked Lady Summerson too much to go back on her word.

Charles sensed her hesitation and knew what caused it; she didn't want to go because of him. "I probably won't attend. My mother holds these parties periodically—she invites all of Lucy's beaus, thinking that the best way to get one of them to propose is to put them all together and see who survives the longest. It's quite frightening, really."

Beatrice grinned, relaxing. "I can see why she and my aunt are friends, then. Louisa is desperate that I marry, although if it's just your sister's first season, I can't see that she has much reason to worry. Is Lucy your only sibling?"

Beatrice noticed a slight tightening around his mouth before he answered. "Yes, she is." He said nothing for a moment. "How about you? I know your brother vaguely…he was a few years behind me at school."

, "Yes. Ben…he's five years older than me. Every time I get annoyed at Louisa for worrying over me so much, I'm just thankful that I'm not Ben. She considers him a lost cause."

Charles grinned. "Nothing wrong with lost causes, you know."

Beatrice refused to make eye contact. He was much too charming when he grinned like that. "Yes, well, I'm the oldest after Ben, and then comes Eleanor—she's sixteen. And after Eleanor is Helen. She's thirteen and, according to my aunt, will be the death of us all."

"I take it Helen is a troublemaker?"

Beatrice nodded, for the moment forgetting that she had ever felt uncomfortable around him. "Definitely. It comes from being the youngest, I think. Our mother died right after she was born and Helen has been allowed to run a bit wild." Beatrice blushed when she finished, not having meant to say so much. "Sorry. I don't mean to go on so."

"No, it's all right," Charles said, thinking that she looked lovely with the sun lighting her face. Her happiness was contagious, and he couldn't help smiling. "You're very close to your siblings, I think."

She smiled back. "I am—I'm close to everyone in my family, for that matter, although we're all quite different."

As they reached the end of the path, Charles didn't know what possessed him to utter his next words. "I used to have a brother."

She looked up at him in surprise. "I'm sorry. I didn't know that."

He shrugged. He never talked to anyone about his brother. The subject brought back too many painful memories. "It's all right," he said. "He died a long time ago."

"May I ask what happened?" Beatrice murmured hesitantly.

His expression was guarded. "He was two years younger than me…his name was Mark. He and my father were driving up to visit me at Eton, and they had an accident on the way. I was fifteen."

Beatrice unconsciously laid a hand on Charles's arm. "I'm so sorry…I didn't know. Don't continue if it's too painful."

He looked away. Now that he'd started, he couldn't just stop. "It's all right. Mark was killed instantly. My father was brought to Eton—the accident happened quite close to school—and he survived for another week."

Beatrice didn't know what to say. She had no experience with loss on quite that scale, but she understood. Her mother had died giving birth to Helen, and Beatrice had never quite gotten over her death. She didn't think she ever would.

Beatrice felt Charles's hand on her shoulder and looked up at him, realizing that she had become absorbed in her thoughts. He appeared concerned. "I'm sorry—I've made you sad. I really don't know why I brought that up."

"I don't mind…perhaps you just wanted to talk about it?"

He shook his head. "I *don't* want to talk about it, actually."

Beatrice looked uncomfortably at the gate to the street. "Well…I suppose I should go. Louisa will wonder where I've been."

Charles nodded. "Don't want to make her angry."

They passed through the gate and crossed the street, the dogs behind them.

"Perhaps I'll see you later on this evening," he said as they reached the other side.

She turned around. They were in front of Louisa's house and Beatrice didn't want to linger. Hoping her voice didn't reveal her nervousness, she asked, "This evening?"

"I assume you're going to the Dalrymples' dinner party. Am

I wrong?" Charles had been invited to the event weeks ago, but hadn't actually planned on attending until now.

"Oh. Yes. I mean, no, you're not wrong."

"Well, then, I shall see you there."

Chapter Eight

Several hours later, Beatrice was almost ready to sigh in relief. Dinner had come and gone, and Charles had not appeared. She had been all but wringing her hands, during supper, expecting him to materialize at any moment. Louisa had shot her several dirty looks for her inattentiveness, but now, at this late hour… perhaps Beatrice could stop worrying. Charles had probably changed his mind about coming. She hoped so, or at least tried to convince herself that she did. She knew, however, that if she were honest with herself, she'd have to admit that she was bored without him and that her anxiety that he *wouldn't* show surpassed her anxiety that he would.

Luckily, she wasn't in the mood to be honest.

It was about ten o'clock, supper had just ended. The men remained in the dining room to drink their port and the ladies had retired to the sitting room where, for the most part, they were discussing the men.

"—well, I would have said yes, Bea, but I simply *cannot* be a pauper. I mean, a title is fine, but a girl must draw the line somewhere, mustn't she?"

Beatrice nodded weakly in response to Georgina Emerson's incessant chatter. Beatrice let her gaze wander around the room as her mind began to wander, as well. She wished the men would finish up. That was the only thing that would drag Georgina away from her…that or a second round of dessert.

Lady Summerson caught her eye from across the way and waved. She began making a beeline toward her.

"Hello, Beatrice! Georgina." A smile for the former and a rather curt nod for the latter accompanied her greeting before she turned toward Beatrice. "I'm sorry to interrupt, dear, but I was hoping to see you this evening. I promised to introduce you to Lucy, remember? Would you please excuse us, Georgina?"

Miss Emerson nodded meekly, cowed by the woman's commanding presence. Lady Summerson quickly whisked Beatrice away to the other end of the room.

"I hope you don't think me presumptuous, but you seemed to be in need of rescuing."

Beatrice smiled. "Well, a bit."

"You'll have to pardon me for having a less than favorable opinion of Miss Emerson. It's just that she was courting my son last year—yes, *she* was courting *him*—and I found her rather grasping. Ah, here is Lucy. Lucy, I'd like you to meet Miss Beatrice Sinclair. She is currently staying with our neighbor, Lady Louisa Sinclair."

"How do you do, Miss Summerson?" Beatrice inquired, curtsying. Up close, Lucy looked even more alarmingly like her brother.

"Call me Lucy, please, and I have been better. Do you know Lord Dudley?"

"Has he declared his undying love for you yet?"

Lucy rolled her eyes comically. "I'm wounded! You mean I'm *not* the only one?"

Beatrice giggled, truly enjoying herself for the first time this evening.

Lady Summerson smiled. "Ah…the life of the unmarried girl. It's hard, isn't it? I had several persistent suitors myself."

Lucy rolled her eyes once more.

Her mother just patted her hand and continued. "Although my daughter finds that hard to believe. You know, Beatrice, I was hoping to introduce you to my wayward son, as well, although he hasn't appeared yet."

"Perhaps he is not coming then?" Beatrice hoped that her voice didn't betray her anxiety.

Lady Summerson sighed. "Perhaps he'll stop by later. He and Lord Dalrymple have been friends forever. They're beyond politeness."

Beatrice nodded, trying to seem disinterested. She supposed she should inform Lady Summerson that she'd already met her son, but wasn't sure, at this point, how to work that tidbit into the conversation. She was saved from her deliberations, however, by Lady Dalrymple, who announced that the men had finished their port and that there would be music in the drawing room.

Lady Summerson scurried off to visit with another friend, and Lucy took her place, linking arms with Beatrice.

"Shall we?"

Beatrice nodded, asking as they made their way to the drawing room, "So have you been meeting with much success this season?"

Lucy sighed forlornly. "Frankly, it's not at all what one is led to believe as a girl. I cannot imagine how you did it so many times."

Beatrice blushed profusely.

Lucy gasped, appalled by her rudeness. "I'm sorry. I can't believe I said that, Beatrice."

She surprised Lucy by laughing. "Well, it is common knowledge, isn't it?"

"That this is your fourth season? It's not common knowledge, although it *is* known. Don't be embarrassed, though. I *rather* respect you for it. Do you not want to marry?"

Beatrice decided to be frank. "Yes. I just don't want to marry someone like, well, our friend Dudley, for example."

"Surely they aren't all like Lord Dudley, are they?" Lucy looked a trifle alarmed at the prospect. "Do I have nothing to look forward to?"

"No. No, that isn't what I meant. I liked several of my suitors quite well. I just couldn't imagine marrying any of them. It should almost be easier if I needed a title or money from a marriage. But I've never been pressured into marrying quickly and, well, as you can see, I haven't."

"But you do want to?"

Beatrice nodded. "Definitely…if or when I find someone who appeals. But I'm more determined this year to find a suitable match. In the past I think my goals have been a bit unrealistic. I do want children, you see—"

"Oh, damn." Lucy cut her off, looking quite annoyed.

"What is it?"

"Sorry to interrupt. Charles. My brother has just shown up. I was really hoping he wouldn't come tonight. I love him dearly, but he glowers at all the men who dance with me."

Beatrice's gaze flew about the room, searching for Charles. He appeared to be looking around the room, as well, probably searching for his mother, or Lucy, or perhaps Lord Dalrymple….

The moment his eyes lit upon her, Beatrice knew how wrong she'd been. He stopped searching, and for a brief moment, his gaze never faltered, never swayed. Beatrice felt a current of sensation almost overtake her, and forced her eyes away.

Unfortunately, Lucy was *extremely* observant. "Oh, I say, Beatrice, he really shouldn't look at you like that. Someone is sure to notice."

"Who is looking at me? Like what?" Beatrice prayed that she could get out of this predicament by feigning ignorance.

She could not. "Don't play the fool, Beatrice. My brother is looking at you as if you were a big, juicy steak. Here, stand behind me so everyone will think he's looking at me." Lucy grabbed Beatrice and pulled her to her other side, blocking her from view.

Beatrice didn't point out that Charles would hardly be looking at his sister with such interest. But arguing with Lucy might only draw more attention their way.

Lucy turned to her to whisper, "I thought you said you didn't know my brother…didn't my mother say she wanted to introduce you to him? You didn't contradict her, did you?"

Beatrice inwardly groaned. She liked both Lucy and her mother very much and didn't want to seem dishonest. "Um, you see…"

Lucy didn't wait for her to complete her thought, but dragged her across the floor, saying, "He probably only stared because he didn't know who you were, Beatrice. Men are like that—anything novel interests them. I have the perfect solution—I will introduce you to Charles myself."

Beatrice tried to pull away her arm. "Oh, no, I'm sure he has other obligations—"

"Nonsense."

Beatrice wanted to protest, but could think of no plausible *and* polite objection. If she announced that she had already met him, Lucy would wonder why she hadn't said so in the first place. Beatrice was also concerned that Charles would unwittingly reveal this information. After all, nothing had happened, really, at least by his rakish standards. In truth, Charles probably thought very little of their essentially innocent meetings. Certainly they couldn't have left him as flustered as they'd left her.

She crossed her fingers as she neared her social doom.

Lucy, sensing her apprehension, squeezed her hand before smiling at her brother. "Miss Beatrice Sinclair, I'd like you to meet my brother Charles."

Charles bowed slightly, and Beatrice had the ridiculous urge to hide her hands behind her back lest he should think to kiss them. But before she could act on this impulse, he bowed over her hand and placed a light, proper kiss on her knuckles. It took all of two seconds, but she felt it to her very toes.

"Pleasure to meet you."

"Miss Sinclair is staying with her aunt, Lady Louisa Sinclair."

"For that, Miss Sinclair, you have my sympathy," he said with a grin. "Perhaps you'd care to dance?"

Beatrice sensed the wicked laughter behind his eyes and looked desperately around the room, hoping for some sort of salvation. There was none to be found.

"Oh, do, Beatrice," Lucy urged. "I have to go chat with my mother anyway."

Beatrice had no choice. She met Charles gaze and nodded slightly. She put her hand on his arm and he led her onto the dance floor. Then he took her palm in his and placed his other hand on the small of her back. Beatrice just stood there, feeling as if her body were weighted down with lead.

"You know, Miss Sinclair, that *is* your cue to move. If you want to dance, that is. We could just stand here, if you prefer."

Beatrice shook her head. "Sorry. I was thinking of something." She took a step forward and landed firmly on his toe.

"Oh! So sorry," she said again.

Charles smiled and leaned in close to say quietly, "Are you nervous?"

Her stomach dropped. He was much too near for her peace of mind. She simply said, "No."

"Are you a terrible dancer then?"

Beatrice knew he was only ribbing her, and relaxed. She smiled this time when she answered, "No," and in the next instant found herself swept up into a waltz.

They danced for a while without speaking—Beatrice was concentrating on ignoring the heat that emanated from his large, firm hand and seeped through her thin silk gown.

Charles spoke first, "So why are you nervous?"

"I told you I wasn't."

"You were lying," he said, his gaze wandering across her face and drifting down to focus on her mouth.

Beatrice blushed uncomfortably under his scrutiny. "I did lie, but not about being nervous. I *am* a terrible dancer." And with that, she promptly stepped on his toe once more, only this time on purpose.

He yelped, causing a nearby couple to look at them in alarm. Her blush deepened.

"I guess I deserved that," he said without looking the least bit remorseful.

"Deserved what?" she asked, blinking innocently.

"You're an even worse liar than a dancer. You stepped on my toe intentionally."

Beatrice pretended to be affronted by his accusation, although in fact she was beginning to enjoy their banter. She reprimanded him with mock severity. "Lord Summerson, I did no such thing. I am offended that you would even suggest it."

"Call me Charles."

The sudden, intense look in his eyes caught her off guard. "I beg your pardon?"

The look vanished. "I said for you to call me Charles. It's my name. I don't particularly care to be called Lord Summerson, especially by friends."

Am I his friend? Beatrice asked herself. To him, she said, "I'm not your friend. We've had several pleasant enough conversations, but I've only just met you."

He sighed. "Are you always this literal?"

"Are you insulting me?"

"Yes," he said, swinging her around so that she ended up a bit closer to him than she had been before. A bit *too* close, really. "But I would rather be your friend. May I call you Beatrice?"

She wondered what, exactly, he meant by the term "friend." She had little doubt that his present definition of the word was a far cry from the one she was used to.

However, she wisely refrained from questioning him too far on semantics, knowing that to do so would only start her blushing again. All she could do was answer him. "I suppose you may use my Christian name, but that is only because I have given the rest of your family leave to do so and don't want to seem rude…it doesn't mean that I am your 'friend.'"

"That's most generous of you, Beatrice. Then since we're *not* friends, may I ask you a rather rude question?"

She blinked. "Excuse me?"

Charles's green eyes sparkled devilishly. "Why aren't you married?"

"A great many people aren't married," she retorted defensively. "I could be asking you the same question."

"Yes, but I don't want to be married. The fact that you're in London for the season implies that you don't share my sentiments. What's stopping you? You're intelligent and amusing, not to mention," he added quietly, his eyes darkening, "the most beautiful woman in town. Are you sure you really want a husband?"

Beatrice colored again. "Are you proposing?" She knew that she shouldn't have asked him this question. He was only toying with her, and there was no telling what sort of outrageous answer he'd give—yet the question had slipped out all the same.

Charles leaned in closer yet again, this time to whisper in her ear. "Not marriage."

She pulled away, flushed and flustered. "I…I have to get back to my aunt."

He still held her tightly. "The dance isn't over yet, sweet. If you leave now you'll cause people to talk."

She shook her head. "I don't care if they talk. Let me go."

Charles shrugged slightly, bowed and left the dance floor.

Ignoring the curious glances cast her way, Beatrice turned and walked in the other direction, searching for her aunt to plead sick.

* * *

Lady Summerson had just taken a solitary seat along the side of the room, ready to enjoy a brief respite from the endless gossip that always attended a large ton gathering. Her gaze, warm with satisfaction, followed her son and Beatrice as they moved across the floor.

Her peace didn't last long, however. Louisa's hawk eyes spotted her from across the room, and she marched over clearly on a mission.

Louisa got right down to business. "Emma, when will your son's town house be ready for reoccupation?"

"I beg you pardon?"

Louisa cleared her throat. "Do not misunderstand me, Emma. I like Charles quite well, but…perhaps you're unaware that he's been paying undue attention to my niece."

Lady Summerson looked surprised. "I'm sorry?"

"I discovered him leaving my house last week. Claimed he'd come over to lend Beatrice a book." Louisa snorted with disgust. "I haven't the faintest idea what to make of it, but I find this sort of behavior highly erratic and unacceptable."

"But…" Lady Summerson searched for words for a moment. "I wasn't aware that he even knew Beatrice until this moment."

Louisa arched a thin, silver brow. "What do you mean by *this moment?*"

"Well…" Lady Summerson explained carefully, "they *are* dancing together."

Louisa spun around and scanned the crowd. Sure enough, Beatrice was waltzing with Charles Summerson. Waltzing a little too closely, for that matter. Louisa's eyes narrowed and her lips tightened until they all but disappeared.

Lady Summerson tried to draw Laouisa's attention away from the dancing couple. She asked, "Where do you suppose they met?"

"Larrimor's Bookshop, so your son informed me as he was

leaving my home. Although I trust Charles about as far as I can throw him. He might have met her somewhere else."

Lady Summerson had to protest. "Now, Louisa, I can't allow you to say such things. Charles would never lie. Especially to you of all people."

Louisa shrugged. "Well, he met her somewhere or other. Lady Markham just finished informing me that she spotted them walking together in the park this morning, although she's blind as a bat and not at all reliable. Perhaps no one will believe her."

"Really." Lady Summerson wondered why Beatrice hadn't mentioned either of these meetings. Had something happened between them that she wanted to conceal?

"You know," Louisa remarked offhandedly, her eyes glued to the dancing couple, "I suspected that you were behind it—that you had encouraged him to seek her out."

"I did no such thing!"

Louisa sighed and turned around. "It was just a suspicion, Emma…I know you've been hoping he'd marry, and I *also* know that lending young debutantes novels and ushering them about the park hardly falls under your son's usual pattern of behavior."

Lady Summerson pursed her lips and thought for a moment. "This is most perplexing. Perhaps Lucy will know something about it…she's coming this way."

Lucy approached them, completely unaware of the hornet's nest she was entering. "Hello, Louisa. Hello, Mother. I was actually hoping to speak to you, *Mother*."

"Well, we'd like to speak to you, too. You and Charles are close…do you know why he lent Beatrice Sinclair a book?"

"And made a public spectacle with my niece in the park?" Louisa added.

Lucy's eyes grew wide. "I'm sorry?"

Her mother sighed. "I take it from your expression that you know nothing about it, then."

"Well…" Lucy began, "you did tell me to…observe things, Mother."

"What are you talking about?" Louisa asked sharply. When Lucy didn't answer immediately, she turned to her mother. "What is she talking about?"

Lady Summerson blushed. "Well, Louisa, you see…I liked your niece from the moment that I first met her…and I thought my son might like her, as well."

Louisa snorted. "It's safe to say that you were right, Emma."

"Oh, come now. You know how important it is to me that Charles marry soon…or, God willing, at least eventually. I'm allowed to hope."

"So you introduced them?"

Lady Summerson shook her head vehemently. "No! I didn't. I merely invited your niece to my dinner next Saturday."

"Beatrice informed me, although I now plan to revoke my consent."

"But she *must* come, Louisa. Charles will be there, but I plan to have other eligible young men there, as well, and it would only be to her benefit."

"I see," Louisa said, not looking as if she saw at all. "But that doesn't answer my question. What did Lucy mean when she said she was 'observing things'?"

Lady Summerson wasn't quite sure how to approach this sticky subject. "Well…Lucy has greater access to the opinions of young people, and I only asked her to find out something of Beatrice's reputation, just because—"

"Just because you heard this was her fourth season."

"Well…"

"Oh—" Louisa held up her hand "—no need to explain. I can hardly blame you, Emma. I'm sure you were wondering what's wrong with the girl that she can't find a husband after all this time. I'd be just as suspicious."

"If you consider all that she has in her favor, Louisa—beauty and fortune and intelligence—her lack of a husband does seem rather conspicuous."

Louisa sighed with resignation. "It does. I just can't figure her out. She *does* want to get married, I assure you. She just can't seem to find someone to suit her."

Lady Summerson placed an understanding hand on Louisa's arm, and Lucy took this as her sign to leave.

"Well, I'm sorry I couldn't help you more—"

Her mother removed her hand from Louisa's arm and grabbed Lucy's instead. "In a moment, Lucy. You haven't answered Louisa's question yet."

"Question?"

"Charles's meetings with Beatrice can hardly be mere coincidence."

Lucy knew she was done for. "I only did what you told me to, Mother. You wanted me to find out more about her, so I sent my maid over to see what she could find out from Lady Sinclair's servants."

Louisa sputtered in disbelief. "You *what?*"

"They would hardly be privy to her reasons for not marrying, Lucy. That was all that I wanted you to discover," Lady Summerson reminded her daughter.

"I *know* that, Mother," Lucy exclaimed. "I was merely doing my best."

"Well, what did you learn?"

"Almost nothing beyond who her family is and where they come from. Really just the sort of stuff anyone in society would be privy to."

"*Almost* nothing?"

"Well, it was mentioned that she goes to Larrimor's Bookshop every Tuesday. At two."

"You didn't tell Charles to seek her out, did you?" Louisa asked.

"Well, I wasn't going to, but then the oddest thing happened. He asked me if I knew who she was. Completely out of the blue.

Said that he met her when he returned from Lady Teasdale's ball and that he was interested in her."

Delight slowly spread across Lady Summerson's face.

Louisa looked horrified. "So you told him how he could get to know her better?"

"Well, I wouldn't have, Lady Sinclair, except…"

"Except what, dear?" her mother asked encouragingly.

"Except I was so surprised that he wanted to know. Charles doesn't have to seek out women—they come to him in droves. So for him to be willing to go out of his way—"

"Yes!" Lady Summerson squealed excitedly. "I thought so! I knew my instincts were right."

"What on earth are you blathering about?" Louisa asked.

Lady Summerson answered with a triumphant glow in her eyes. "My son, Louisa, is interested in your niece."

"Of course he is. That's what we're talking about, remember?"

Lady Summerson ignored her sarcasm. "There's no 'of course' about it, Louisa. Charles has no shortage of female companions, but he never seems to be totally interested in any of them. I think it should be encouraged. And before you protest, let me point out that they both need to get married."

"Except your son doesn't seem to be aware of that fact."

"But when he finds the right woman… I wonder why Beatrice didn't mention having met him?"

"Maybe I can find out?" Lucy offered. She didn't really want to act on this plan, but she definitely did want to quit the conversation.

Her mother jumped on her suggestion. "That's a brilliant idea. You can visit her tomorrow. Would that be all right, Louisa? Seeing as something already seems to be happening—"

"Oh, do whatever you like," Louisa muttered. A small corner of her heart found the idea as appealing as Lady Summerson did, but she was too stubborn to admit it. She'd always been exceedingly fond of Charles. "So, who else is invited to your party?

You said that there would be several eligible young men present."

"I exaggerated a bit. I've only planned a small gathering of Lucy's suitors. I could send out some last-minute invitations.…" Lady Summerson offered reluctantly.

Louisa harrumphed. "I will not allow my niece to attend unless you assure me that there will be at least a few prospective matches present."

"Actually, Mother," Lucy added, "that might not be such a bad thing. Charles is competitive, and perhaps seeing that he isn't the only one interested in Beatrice—"

"But I'm not sure if Charles is the sort to succumb to jealousy, dear," Lady Summerson interjected rather sadly.

"Then we shall know that his interest in Beatrice is purely superficial, and that will be the end of it," Louisa stated firmly.

Lady Summerson nodded thoughtfully, a slow smile brightening her face. "I think it's actually quite brilliant, Louisa. Lucy, when you visit Beatrice tomorrow, you must also find out who her prospects are. We'll invite them all."

Louisa snorted. "Good luck. What prospects?" Sighing resignedly, she turned to go. "It's time for me to be off, and as I recall, you needed to speak to your mother, Lucy."

Lucy nodded, but as Louisa walked off, she said, "It's nothing important now, Mother…I was just going to tell you about the way that Charles was looking at Beatrice. I've *never* seen him look at any woman like that."

Her mother opened her eyes wide in alarm. "I should hope not! I hope nobody noticed or there'll be dreadful talk. Hmm, where are they now?" She began to scan the dance floor.

After a moment, she groaned. "Oh, no."

"What is it, Mother?" Lucy asked.

"I do believe your brother just abandoned her in the middle of the dance floor. Please don't let Louisa have seen that or we can forget about our plan."

Chapter Nine

The very next day, Charles decided to return to his own home. The work wasn't quite complete yet—but he didn't care. He could tolerate the noise more easily than he could tolerate another restless night at his mother's.

The knowledge that Beatrice was next door was driving him crazy. He'd dreamed about her—her golden hair spilled out across her pillow, her rumpled bedsheets, her drowsy, amber eyes… Charles swallowed, feeling the blood rush through his body.

This had to stop.

He hoped that by putting some distance between them—even just a few blocks—he would be better able to control himself. Perhaps when he returned home, he'd finally be able to sleep.

He certainly couldn't afford to have a repetition of last night. The moment he'd seen Beatrice at the Dalrymples' party, the urge had come over him yet again to scoop her into his arms, carry her into the nearest empty room and have his way with her.

Charles cursed. He seriously had to reconsider his plans. At first, he'd thought very little about seducing Beatrice; that is, he'd thought about it a lot, but he hadn't experienced any moral dilemmas over it. He'd assumed that, after three seasons, she must have some experience with men. But after last night, after her deep blushes, after the way she reacted when he'd leaned in close to whisper in her ear...he wasn't so sure she had any experience at all.

This realization, however, didn't deter him. Instead, the thought of her innocence sent his blood surging even more. He knew that marriage was her goal, and he damn well wasn't going to marry her, but he still wanted her as he'd never wanted a woman before. The thought of giving up the chase and letting someone else have her...he couldn't endure it.

Charles looked at the clock on his desk. It was nearly ten and he had yet to leave his room. He wished that there was some way for him to leave without informing his mother; she would surely have something to say about his behavior the night before.

But there was no help for it. He shrugged on his coat and headed downstairs. When he finally found his mother reading in the study, she seemed annoyed as she looked up from her book.

He began cautiously. "Well, Mother, my house is ready and it's about time I got out of your hair."

She snorted.

Charles didn't know how to respond. "Well...I suppose I'll be off, then."

"Funny thing," she said. "Louisa was wondering *just* last night when you would be returning to your own home."

Charles had known it was coming. "Lucky for her, I'm leaving now."

"Do you know why she was interested?"

"I'm sure you'd like to tell me," he said with a sigh.

"What, precisely, are your intentions toward Miss Sinclair? It's obvious you like her."

Charles chose his words carefully. "I like her. Why shouldn't I?"

"Are you attracted to her?"

He flushed. "I'd rather not talk about this with you, Mother."

She ignored his wishes. "My guess is that you are. She's beautiful, intelligent—"

"What is your point?" Charles asked defensively.

"My point is this," she said, folding her hands in her lap. "Beatrice is here to get married, and having you sniffing about her heels definitely won't help that goal. So unless you propose to marry her yourself, stay away from her."

"I'm not marrying her," Charles's replied shortly.

"You have to marry someone eventually."

He shook his head slowly, his eyes deadly serious. "I'm not getting married."

She looked as if she wanted to scream, but, admirably, kept her calm. "What about children? You have a title to pass on, if you don't recall."

Charles shook his head again. "I won't have children."

His mother finally lost her temper. She nearly flew from her seat. "I never knew I raised a coward."

"I'm sorry?"

"Oh," she continued, "you're not a coward about most things, I'll grant. You've proved that most adequately. But you're being a coward now."

"Would you care to enlighten me as to why, Mother?"

"Because you're running away."

"Running away from what?"

"Running from a girl who *just* might make you happy. All because you're too afraid of the things that could go wrong." She paused, her eyes searching her son's face. "There are no guarantees in life, Charles. Don't deny yourself happiness and love just because you're afraid it might be taken away."

"I don't know what you're talking about," he said, his expression masked. He turned to leave. "Besides, I really must go."

His mother shrugged. "Charles, don't be angry. I probably shouldn't prod you so, but I worry sometimes. I just want you to be happy."

He crossed the room to give her a hug. "I am happy, Mother. Don't worry."

As Lady Summerson watched the door close behind her son, she couldn't help it. She worried.

Lucy visited Beatrice later that day, feeling like a rat. She would have visited anyway—she truly liked Beatrice—but she also had strict orders to carry out her mother's agenda. Neither she nor her parent had missed that Beatrice mysteriously "took ill" and decided to leave after her waltz with Charles. Lucy was dying to find out what had happened. *Something* was afoot.

After announcing her, Humphries led her into the sitting room. Beatrice was seated in the middle of Louisa's slipcovered settee, writing something in a book. *She didn't look at all ill.*

Beatrice closed her book and rose with a smile. "Lucy! So nice of you to stop by."

"I didn't have a chance to talk to you last evening after—"

"After I escaped?" Beatrice asked wryly, resuming her seat and motioning for Lucy to join her.

"Charles didn't do anything he shouldn't have, did he? He *always* does things he shouldn't…. I just hope that isn't the reason you left so early."

It was, but Beatrice didn't care to discuss it. "No, he did nothing improper, Lucy. I hate to have given that impression. I had a headache, and…well, the only reason I was there was because Louisa was certain that several of my suitors would be in attendance. However, as they weren't, she didn't mind my leaving early."

Lucy raised her eyebrows. "Oh? I didn't know that you had any serious suitors."

Beatrice laughed. "I don't—Louisa just insists on calling them that."

Lucy had no idea that her task would be so easy. "If you don't mind my asking, Beatrice, who are they?"

"Randolph Asher and Douglas Heathrow. Christopher Winters, too. Although I declined his proposal three years ago. I'd hazard he still despises me, but Louisa thinks I could change his mind."

"Do you want to?" Lucy asked.

"No," Beatrice sighed ruefully. "Not in the least."

"Well, my mother's invited Asher and Heathrow, and some other eligible gentlemen, as well. She's even invited my brother's friends, and they're not the sort to attend Almack's…but they're dashed good-looking." Lucy crossed her fingers. Her mother hadn't yet invited Asher and Heathrow, but their invitations would go out the second Lucy relayed the information. Hopefully they would accept!

Beatrice smiled. "Lucy? Remember how you asked if I'd met your brother before?"

"Yes…"

"Well, I had. I met him on my way out the door to attend Lady Teasdale's ball…as he was coming back. I didn't know who he was, though, and I didn't know that he was related to your mother when I agreed to attend her dinner. And last night, I wasn't quite sure how to tell her."

Lucy smiled reassuringly, grateful that Beatrice had proved her honesty, even as she tried not to feel too traitorous for concealing her prior knowledge of their earlier meetings. "Think nothing of it. With the way my mother and I were jabbering at you, it's a miracle you got in any words at all."

Lucy left an hour later, and Beatrice felt relieved for having told her *most* of the truth about her previous meetings with Charles.

Alone once more, she began to write. She'd yet to find a sensible man who made her heart race, but at least Charles gave her material to write about. As long as she could keep her fantasies confined to pen and paper, she had no need to worry.

Chapter Ten

Beatrice was extremely nervous as she rang the Summersons' doorbell on Saturday evening. She had begged Louisa to come with her, but she'd declined. For once Beatrice felt she needed her aunt's support.

The butler ushered her inside. A footman took her coat and she stood there for a moment, smoothing her green silk gown and glancing around the front hall.

"Beatrice! I'm so glad you've come!" Lucy greeted her as she walked down the steps. When she reached Beatrice, she gave her a hug and whispered, "I had a few doubts whether you would appear or not. After our conversation the other day, I thought you might have another headache."

Beatrice blushed. Lucy had seen through her thin explanation and knew that Charles had acted most improperly. "I should hate to disappoint your mother."

"And me, as well, Beatrice. You know, this is the first time I've been downstairs all evening. I was having the worst time with my hair. Does it look all right?" Truth was, Lucy had been waiting at the top of the steps for Beatrice to arrive so she could speak to her.

Beatrice was grateful for the way Lucy helped her feel more

at ease, and she truly meant it when she said, "Lucy, you couldn't look lovelier."

"And the same to you." She leaned close to whisper conspiratorially, "Randolph Asher is here, as well as Lord Heathrow. They both asked about you *first thing* as they entered the house."

Beatrice furrowed her brow. "But I thought you hadn't been downstairs yet."

Lucy silently cursed herself for making that slip. She *hadn't* been downstairs, but she had been eavesdropping from the landing. "My mother mentioned it when she came to my room to see what was taking me so long."

"Oh."

"Shall we?"

Nearly all the guests were assembled inside the drawing room. As usual, Beatrice was late and one of the last to arrive. Although she didn't mean to, she immediately started searching the room for Charles. She knew that he'd returned to his own home, and he'd mentioned in the park that he might not attend. Until that very moment, she had clung to the possibility. Suddenly, faced with the prospect of spending the entire evening without him, Beatrice didn't quite know how she felt. She was still angry with him for his outrageous behavior, but her anger wasn't so much the result of his inappropriateness as it was the result of her reaction to it. Charles was off-limits, and she'd best keep that fact in mind.

Her search was rewarded soon enough. He stood by a window along the side of the room, not talking to anyone and looking as if he was in a foul mood. But even glowering slightly, he still caused Beatrice's breath to catch in her throat. He looked so fine in his evening togs, his formfitting velvet coat emphasizing his broad shoulders and narrow hips. Absurdly, Beatrice had the urge to walk right over to him and run her hands across his chest to see exactly what that velvet felt like.

Of course, that was about the last thing she would do. Having located him, she turned away, not wanting anyone to notice the direction of her gaze.

Lucy ushered her to a small group of people at the far end of the room. "I want to introduce you to Jack Davenport. He's dashed good-looking and quite charming. He's been my brother's best friend for as long as I can remember, and if he weren't like a brother to me, as well, I'd set my cap for him myself." Lucy crossed her fingers as she said this. Jack was rarely in town, and it had been years since she'd seen him. But Lucy was a take-charge sort of girl, and she had taken the liberty of sending him a note to inform him of Charles's interest in Beatrice and to request that he make a point of flirting with her. Of course, Jack probably wouldn't need any prompting, rake that he was. But if he knew that it would irritate Charles, he'd be sure to make the extra effort.

Beatrice looked at the man in question, and had to admit that he was quite handsome. He was tall, broad shouldered, and had light brown hair that was just a shade too long. As he turned around to greet Lucy, his hazel eyes warmed perceptibly.

"Jack! I haven't seen you in ages—have you been on the Continent all season?"

Jack smiled, his eyes crinkling slightly around the corners. "I have, Lucy, although it's top secret." He turned an appreciative gaze to Beatrice.

Lucy noticed and grinned. "Oh, how very rude of me. Miss Beatrice Sinclair, I'd like you to meet Mr. Jack Davenport."

"The pleasure is all mine, Miss Sinclair," he replied, bowing gracefully and kissing Beatrice's hand.

Before she could do anything more than blush, a deep, familiar voice came from behind her. "Jack, I've been looking for you. Mind if I have a word with you?"

Lucy narrowed her eyes. "Why, that's very rude, Charles. You haven't even greeted Miss Sinclair."

Charles glared at his sister before smiling tightly at Beatrice. "Good evening, Miss Sinclair."

Jack turned his attention back to Beatrice, putting on his most charming face. "Ignore him, Miss Sinclair. Sometimes my friend is a bit lax in his social graces."

"Jack…" Charles's voice had lost all humor.

Jack sighed. "You'll have to excuse me, Miss Sinclair. This, apparently, is extraordinarily important." And with that, Charles led him away.

Lucy broke out in giggles and Beatrice just stood and stared in bemusement.

"I wonder what that was about," she said.

Lucy smiled. "Who knows? Jack seems quite taken with you, though."

Beatrice looked at her doubtfully, thinking he'd actually seemed quite taken with Lucy. "I imagine he reacts that way to most women."

"I guess I needn't tell you to be careful, then."

Beatrice smiled and shook her head. Jack was handsome and charming, but he didn't make her insides quiver like someone else did.

"Would you mind excusing me, Bea?" Lucy asked. "My mother is making a face at me. She must have something to tell me. Besides, Lord Asher is headed your way."

Randolph Asher was crossing the floor with a warm, purposeful smile on his face. Bea smiled back. Asher was thoughtful and kind. Of course, she'd never found herself wondering what his mouth would feel like pressed against hers, but Beatrice reckoned that sometimes that wasn't such a bad thing. Asher was real and sensible. Charles was not.

Beatrice stepped forward to chat with Asher, and Lucy scampered off to meet her mother; within minutes, they were firmly ensconced in a tête-à-tête, chattering excitedly about how brilliantly their plan was working already.

In the study, Charles poured Jack a glass of claret. They'd been best friends since they'd lived next door to each other at Eton, and for most of their adolescence they'd been inseparable. After university they'd toured the Continent together. Jack's proficiency with languages had brought him into involvement with the War Office, and he'd recruited Charles to work informally for the office, as well. Although Charles had left that work over two years earlier, Jack continued his involvement. He spent the better part of the year abroad, and Charles hadn't seen him since he'd quit. He supposed, however, that Napoleon's recent defeat might keep Jack in England for the near future.

But best friend or not, Charles still wanted to hit him on the head with a large, blunt object.

"…quite pretty, isn't she?" Jack was saying, a familiar gleam in his eye. "If I'd known there was anyone like her out this season, I'd have returned to London sooner."

Charles tried to contain the anger swelling up inside him. "I don't think Beatrice Sinclair is your type, Jack."

He looked confused. "I beg to differ. She seems exactly my type."

Charles stared down at his knuckles, which were turning white as he gripped his snifter. "I'm not talking about the way she looks—I meant that she's looking for a husband, and unless you've had a drastic change of heart, that doesn't describe you." He ignored the fact that he could be castigating himself for the same thing.

Jack sighed. "She'd almost be worth the complication, though, wouldn't she?"

"Complication? You mean marriage?" Charles asked, alarmed.

"No, ass," Jack explained impatiently, "I meant the complication of pursuing a debutante *without* the intention to marry. She'd almost be worth it, don't you think?"

"No," Charles said shortly, wanting to plant his fist in Jack's face, "I do not. Spend a few more minutes talking to her and you'd see exactly what I mean. She's blasted annoying, not to mention she affects some sort of a lisp. And her teeth are crooked." He paused for a second. "Better yet, don't talk to her. Just take my word for it."

Jack stared. "I hadn't noticed any of this."

That's because she's bloody perfect, Charles thought, before adding, "Trust me." He felt guilty maligning Beatrice's character so, but he could think of no other way to keep Jack away from her. He'd been worried about it since he'd learned that his friend would be in attendance—Jack was handsome and charming, and women consistently made bloody fools of themselves over him.

Come to think of it, his mother had invited several of his friends to her gathering—all charming and unscrupulous wastrels who would have no qualms about seducing innocent females, namely, Beatrice Sinclair. Charles didn't have the faintest idea why she would have done that—he'd been expecting to spend the evening surrounded by a bunch of Lucy's milk-faced suitors, and he would almost have preferred it. At least that way he wouldn't be tense all evening, wanting to pummel any man who looked at Beatrice sideways.

Jack had settled back into a deep leather chair. He swirled his drink around in his glass and inquired, "So what was it that you needed to talk to me about?"

Charles didn't have a bloody thing to talk to Jack about, other than what they had just discussed. But they did have a lot of catching up to do…. "It's been almost three years," he stated pensively.

"Was never the same after you left."

Charles raised his eyes, immediately defensive. "Hadn't any choice. It'd be different if my father or brother were still alive, but after what happened… Without me it'd just be my mother and Lucy. I've never exactly been an ideal son, but—"

Jack nodded, cutting him off. "No need to explain. I'd have done the same thing. How's your neck, by the way?"

Charles raised a hand to the scar at his throat. "Healed a long time ago."

"Richard Milbanks is probably dead."

Charles looked up sharply but his expression remained unreadable. Slowly, he replied, "I figured as much."

Jack nodded. "Ship went down in the North Sea. Not that you'd have to worry, anyway. That traitor lost the ability to return to England."

Charles shrugged. He didn't want to discuss it. Milbanks had worked alongside him at the War Office, trying to suppress smuggling along the coast. Charles had trusted him with his life. Then late one night they'd approached an unknown vessel, their ship already loaded with confiscated cargo. It should have been a routine inspection, and his guard was down—he certainly hadn't expected Milbanks to pull a knife from his pocket and try to slit his throat. The rogue had nearly succeeded, and as Charles lay bleeding on the deck, his ship was seized, its cargo unloaded. Semiconscious, he'd watched Milbanks board the other vessel. Turned out Milbanks had decided smuggling was a more lucrative business. Charles's last mission for the War Office had been seeing that he was captured and hanged. Unfortunately, while awaiting the gallows, Milbanks had escaped.

Charles had felt impotent. He'd nearly died that night, and he wanted to hunt Milbanks down and bring him to justice. But the knowledge that he'd be risking his life again, that this time he might not be so lucky, had made him pause. His family knew nothing of his brush with death, but Charles couldn't ignore his responsibility to them.

That was what he told himself, anyway, but he knew his reasons were more complicated than that. Although he had pretended to shrug the incident off, it had affected him deeply. He felt like a coward to admit it, but he was terrified of dying. And knowing that Milbanks might still be out there... When Charles had sent him to the gallows that had made it personal, and he fully expected Milbanks to seek revenge.

Charles had already heard that Milbanks's ship had been gunned down, but of the twenty bodies recovered, Milbanks's had not been among them. Charles couldn't put the memory behind him, not until he knew for sure that his enemy was dead.

"Charles?" Jack asked.

He glanced up, having become absorbed in his thoughts. "Sorry?"

"I said I could probably find out if he's dead for certain."

Charles considered this offer for a moment. Finding out that Milbanks was dead would give him peace of mind like nothing else, but learning that he still lived would only make his problems worse. It was better not to know.

"No, Jack. It's all in the past."

"Well, if that's true, then you shouldn't care if I write a few letters to find out. Confirmation, one way or the other, won't bother you."

It would bother Charles very much, but he couldn't argue with Jack without letting on. Tightly he conceded, "No, Jack, it won't bother me at all. Do what you like."

Jack didn't miss his friend's discomfort. "I see. Mind if we rejoin the party?"

Charles just nodded, still distracted. He was in too foul a mood to feel any enthusiasm about socializing. He felt like going home and stewing in his study. Better yet, he felt like dragging Beatrice home with him, making love to her and then stewing in his study.

When they returned to the party, the guests were going to the dining room. Charles and Jack followed, and Charles tried to locate Beatrice. He relaxed when he saw she would be seated directly across from him, but his satisfaction quickly died. To Beatrice's left sat Randolph Asher, his head already bent toward hers in conversation. Jack, grinning wickedly, was seated to her right. Charles wondered if his mother was trying to punish him.

He, unfortunately, was flanked by the Pendleton sisters: Priscilla and Lavinia respectively. Singly, their simpering was hard to take, but combined, they embodied everything he hated about London society. Charles had to strain to hear what was being said on the other side of the table, so constant and grating was their chatter. At one point, he got so frustrated that he nearly turned to Lavinia and asked her to shut up and eat her blasted soup. However, he still would have found it difficult to hear the conversation across the table; both Jack and Asher were vying for Beatrice's attention, and they were hardly interested in inviting others into the conversation.

Charles let out a grateful sigh when the dinner finally ended, but his thanks were fleeting. After cigars and port, the men rejoined the ladies in the drawing room. No one would leave for Lady Parberry's ball until nearly ten o'clock, so that meant that he would have to suffer through almost another hour of socializing.

After five minutes, he wanted to strangle his sister. Charles tried to approach Beatrice several times, but every time he got near, Lucy would drag her away, or worse, invite Asher or Jack or some other wastrel to join in their conversation. Charles hadn't spoken to her the entire night, beyond his curt greeting, but he wasn't about to make a fool of himself trying to get her attention. Determined, he decided to hide out in the study until the guests began to filter out, heading to Lady Parberry's.

He entered his retreat, poured himself a hefty glass of brandy and took a seat, trying to relax. But the noise from the party trickled in, making relaxation impossible. Whenever he heard Beatrice's musical laugh, his body tensed, and he immediately began to wonder what she was laughing at, or whom she was laughing with.

It was too much. Charles had learned long ago that a little bit of cold air went a long way to cool his emotions. He picked up his drink and slipped out onto the terrace. He wouldn't be able to hear the party from there, and as the evening was quite chilly, he expected he'd be perfectly alone.

Chapter Eleven

The half-moon cast a pale glow on the stone terrace. A low wall enclosed the terrace on all sides, except for the short flight of steps that led down into the shadowy garden. Charles didn't venture out very far, where he might be visible from the windows of the house. Instead, he leaned against the back wall, where he could remain undetected.

He didn't know the last time he'd felt so confused or, oddly enough, alone. He didn't even know *why* he felt this way. He'd always been able to separate the women in his life into two neat categories: those in his family, whom he loved and would protect with his very life, and those he bedded, whom he desired, seduced and left. But Beatrice didn't fit into these categories. He wanted her so badly that he could hardly look at her without becoming aroused, and yet he enjoyed her company like that of an old friend. It was a novel concept, really, and worst of all, Charles couldn't discuss his feelings with anyone. They were too private.

His thoughts were interrupted by the creak of one of the terrace doors opening, momentarily spilling a path of light across the flagstones. Charles pressed himself closer against the house, hoping that whoever it was would decide it was too chilly and return inside. He didn't feel like exchanging pleasantries with anyone.

Several soft, hesitant footsteps echoed across the stone floor, and he craned his head to look.

His breath caught in his throat.

It was Beatrice, almost ethereal in the moonlight. She had her back to him, and looked neither to the left nor right as she walked to the terrace wall. There, she paused, putting her hands on the balustrade and leaning forward slightly to peer into the garden. It was too dark for her to see anything, really, and she straightened, reaching her arms behind her head to stretch. She sighed quietly and lowered her arms, rubbing them to ward off the night's chill.

Charles didn't know what she was doing out here, and he refused even to hope that she had come seeking him. He immediately decided that unless she turned around and saw him, he wasn't going to reveal himself. He didn't think he'd be able to control himself if he were forced into conversation with her; his emotions were running that high.

But she did turn around.

For a moment, Beatrice still didn't notice him. She took a seat on the wall, her eyes not really focusing on anything in particular. Apparently, she was just as deep in thought as Charles had been. He took a step forward, helpless against the urge to close the gap between them. He moved quietly, but the dull sound of his shoe hitting the hard stone floor was audible nonetheless. She looked up.

Their gazes met, and for several breathless seconds they just stared, drinking in their fill. Without taking his eyes from hers, Charles stealthily began to move toward her.

That brought Beatrice out of her spell. She rose immediately. "Lord Summerson—"

"Charles," he reminded her, still moving forward.

"Charles, please, don't come any closer. If I should be discovered with you—"

He just kept approaching, and he didn't stop until he was mere inches away from her. She had backed up as far as possible. Her calves pressed into the stone wall behind her, and she held her hands up, as if to keep him at bay. But then something happened.

As if in a trance, Charles reached out to cup her face, his eyes still on hers. Then, with a gentleness that he wouldn't have thought himself capable of, so hot and pulsing was the blood in his veins, he gently slid one hand behind her head and through her hair, to caress the back of her neck. With his other hand, he traced a path to her mouth, and with the slightest pressure, brought her forward to meet his lips.

Beatrice's protest died. Her hands, so ready to push him away, suddenly reached for the lapels of his coat, pulling him closer. She didn't know what she wanted, exactly, but she knew that she urgently desired to have his body pressed up against hers, that she wanted to feel every hard inch of him surround her. And when their lips met, it sent a thousand electric sparks coursing through her body.

It was hardly a kiss at first, at least not like one in Charles's realm of experience—as soft and hesitant as butterfly wings, but hot and sweet like nothing he knew. Her lips were closed, in inexperience, but her eyelids dropped in innate response. She leaned into him, and the feel of her smooth body, the subtle scent of her hair…

Charles groaned, desperate to kiss her more fully. He brushed a fingertip against the corner of her mouth and whispered gruffly, "Open your mouth, Beatrice."

Instead, her eyes flew open, her soft gaze slowly focusing on his face. For a minute, she'd lost track of everything: time, place… She began pressing her hands against his chest, pushing him away. "Please, Charles—someone will see us."

He didn't step away. Instead, before Beatrice had an opportunity to protest, he picked her up in his arms and started carrying her toward the steps to the garden.

"Charles, put me down," she said, trying to sound firm but knowing that her voice quivered slightly.

He shook his head and put his mouth right against her ear to whisper, "No. You're perfectly right—someone would see us."

Beatrice shivered, the gentle touch of his lips on her ear sending jolts of pleasure down her body. She had no time to comment on his logic before they were down the short flight of steps. He didn't stop right away, but carried her several feet into the garden, where they would be enveloped in shadow. When he reached a large oak tree, Charles slowly eased her to the ground, letting her slide down the length of his body. He kept his hands on her shoulders, sensing that if given the chance, she would run.

"Charles, I will scream if you don't let go of me." Her voice trembled even as she said this. She wasn't scared of him—she knew that if she insisted, he would release her. No, the frightening part was that she didn't *have* the will to resist. Deep inside of her, a niggling voice told her that if she left now, she'd regret it forever. She wanted to feel him pressed up hard against her body once more. She needed to feel his warm mouth on hers.

Charles put his fingertip to her lips. "Don't. I just want to taste you."

Beatrice blinked. She'd never heard words like that before. Truth was she'd never been kissed before that night; the few chaste pecks she'd received in the past hardly qualified after what she'd just experienced. She wasn't quite sure that she even knew what he meant by "tasting" her, but the possibilities thrilled her, sending her stomach dancing and setting her skin afire.

Beatrice knew she should run for her life. She knew that as much as she might regret it if he didn't kiss her again, she'd also regret it if he did. The memory of tonight would be permanently seared into her brain, and she would compare every kiss that she received from there on out to Charles's.

But instead of running, she just waited for what would come next.

Charles wanted to shout in satisfaction when he saw her acquiescence, revealed to him only by the slight parting of her lips and the darkening of her eyes. He'd been afraid she would bolt, and he knew that if he didn't thoroughly kiss her in the next minute he'd explode. He hadn't expected her to be so inexperienced, though. To judge by the way she kissed him, he guessed she'd never been kissed properly before. That possibility, for reasons that he didn't care to explore, satisfied him like nothing else could have. His body responded, as well, straining painfully against the confines of his breeches.

Charles bent his head again, slowly this time, giving her every opportunity to change her mind, and relishing the fact that she didn't. He caressed her cheek with the pad of his thumb, watching for any sign of uncertainty on her part. Beatrice didn't flinch, and he pressed his lips to hers once more.

This time, the kiss was different: still gentle, but now more urgent. Charles licked her lower lip in a silent entreaty for her to open her mouth. When she didn't understand, he leaned in closer to suck her lip and nip it slightly; when she gasped in surprise, he took advantage to claim her fully.

Her gasp turned to a moan as his tongue met hers, circling, teasing, driving her wild. Beyond rational thought, she reached for his head, running her fingers through his hair and bringing him closer. Beatrice wanted something, she just didn't know what….

Her moan seemed to incite something inside Charles. His kiss intensified, and with a groan, he lifted her into his arms once more. This time, however, he wrapped her legs around his hips, hiking up her skirts slightly as he did so to accommodate him fully. He took several steps forward, then pressed her back against the large tree, his frantic lips never leaving hers.

Beatrice had stopped thinking. All she could do was feel: the heady, foreign sensation of his hardness pressed against the most intimate part of her body; the shock waves made by his mouth as he trailed hot kisses down her chin and along her throat. His mouth stopped at her demure neckline, just above the gentle

swell of her breasts. Then, with Beatrice nearly melting in pleasure, he tugged at the fabric with his teeth until one of her breasts
was bared. She gasped at the shock of seeing her nipple, em-
barrassingly alert, only inches from his mouth. She tried to pull
back, but Charles leaned forward swiftly, his mouth closing over
her, his tongue spiraling over the taut peak of her breast.

She forgot to pull away. Her body literally exploded—at least
that was what it felt like—as he sucked and teased, the gentle
abrasion of his tongue affecting her in her deepest core. Pleasure came over her like a wave, beyond her comprehension.

Charles heard someone calling his name, but the danger only
vaguely registered at first. Ever since he'd first seen Beatrice, he'd
thought about kissing her mouth, her neck; he'd thought about
the pink crests of her breasts begging him to kiss them, as well.
Now that he had her in his arms, her pleasure so natural and intense, he wasn't about to stop. He thought he'd die if he stopped.

"Charles?" The voice came again. "Are you out here? Your
mother sent me looking for you." It was Jack, calling from the
terrace.

Charles groaned against Beatrice's breast before tearing himself away and lowering her to the ground. "Damn," he muttered.
"Beatrice?"

"Hmm?" She was still absorbed in her newly awakened feelings, and he cursed again, seeing her heavily lidded eyes and
swollen lower lip.

"Beatrice—we have to stop. Jack is coming."

Awareness came back to Beatrice like a bucket of cold water
dumped on her head. With a horrified cry, she dashed behind a
nearby rhododendron, just before Jack came down the steps and
around the corner.

He looked at the rustling shrub with amusement. "I say,
Summerson, what are you doing out here? Your mother is rav-
ing in there about ungrateful sons—quietly, mind you. The guests
are heading off to Lady Parberry's. Are you coming along?"

"I just stepped out for some air, Jack. Tell her I'll come in a moment."

His friend nodded and was about to leave, but his internal devil got the better of him. "By the way, have you seen Miss Sinclair? Your mother said that she…stepped out for some fresh air, as well."

Charles made no response.

"I see," Jack drawled. "Well, if you happen to chance upon her, you might inform her that your mother is looking for her." And with a knowing grin and a wink, he headed back to the house, taking the steps two at a time.

Charles cursed. Beatrice groaned unhappily from the bushes.

He moved over to help her out. "Terrible timing, wasn't it?" he asked as he held out his hand to her. "Jack is never one to be subtle."

Beatrice just glared. She ignored his hand and rose on her own.

Charles put his hand on her arm, and his voice dropped to a whisper. "We can continue this later, you know. We can leave the ball early. We don't even have to go at all…."

Beatrice didn't answer. Her fury so overwhelmed her she couldn't utter a word. She slapped him across the face with all her might, picked up her skirts and dashed through the garden without a backward glance.

Charles stood for a moment, watching her go. He gently touched his face where her palm had connected, before turning around and heading back to the house.

Back in the safety of her aunt's house, Beatrice paced her bedroom floor. Louisa had long since retired, although Beatrice had seen her briefly when she'd first returned to the house, breathless and disheveled. Louisa had been shocked by her appearance, but her shock had been quickly replaced by extreme annoyance when Beatrice informed her that she was not going to Lady Parberry's. Louisa, too irritated to argue shot her a fulminating glare, harrumphed loudly and stalked off to bed, muttering all the way.

Beatrice paused to look in her dressing mirror as she paced passed it. Her hair tumbled over her shoulders in disarray, and her gown was slightly torn at the neckline. Worst of all, a small piece of bark had rent her gown, and remained lodged in the fabric at her shoulder. Thankfully, she hadn't run into anyone as she left the party, for there would have been no doubt in their minds as to what she had been doing.

Of course, she mused as she resumed her pacing, there had been little chance of running into anyone as she left the party, seeing as she hadn't gone through the house. No, she'd exited directly through the garden, hiking up her skirts to scale the high stone wall that separated the Summersons' house from Louisa's. It was actually during this process that the majority of the damage to her gown and hair had occurred.

Beatrice plopped down on her bed, lying dejectedly on her stomach. She hoped that Lady Summerson and Lucy, not to mention all of their guests, weren't too suspicious of her whereabouts, and she felt bad for vanishing without a proper goodbye. Once she'd arrived home she'd sent Humphries to inform Lady Summerson that she had suddenly fallen ill and would not be going to Lady Parberry's ball. Even if she *had* felt like taking the time to repair her appearance, she wouldn't have been able to do a thing about her mess of nerves and emotions. Nothing would ever be the same after that evening. Charles's kiss had churned up all sorts of feelings she had never before experienced, and now…

In addition to being upset and confused, she was furious. How dare he toy with her? Perhaps Charles didn't understand her desire to marry, not being plagued with such an inclination himself, but she couldn't help but ask herself what she was supposed to do now. Just when she was beginning to accept that love wasn't really about racing heartbeats and passion, but rather about two sensible people forming a life together, *this* had to happen. Charles had aroused feelings in her that she'd never even known existed; now she would never forget them. How could she settle for someone like Randolph Asher after knowing what it was like to be held in Charles's arms?

Suddenly, a horrible feeling spread over her. It was one thing for her to worry that she might not be able to settle for Asher, but another entirely for her to consider that *he* might no longer want her. Judging from Jack's words, her disappearance into the garden had aroused at least a few people's suspicions. After all these seasons, she wasn't naïve; girls were ruined for less.

Beatrice groaned and buried her head in her pillow. There was little she could do about it now. Tomorrow was a new day, and by the end of it—with luck—she'd be happily home in Hampshire. She definitely couldn't stay in London after what she'd just experienced.

She wondered if Charles had gone to the ball.

Probably not. She could only hope that he was sitting at home as angry as she was, although she was probably just one in a long line of females who had found reason to slap his arrogant face.

Her fury unabated, Beatrice lifted her head from her pillow and scowled. What she wouldn't give to tell him what she thought of him. Now that she wasn't standing right in front of him anymore, a hundred insults came readily to her mind. If only she hadn't been so tongue-tied with anger and shame, she would have told him in situ. Now, since she had already pretty much determined to leave London in the morning, she'd all but lost her chance.

Or had she?

In an instant an idea occurred to her, both so tempting and foolhardy that, hothead that she was, she jumped on it immediately. Why not go speak her piece? This would be her only chance, after which she'd probably never see him again. Since she was leaving in the morning, what did she have to lose? She knew Charles lived in Belgrave Square, and she was certain that she could find the exact street number in Louisa's address book.

Before giving herself a chance to talk herself out of this lunacy, Beatrice jumped from her bed, ready to act. She hadn't removed her gown yet, so she merely had to slip on her shoes and coat.

Stealthily, she padded downstairs and headed to the study, where Louisa kept her address book. Beatrice skimmed ahead in it to "Summerson, C." and was quickly on her way.

She was accustomed to walking great distances by herself in the country, but in London it wasn't done for a lady of quality to walk alone, not to mention in the wee hours of the morning. A tiny voice in her head reminded her that it wasn't proper for ladies to pay unchaperoned visits to a bachelor's residence at *any* time.

Beatrice walked briskly, her steps fueled by anger. As she rounded Park Lane, she began mentally rehearsing what she would say to him. She would keep it short and to the point; lingering on his doorstep or, God forbid, entering his house, would only bring disaster. No, she would pound on his door, demand to see him and state her business. Then, before he knew what had hit him, she'd leave.

He'll probably laugh, she told herself derisively. Great guffaws at my expense. Who could blame him, with her standing there on his doorstep, scolding him like a harpy, and then dashing off for dear life?

Beatrice stopped dead in her tracks. She couldn't do this. The more she thought about it, the more she realized how completely idiotic her scheme was. She'd look foolish. Charles would laugh at her...or even worse, he'd continue where he'd left off earlier in the evening *after* laughing at her.

She took a deep breath, feeling reason enter her body. Shaking her head, she turned to go back home; she might not have accomplished her goal, but the walk had cleared her head. She'd be better off putting Charles Summerson—and thoughts of revenge—well behind her.

Consoling herself with the idea that one day she would probably be able to laugh about her impulsive reaction, Beatrice began to walk home.

She had taken only a few steps when she noticed a flicker of movement in the shadows behind a nearby hedge. She paused, waiting to see if it would come again. Nothing happened, and she took another step forward. But the second her foot hit the ground, the motion came again, this time more noticeably. Her breath caught in her throat in fear, and she stood completely still as the lumbering shape of a man emerged in front of her.

Chapter Twelve

Charles didn't know when he'd become such a complete ass. What had he been thinking? Even as he asked himself this question, he answered himself: he hadn't been thinking. He'd merely seen her there, looking so beautiful, and he'd known that he had to at least kiss her. The whole thing had been quite beyond his control.

He cursed himself for a fool yet again that evening, and lay back on his chaise longue, trying to relax. The ridiculous piece of furniture was part of the new decor, and he was too damn tall for it, so he cursed his decorator, too.

Charles lay uncomfortably for another moment, knees bent, staring at the ceiling and drumming his fingers. Finally giving up, he rose. Every muscle in his body was tense, and he realized that it would be impossible for him to relax that evening. He began pacing the study floor.

He hadn't gone to Lady Parberry's with the rest of his mother's guests knowing that Beatrice wouldn't be there. Instead, he'd ignored his mother's disapproving glare and headed home. She knew, or at least suspected, what had been going on in the garden, and he was sure to hear about it the next day.

Silently, he vowed that he'd get up for an early ride the next morning, followed by a trip to Gentleman Jackson's. That much activity and physical abuse should clear his head. If not, he was doomed. But for the time being…

Charles decided that he needed to take action sooner. He had to get out, and he didn't care where he went. He needed a strong drink and perhaps a good fight; nothing would be better for his condition than a barroom brawl. He threw on his coat and left. He didn't even bother calling for his coach. There were hacks often enough around Belgrave Square, even at this late hour, and he'd be sure to find one willing to convey him to a rougher side of town.

However, Charles had no success finding a hack that evening. With a frustrated curse, he began to walk. It was then that he saw her.

He'd only gone one block from his house when Beatrice Sinclair, striding purposefully in his direction, rounded the corner. Without thinking, he quickly stepped behind the elegant stone gatepost of one of the mansions nearby.

He waited and watched, wondering where she was going. Although she appeared to have been headed straight for him, that was unlikely to have been her intention. After what had just passed between them, Beatrice would have to be a fool to follow him to his house, and that was one thing that he was sure she was not. He couldn't imagine where she would be going at this time of night by herself, however. *Reckless chit,* he thought. When he revealed himself, he'd see that she was sent home posthaste.

While he watched, she suddenly stopped. After a moment, she turned around as if to head back in the opposite direction. Charles stepped out from behind the gatepost, determined to catch up to her and at least walk her back to her house. She'd protest, he was sure, but it was unsafe for her to be walking alone.

But before he could take a step forward, Beatrice paused once more. Her back was to him, but he could see that her head was turned slightly to the right, facing the shadows surrounding a large mansion. Charles could sense the tension in her.

A large, shabbily dressed man stepped menacingly out from behind a hedge, not ten feet from her. Charles's blood chilled as Beatrice took a step back in fear.

It demanded every ounce of control that he possessed to keep from charging down the street and lunging at the man, but he suppressed that impulse. In the time it would take to reach her, the man could inflict any sort of harm. Instead, Charles stepped quietly back into the shadows, hoping she wouldn't do anything rash.

From his hiding place, he listened closely, waiting for his opportunity. He was positioned about thirty feet behind Beatrice, but the man's slurred speech carried in the silent night air. "Well, what 'ave we 'ere? Are ye lost?"

Charles watched as she stiffened in fear and shook her head, taking another step back. Her retreat brought her slightly closer to him, and he tensed in anticipation.

"Ye look lost to me, miss. I kin 'elp ye find yer way fer a small fee." The man stepped closer, and Charles could see the lecherous gleam in his eyes.

Beatrice took another step back. "I'm not lost, sir, and I have nothing on me."

The man chuckled menacingly. "Beg to differ, m'lady. Ye 'ave plenty to offer." With these words, he lunged, grabbing her by the arms and pulling her close. She cried out briefly before the man snaked out his hand to muffle her. Beatrice responded by kicking him in the shins, and in the ensuing struggle she was knocked to the ground. Charles rushed out from his hiding place, throwing the man off balance and tackling him.

As the man sprawled on the pavement, groaning, Charles knelt down beside Beatrice, scanning her face for any sign of injury. He said nothing, but she nodded her head to assure him that she was all right; she felt shaky and frightened, but she knew that her fate could have been far worse. Charles put a hand on her shoulder and nodded back. He rose, but not before shooting her a look that promised dire retribution if she dared move. For once, she didn't argue.

Charles turned his attention back to the man. As he leaned over him, the fellow began to scuttle away, but Charles pulled him up by the front of his shirt.

Once they were at eye level, the man began blubbering. "I didn't mean no harm…I was just gonna lift 'er purse…."

Charles looked at him in disgust, sent a solid punch to his jaw and let the man fall back down to the ground in an unconscious heap. Then, with no further ado, Charles turned around, scooped up a stunned Beatrice into his arms and began walking down the street toward his house.

She was too surprised to say anything for a moment. When she got her voice back, she was every bit as angry as she had been earlier. "Put me down, Summerson!" she whispered furiously.

Charles ignored her and kept walking. She struggled, but he just squeezed her tighter.

"Charles," she said through clenched teeth, "put me down. Please."

He paused. "Promise not to dash off?"

Beatrice thought for a moment. Dashing off had been precisely her intention, but she knew that he wouldn't set her down unless she promised, and she wasn't one to break her word. "All right," she grudgingly acquiesced. "I won't. But will you tell me where you're taking me? I have to go home."

He lowered her to the ground slowly. "You can go home, but you can't walk there. I live just three houses away, and my coachman can take you back."

Beatrice stood up straight and winced as pain shot up her leg.

"What is it?" he asked with concern.

She grimaced. "My ankle."

"Think you can walk on it?"

"I think so," Beatrice fibbed. Her ankle throbbed in pain, but she'd be damned if she'd allow Charles to carry her along Belgrave Square. "Are you just going to leave him there?"

He looked back at the footpath. "Yes. I have to get you home, and he'll be out for a while. Once he comes to, he won't remain in the neighborhood." Charles began leading Beatrice down the street. Or he tried to, at least. She didn't budge.

He turned around, giving her a fulminating glare. "Is there a problem, Beatrice?"

There was a problem—a very big problem, as a matter of fact. She did not want to go to his house, never mind the fact that she'd originally intended to do just that. Now that her head had cleared and her temper had cooled, she hated to admit her foolishness, even to herself. She didn't care if Charles had saved her hide or if he was only trying to be helpful. She still didn't trust him and, quite frankly, she didn't trust herself around him, either. She'd already made enough of a mess of her life that evening.

However, there was no way that she would admit to him her reasons for being out so late. "There's no problem, no…. I was just wondering if perhaps we could look for a hack instead."

"I hate to inform you, Beatrice, but you're not going to find one this evening. Besides, my house is not even a block away."

Assuming that she had seen reason, Charles turned and tried to walk away once more. Still she didn't move.

When he turned around this time, he'd finally lost his patience. "What is the matter now?" he asked tightly.

"I…I would rather walk home."

Charles looked at her for one moment before flatly stating, "No."

She opened her mouth to protest once more, but wasn't given the chance. Before a single word passed her lips, Charles surprised her with a lecture. "What the hell do you think you were doing out here alone? Have you completely lost your wits?"

Beatrice blinked in surprise. She'd known that he was annoyed, but she had no idea why he would be so angry. Probably because her presence had interrupted his undoubtedly debauched plans for the rest of the evening. "My wits?"

"Yes. Your wits. Your common sense. Has it totally abandoned you? What *were* you doing?"

Beatrice couldn't admit the real reason, so she stubbornly raised her chin a notch. "I couldn't sleep."

Charles stared at her in disbelief and ran his hand through his hair with frustration. Then, having had no luck in getting her to walk on her own, he picked her up once more, this time tossing her unceremoniously over his shoulder.

"Let me down!"

"I'd be quiet if I were you, Beatrice. I see Lord Hastings coming down the street. You wouldn't want him to know who you were, would you?"

Beatrice bit her tongue and buried her face in her coat. She'd met Lord Hastings on several occasions, and he was certain to recognize her. She didn't know why it mattered, though—surely the sight of Charles walking along Belgrave Square with a woman over his shoulder was scandalous enough on its own. Hastings would probably demand to know what was going on.

Or maybe not. As they approached the man, Charles stopped. Beatrice felt him nod in greeting as if nothing were amiss. "Good evening, Hastings."

"Evening, Summerson. I say, lad, what's that you're carrying? Or should I say who?" Hastings began chortling at his own wit. Beatrice was disgusted.

Charles chuckled along, and she vowed that he would pay. "My mistress…I'm afraid she's quite drunk. Can't walk."

"Foxed, is she? That's naught to be afraid of at all, my boy. I'd say it's quite fortuitous," Lord Hastings responded, chortling once more.

"So it is, Hastings. You'll understand, then, if I bid you good-night."

"Ho, ho, indeed. I don't blame you…it's what I'd be doing myself if I were your age."

Beatrice felt Charles nod once more, and they continued down the street. After about twenty paces they turned and began the short ascent up the steps to his house.

She craned her head, trying to make out any details of his home, but next she knew they were in the dark and silent foyer. He closed the door behind them, and then carefully lowered her to the floor.

"Easy now—you don't want to make that ankle any worse," he said quietly.

Beatrice nodded, and promptly kicked him with her good foot.

She immediately regretted her action. Charles winced slightly, but that was all. Instead, he took a step closer, his eyes narrowing.

Unnerved by his predatory gaze, she stepped back, moving closer to the door.

Charles let his gaze wander deliberately over her body. "No need trying to escape, sweetheart. I'm not going to hurt you. Why would I do that when there are far more pleasurable things I could do to you instead?"

She gulped, her skin burning and her stomach dropping to her toes. She had to get out of here. In a small voice, she said, "I'm sorry I kicked you. Can I go home now?"

Charles made no move to comply. "Not so fast," he said, brushing a loose strand of hair away from her eyes. "You still haven't told me why you were out walking so late."

"I don't know…I was restless. I didn't realize how far I had strayed."

Charles's green eyes practically burned as they looked into hers. "I'm not sure that I believe you. But I'm glad I found you."

He knew. Beatrice was sure of it. She could see it in his eyes, in the way they smoldered, as if he could read her thoughts. He knew that she had been out, maybe not looking for him, but because of him. He knew that their earlier meeting had disturbed her, and that even now she was thinking about the feel of his lips against hers.

He took another step closer, leaving a mere inch of space between them. His eyes still burned, but with the heat of passion now, not anger. She swallowed when he said, "It would be so easy, you know, for you to stay."

Beatrice shook her head, unable to take her eyes off him. She wanted to stay. She wanted to know what the feelings deep inside her meant, and sensed that Charles was the only one who could show her. He was the only one who'd ever made her feel this way, and a small, shocked part of her could admit that curiosity as much as anger had brought her to his house this night.

But she knew that she had to leave—or she'd be caught in his web. "I can't."

Something—some kind of desperate need—passed across his face. "But you want to."

"No."

"Stay." Charles had never pleaded with a woman before, but now he was unable to do anything but. Just a few hours ago, his body had been rampant with desire, and now that he had her, he didn't want to let her go. He trailed his hand down her face, using just his knuckles to feel the smoothness of her skin. He leaned his head in close, drawn to her lips as if by a magnetic force. And when their lips connected…

Charles moaned, giving in to his desire and kissing her with a suddenness and a strength that he was powerless to control. He moved closer, pressing Beatrice back to the door, running his hands through her hair and spilling hairpins onto the floor.

For a moment, she allowed herself to revel in his kiss, her eyelids fluttering shut as she groaned in pleasure, in frustration, in need. His tongue circled, teased and thrust, and her body sang in response. She wanted Charles Summerson without knowing exactly what she wanted from him; all she knew was that she wanted to touch him, to run her hands along his hard chest and through his hair. And she knew that she wanted him to touch her in return, to relieve the throbbing deep within her.

That was why pushing him away was the hardest thing she had ever done. "I can't," she whispered raggedly, hating the words as she uttered them, but knowing they must be said. She couldn't sacrifice herself for one night of pleasure, and that was exactly what she would be doing. There was nothing she'd like more than to lose herself completely in the moment of passion, but Beatrice knew that it wouldn't *really* be just a moment. If she were to make love to Charles, her whole life would change forever. His life, however, wouldn't change one wit, and Beatrice clutched that fact for dear life.

"I...I have to go."

He shook his head slowly, his eyes still dark, his hands still deeply entwined in her hair. "Why do you stammer?"

Because you make me lose control. "I'm just tired, Charles. Please let me go."

He didn't release her right away, but he knew she was right. Making love to Beatrice was the greatest temptation he'd ever faced, but he had to deny it. He wasn't going to marry her, but he respected her, he liked her, and he couldn't ruin her chances to find happiness. She just wouldn't find it with him.

Charles released her suddenly and took a step back, needing the distance, but hating the rush of cold air where her warm body had been. He put his hands in his coat pockets so he wouldn't be tempted to reach for her again. "All right, then," he said, forcing a coolness into his voice that he didn't feel.

Beatrice stood for a moment, not quite sure what to do. Getting what she asked for so easily only made her realize how much she didn't really want it.

"Aren't you going to leave?" he asked, his tone intentionally clipped and polite. For his own sanity, he needed her to go, and he didn't care if he hurt her.

She colored. "I should," she said, turning to do so, without meeting his gaze.

Charles put his hand on the door to stop her. "Wait. You can't walk home, Beatrice. Have a seat," he said, motioning to a mahogany chair. "I'll have my coach sent round."

She nodded and sat as he left. She felt deeply uncomfortable, sitting there so nervously in his masculine hall. The chair had no arms, and she folded and unfolded her hands in her lap. She listened attentively for his return.

Charles never came back. Instead, after about ten minutes, the front door opened and a sleepy, surly coachman peered in. "Coach is out front when you're ready, miss." He left as suddenly as he appeared.

Beatrice looked around the hall, wondering if she should wait for Charles. But after a moment she knew that he wasn't coming back.

She should have been glad. Instead, she wanted to cry. She felt as if she'd just been dismissed. She rose stiffly, hoping bitterly that she'd never have to see him again.

It was still dark outside, although the first traces of dawn were beginning to streak the horizon. As Beatrice closed Charles's door behind her, the sound of whistling drew her attention several houses up the street. Jack Davenport was standing in front of a large house, his head bent as he fumbled for something in his waistcoat pocket. She watched him dumbly for a moment, realizing that it must be his house, and that he was looking for his key. Her feet felt as if they were made out of lead, and she couldn't move.

Jack lifted his head, and his whistling died on his lips when he noticed her standing there on Charles's steps.

Her feet suddenly worked—better, in fact, than they ever had in her life. Ignoring the carriage completely, oblivious to the pain in her ankle, Beatrice dashed off into the darkness, heading for home.

Jack's laughter echoed in her head the entire way to Park Lane.

Chapter Thirteen

Beatrice didn't stick around to see if any scandal erupted. Early the next morning, she informed her aunt that she was leaving. Louisa was outraged, but Beatrice put her foot down, citing exhaustion, frustration and the strong desire to grow old quietly and alone in Hampshire, keeping her father company and, perhaps, helping him breed foxhounds. By noon, she was in her carriage, swiftly heading south.

She sighed as she watched the scenery pass outside the window. She'd been sitting in her carriage for several hours now. As the city receded farther, the landscape grew friendlier and more familiar. The sky was bluer, the grass more green….

Unfortunately, her mood only seemed to worsen the more time she had to stew. She couldn't remember having felt so furious before. Charles Summerson, for purely selfish motives, had probably sabotaged her reputation and ruined her chances of ever marrying…at least if word of last night ever got out. If the fact that they had vanished into his mother's garden together didn't raise enough eyebrows, there was a very strong chance that her idiotic visit to his house would surface. Lord Hastings hadn't recognized her, but Jack Davenport certainly had. Jack was Charles's best friend, but that didn't mean he wouldn't tell tales.

After all, it wasn't as if Charles's reputation would suffer. Quite the contrary—that sort of scandal tended to improve a man's reputation. Beatrice would simply be perceived as another notch in his bedpost.

Over and over in her head she could hear him say, "But you want to." *But you want to.* She *wanted* to scream. She *wanted* to hit him for his selfishness. Oh, Beatrice knew it could have been worse. He could have taken her virginity…hell, she'd been ready and willing to give it to him.

She took a deep breath and tried to relax. Much as she'd like to scream, she couldn't do so without worrying her driver, and hitting Charles, for the purely logistical reason that he was back in London, was out of the question. With no other outlet, she turned to her journal.

She reread everything that she had written over the past month and began crossing out entire pages with a vengeance. *Sentimental drivel.* She vowed at that moment not to look at it again. Her journal hadn't been one whit of help, anyway. In fact, she had gotten into even more romantic trouble this season than ever before. Beatrice shoved it, without a second thought, into the reticule on the seat beside her. Satisfied, she closed her eyes and let the swaying motion of the carriage lull her to sleep.

She arrived three hours later, the familiar jostling of the carriage as it turned up their long drive waking her from her nap. She eagerly sat up, her eyes drinking in every detail of her home as she passed: the winding stream, the apple orchards, the gentle rolling hills on the horizon behind the house…. She sighed deeply, thinking that there never was a more beautiful place to live. Growing up, Sudley had been the perfect fuel for her imagination: she had seen dryads in the trees, fairies in the forest at night and a troll under the bridge over the stream.

She took a steadying breath as the carriage pulled to a stop in front of the house. As she stepped from the conveyance, she expected Eleanor and Helen to come barreling out of the house for a hug. Within minutes, if she were lucky, her father's precious foxhounds would be swarming around her, barking and begging for food, with her father not far behind.

Of course, this time no one would be expecting her, and she dreaded the questions that her family would inevitably ask.

As Beatrice began to walk toward the house, a small, beaming face appeared in an upstairs window as if on cue.

"Hallo, Beazie!" thirteen-year-old Helen shouted down. "I thought you weren't coming back until you were married. Where's your husband?"

Beatrice grinned back and waved at her younger sister. "A wicked witch turned him into a frog, Helen. He awaits only your kiss." Beatrice had missed her youngest sister dreadfully while in London. Very soon, however, she knew that she would have had her fill of her impish sibling; in fact, if she did end up living at home indefinitely, she would be spending at least another five years with Helen.

That is, Beatrice thought to herself with a rueful grimace, if Helen didn't run off with a band of gypsies. One could never discount such events with her.

"Pity," Helen said with a grin. "Father won't let me do any kissing." Beatrice was quite tempted to inquire why their father would have constituted such a rule, but thought better than to ask.

Eleanor rounded the corner of the house just then, her nose buried in a book. When she finally looked up and noticed Beatrice, her eyes grew wide. "Bea! What are you doing here? I thought you'd be in town for another month at least."

Beatrice shrugged, smiling at her. "That's not the greeting I expected, Ellie…but to answer your question, I decided to leave early. Nothing was much different from my past seasons, and Louisa was beginning to get quite demanding."

Eleanor nodded sympathetically, her own two weeks in town with Louisa having taken their toll. Her sympathy quickly faded, however, and her eyes glowed with devilish humor. "That's all? There must have been more to it than that, for you to return home without prior notice. Do tell, Bea—was a delicious scandal involved?"

Helen craned her head as far out the window as possible without falling.

Beatrice would have blushed about this subject with anyone but her sisters. "No scandal at all, you ninnies. Helen, get back inside this instant. I need to have a word with Father."

Eleanor looked at her sharply. "You all right, Bea? Father's in quite a mood."

She nodded. "I'm fine…I just wanted to tell him that I'm home."

Helen leaned out the window again. "He's going to kill you, Bea."

"And why is that?" she called back.

Helen grinned. "He's been so happy with you in London for another season, he was even beginning to talk about grandchildren. He'll be so disappointed."

"Ignore her," Eleanor said, shooting Helen a chastising look. She turned to Beatrice and said quietly, "Father's only annoyed because one of the hounds got loose this morning and terrorized Mrs. Jenkins's chickens."

Beatrice frowned. "I hope he got home unharmed."

"He did—Mrs. Jenkins tied a piece of twine around his neck and brought him back personally." Eleanor began to giggle. "Oh, I wish you'd arrived a few hours ago. It was so funny. She stormed the whole way here, and I've never seen anyone so angry before. Poor Father was more worried about the dog than he was about her or her chickens."

Beatrice smiled at her sister's story, relieved to be home. Her father's foxhounds terrorizing the town was about as exciting as it ever got at Sudley, and that was all the excitement she needed after her recent exploits. Romance and adventure were fine for some people, but Beatrice had had her fill. From here on out, it would be quiet living and solitude. Nary an impure thought of broad shoulders would sully her mind again.

Chapter Fourteen

After two weeks at Sudley, Beatrice was bored. After two months, her sisters had driven her completely mad and she was *very* bored. She didn't know if she could take any more. Much as she would have liked to think that she was capable of being sensible and living quietly, the effort of trying to do so proved quite taxing. The quieter her life became, the more rampant her imagination.

She hated to admit it, even to herself, but irritating as Charles Summerson was, she was miserable without him. He was interesting, exciting, and everyone else paled in comparison. Part of her—a tiny part she didn't like to acknowledge—wished that he had written, even though she didn't know what she would expect him to say. That he missed her, too? Hardly—they hadn't parted on the most pleasant of terms.

"Bea?" Eleanor asked from the doorway. "What do you think?"

Despondent, Beatrice craned her head around from her reclining position on the settee. Eleanor had just entered the morning room, her chestnut hair piled artfully atop her head and her blue eyes twinkling. She spun around in her new gown. "Well?"

Beatrice arched an eyebrow. "It's a bit much for a morning, isn't it, Ellie?"

Eleanor looked down at her gown, undismayed. "I know. How do you like it, though? I plan to wear it to dinner on Saturday."

Beatrice just groaned at the mention of Saturday. *Drat Louisa for her interference.* Beatrice had left town to avoid her meddling great-aunt, *among others.* Instead, Louisa had immediately followed her to Sudley, stating that she had the sudden urge to rusticate. Beatrice knew this for a lie; after two weeks, Louisa had grown bored with the countryside and decided that they ought to host a house party. No, Beatrice suspected that the real reason Louisa had followed her was because she wasn't done with her meddling—Beatrice remained unwed, didn't she?

And now she had not only to contend with her great-aunt, but with the rest of the ton, as well; the London season was ending, and society was looking for new diversions. Beatrice only hoped that she *personally* wouldn't be part of those diversions. Her name had miraculously survived its recent brush with scandal, but her ability to stumble into catastrophe was the one constant in her life.

She considered it quite a feat that Louisa had convinced her father to go along with her idea, although Louisa was *his* aunt, as well, and he was as intimidated by her as Beatrice was. Still, their family hadn't hosted a party since Beatrice's mother had died. Her father despised London society and rarely went to town. The last thing he'd want to do would be to invite town to come to him. But try as she might, Beatrice couldn't get him to change his mind.

She returned her attention to her sister. "I love it. You couldn't look lovelier. I'm still surprised, though, that Father is letting you participate. I wasn't allowed to do a single thing until I was fully eighteen."

"It's hardly as if he'd let me have a London season, Bea. He's only letting me come down for dinner, you know, even if I *will* be seventeen by the time of the party. And it's straight to bed after dinner is over. Plus, I told him I'd pitch a fit if I were cooped up with Helen all weekend."

"I'm sure the feeling is mutual, Ellie. Where is Helen, by the way? She promised to ride with Father and me but she never turned up."

"I saw her dash off with George Gregson after breakfast," Eleanor answered with dislike. "I'm sure they're planning all sorts of menace for the weekend…eels in the lemonade and that sort of thing. I wish they'd grow up." George Gregson was Helen's best friend and had been for as long as anyone could remember. He was the local vicar's son, but despite that fact he was also the very devil, and generated more than half of Helen's many scrapes.

Beatrice had a bit more tolerance for Helen's pranks than Eleanor did. "I'm rather looking forward to it. At least *that* should be interesting."

"Are you *at all* excited about this weekend, Bea? I know you're rather jaded from all your experience—"

Beatrice shot her sister an amused look. Eleanor ignored her and continued, "But it won't be that awful. For goodness' sake, you're almost as bad as Ben…lucky thing he'll be out of town or we'd all be miserable."

Beatrice nodded, wishing she could have left with her brother. He'd gone off to the East Indies, where he had some shipping interests, about two months earlier. She hoped he appreciated how lucky he was. If only she could get on a boat and leave whenever she felt like it.

She was actually dreading the weekend to come. In the first place, she had finally accepted spinsterhood as her true calling in life; a doting aunt, perhaps, but a mother she'd never be. She had told Louisa as much, which caused her to throw up her hands in despair. Her father's reaction, when she told him, was less dramatic. He'd merely nodded with resignation and looked to the sky above for assistance.

But Beatrice knew that attending another social event, even if she had no choice because it was at her house, was sure to bring the question of marriage to the forefront once more. Furthermore, Louisa was in charge of the guest list, and she had invited Randolph Asher. Beatrice, for good reason, worried that he would propose. He'd written after she quit London, expressing his concern over her hasty departure and his desire to see her again. Beatrice had written back, considering him a friend and not wanting to seem rude. But he'd written a few more times, as well, and after he had received the invitation to Sudley he'd written yet again, using stronger language than Beatrice would have liked.

Unfortunately, she didn't quite know what to do about the likelihood of him proposing. She had never exactly discouraged his suit, and after all this time, she felt almost obligated to accept. Randolph Asher was attractive, kind and everything, really, that she had been telling herself that she ought to look for in a man. Kissing him might not be like kissing *him,* but she supposed that was preferable in the long run.

"Hello? Bea?"

Beatrice looked at Eleanor, who was staring at her quizzically.

"Sorry, Ellie…did you say something?"

"I merely asked if you truly hadn't met anyone this season."

"I already told you that I didn't." She couldn't talk about Charles with anyone, even Eleanor…her memories were too private and she was still too vulnerable about him. Worst of all, she knew that Louisa had invited the Summersons to the party. Beatrice had wanted desperately to tell her not to invite Charles, but she couldn't have done so without arousing suspicion.

"I know, but you've been acting so bloody distracted recently that I didn't believe you. I'll get it out of you, Beatrice Sinclair. Perhaps you wrote about it in your diary—"

"Eleanor, if you so much as try to look at my diary—"

A tentative knock saved Beatrice from further questioning by Eleanor.

It was Meg, wringing her hands and looking perturbed. "Miss Beatrice, Lady Summerson is here to see you."

Beatrice sat bolt upright. "*Which* Lady Summerson?"

"Lady Lucy Summerson. Shall I tell her you're otherwise occupied?"

Beatrice thought for a moment, panicked. Sudley was located just on the outskirts of Portsmouth, a good sixty miles from London. One didn't just drop by unannounced…. What was Lucy up to?

"No, that's all right. I'll see her…. Tell her that I will be down in a moment."

Meg nodded and left quietly, closing the door behind her.

Eleanor cleared her throat. "Would you like to tell me what that was about?"

Beatrice tried to summon up an explanation but failed. "It's nothing, Ellie. Just someone I wasn't expecting to see…a friend from London. She must be visiting in the area…."

"Mind if I come with you?" Eleanor asked hopefully, knowing that her sister was lying.

"Yes," Beatrice responded decisively, as she rose and walked to the door. "But I shall inform you if anything of note occurs."

As she descended the stairs, Beatrice began rehearsing possible explanations for her sudden departure from town, but she could settle on nothing. When she reached the sitting room door she took a deep breath and resolved to be perfectly frank. She valued Lucy too much as a friend to be otherwise, and hoped she would understand.

Chapter Fifteen

Beatrice found Lucy in the sitting room, worrying the fabric of her dress and nervously sipping tea. When Beatrice entered, she rose from her chair with a start.

"Lucy!" Beatrice tried to sound lighthearted in her greeting. "How good to see you! I'm sorry I left London without saying goodbye—I've been feeling perfectly dreadful. It's just that something came up—"

"Oh, no!" Lucy interrupted, looking every bit as anxious, "please don't apologize, and don't worry about it anymore. I understand completely."

Beatrice paused. She wasn't sure what Lucy had meant by understanding completely. It *was* possible that Charles had mentioned something to his sister. She took a fortifying breath, figuring that she might as well find out. "You understand?" she asked as she sat down in a rosewood chair and motioned for Lucy to do the same.

Lucy perched in her matching chair uneasily and stammered, "Well, I think that I might…I mean, but perhaps it has something to do with my brother. Does it, Bea?"

Beatrice thought for a moment about how to proceed. She wanted to be frank, but she didn't need to be *too* frank. "Not entirely…I don't want you to misunderstand, Lucy. He was interested in…furthering our acquaintance, but nothing happened between us."

"Really?" Lucy asked hopefully.

Beatrice nodded, not wanting to blush, but doing so nonetheless. "He kissed me. That is all." That wasn't even close to all, but that was all she'd admit to. "At any rate, it doesn't matter now. I left London because I realized that there was no one I wanted to marry."

Lucy visibly relaxed. "I'm so glad to hear that he didn't do anything *too* improper. I've been feeling dreadfully guilty."

Beatrice just laughed. "You've nothing to feel guilty about. My brother is every bit the rake that yours is, but it's not my fault."

Lucy paled. "Bea, I have a confession to make."

"You do?" Beatrice couldn't imagine what it would be, but Lucy looked as if she were ready to expire on the spot.

"I might actually be more culpable than you think. After my mother met you, she liked you so much that she wanted to encourage Charles to meet you, too."

Beatrice blushed even deeper, but didn't quite know how to respond to this revelation. And as Lucy guiltily explained to her about how she and her mother had interfered, never once meeting her gaze, Beatrice felt quite numb.

"We did it with the best of intentions…we thought—we still think—that Charles is uncommonly interested in you. And as you needed to get married and he needed to get married…" Lucy trailed off, fidgeting her hands nervously in her lap.

"I see," Beatrice said, not seeing at all. "I guess the plan backfired, didn't it?"

If it were possible, Lucy paled even more. "I'm so sorry, Bea…. I guess we were guilty of wishful thinking, but we really should have just minded our own business. I only hope our interference didn't backfire *too* badly—then I should never forgive myself."

Beatrice forced a smile to her face, not feeling particularly cheerful, but wanting to reassure her friend nonetheless. She forgave Lucy—she shouldn't have meddled, but it wasn't her fault that her brother was such a cad. "Lucy, never think it. It would be impossible to stay angry with you. And rest assured, you haven't been part of my ruination…there *was* no ruination. Just a kiss."

"If you're sure…"

"I am sure. You're coming to our party, aren't you?"

Lucy nodded eagerly. "I'd hoped to, but I wasn't certain you'd want to see me. But now I definitely will." She paused, taking a sip of her tea. "I hope you don't mind my stopping by so suddenly."

Beatrice laughed out loud. "Not at all! I'm delighted, although surprised—"

"I don't blame you. I'm probably the last person you'd expect to see. One of my good friends lives in Hampshire, and I've been visiting her."

"Oh?" Beatrice asked with interest. "Perhaps I know her."

Lucy quickly searched her mind for a name, having invented that excuse on the spot. "Lydia Park. She lives in Winchester, actually, so I'd be surprised if you know her."

Beatrice shook her head. "I'm sorry…I don't know her. But I'm glad you paid me a visit, Lucy. I was thinking just this morning how dull things had become around here. In less than five minutes, you've made my life much more interesting."

"I hope so…. There's one more reason for my visit. I need your advice, Bea."

Beatrice looked skeptical. "*My* advice? Oh, dear, things must be bad."

"No, really," Lucy insisted. "This is something that you know about. I have received three proposals in the last month, all of which I have declined."

"Three? Oh, Lucy, you're in trouble." Beatrice giggled mischievously. "Who are the unfortunate gentlemen?"

Lucy's eyes were wide with distress. "Don't jest. It's awful. I have been proposed to three times by Lord Dudley, and once by the earl of Suffolk."

Beatrice leaned back in her chair and stretched out her legs in front of her, enjoying the topic. "An earl? That's better than I ever did. And, I might mention, Dudley only proposed to me twice. I should be coming to you with questions."

"But I didn't want them to propose! The earl is nearly sixty and Dudley, well…"

"Yes. He's Dudley. No need to explain that one. I suggest that you hide out for a bit, Lucy…wait till they cool off. You don't want to receive any more proposals until you're good and ready, or else you'll acquire a reputation like mine."

Satisfied for the moment, Lucy nodded. But then she had to ask, "So…have *you* received any proposals? Even out here in the country? I don't mean to pry, but it's been over two months since I've seen you…."

"You're not prying at all, and the answer to your question is no," Beatrice admitted with a sigh. "I pretty much decided to give up on it. I don't think I'm meant for marriage—I figure that if I can't find someone suitable after all this time, I never will. But I suspect Randolph Asher might propose this weekend."

"You don't seem excited."

"No? I guess I'm not. I can't imagine spending the rest of my life with him."

"So you plan to turn him down?" Lucy inquired, fiddling with the lace around her sleeve so as not to appear too interested.

Beatrice sighed again, this time a bit more despondently. "I'm not sure…. I don't know if I really have much option at this point. I haven't exactly encouraged Asher, but I haven't discouraged him, either. He'll expect me to accept, and I know that my family wants me to settle with someone eventually…and I'd like children myself. If I turn him down, I don't think anyone will ever ask me again."

"Yes, but that's no reason to marry—"

"I'm not even sure he'll ask, Lucy. It's just a feeling I have," Beatrice interrupted, not wanting to discuss the subject any further.

Lucy caught the hint, but couldn't help but add, "It's just not fair. Why should you have to settle for someone who isn't the man of your dreams?"

"It's the way of the world, I suppose," Beatrice explained, wishing that she could believe that truism herself.

"I suppose," Lucy replied with an equal lack of conviction.

Both girls slouched back into their chairs, musing on the unjustness of it all.

It was nearly ten o'clock in the evening, and Charles was restless and bored. It was the worst kind of boredom, too—though he had lots to do, nothing interested him. He'd tried going out more often, but as that hadn't worked, he'd tried staying in. He'd caught up on his correspondence, made sure his bills were paid in advance, reread Dante.... He'd even installed a dartboard in his study so he could improve his aim *while* he reread Dante and paid his bills.

He knew the real reason for his foul, dissatisfied mood. Had known it, more or less, from the very first moment he'd first laid eyes on Beatrice Sinclair. She'd been on his mind almost nonstop since he'd seen her sprawled out in the grass, and the only way to get her out of his mind, he was convinced, was to have her. Unfortunately, that was not an option. Beatrice was not for him, and she was gone.

Charles supposed he should be thankful that she'd left London, although her sudden flight also made him feel like a cad. He'd caused it, after all. He'd known that she hoped to marry and still he'd pursued her, uncaring of her reputation. He hadn't forced her to do anything she hadn't wanted to do—Charles was convinced of that—but she had been too innocent to withstand his advances. No, he'd had a lot of practice in those matters and he should have left her well alone.

Should have, but couldn't have if his life had depended upon it. He'd wanted her and still wanted her like he'd never wanted a woman before. He only hoped that eventually his desire would ebb and his life would return to normal.

Oddly enough, he missed her—missed her a lot, in fact, and he'd never missed a woman before in his life. For that matter, he couldn't remember having missed anyone, really…except his father and brother, and that was different. They were gone for good.

But so was Beatrice.

Charles stretched out in his chair. She was the most fascinating, beautiful woman he'd ever met. He didn't know why—she just was. There might have been women out there more classically beautiful, more petite, less freckled. But to him, she was perfect, and his boredom stemmed from the simple fact that he couldn't look forward to seeing her. His foul mood stemmed from the possibility that he might *never* see her again.

He was roused from his reverie by a forceful knock at his front door. He rose in alarm when he heard his butler open it and remark in concern, "Lady Lucy! Is everything all right?"

Lucy had been in her carriage for over ten hours that day and looked it. The first leg of her travels had brought her to Beatrice, and the second leg had brought her straight to her brother's doorstep. She hadn't even been home yet. She'd gone directly to his house from Sudley, too alarmed by Beatrice's admission that she was contemplating marriage to Randolph Asher. Truthfully, Lucy hadn't expected her brother to be in at this hour, as it was nearly ten o'clock and he was usually *anywhere* but home at this time of night.

Charles stepped out from his study, a look of concern on his face. "Everything all right, Lu?" he asked.

"Everything is fine, Charles…I'd just like a word with you if you're able."

"I always have time for you," he said.

After he closed the study door behind them, Charles pulled out a chair for her and seated himself behind his desk.

"I say, Charles, you look quite a bit like death warmed over."

He grunted. He hadn't bothered to glance in a mirror yet that day, but he could imagine what he looked like. He'd spent the previous evening getting drunk with Jack, and hadn't fallen asleep until the wee hours of the morning—in a chair in his study. "Thank you, Lu. Speak quietly, if you please."

"Humph." Lucy snorted loudly, sounding remarkably like their mother.

"Surely you didn't come here to tell me I look like hell, did you? Because if that's the case—"

"I have some news that might interest you. I just stopped by to visit with Beatrice Sinclair—"

"Is she in town again?" Charles hoped he didn't sound too interested.

"No. Hampshire." Lucy ignored her brother's surprised look and continued. "I had an important question to ask her. Anyway, she mentioned that she thinks Randolph Asher will propose to her at their house party this weekend."

Charles was silent for a moment, not a trace of his emotions appearing on his face. He felt hollow, cold, and his heart—for an instant—stopped. "And?" he asked baldly.

She threw up her hands in exasperation. "I won't believe that you don't care, Charles! Clearly Beatrice is not in the same class as your other women. You do care for her, don't you? Am I completely wrong?"

He shrugged. "I'm not sure what you're talking about. Beatrice is not one of my 'women,' as you put it. I do care about her…I like her. But I'm not sure what that has to do with Asher." He'd heard rumors that Asher was going to propose, but he'd tried to ignore them. What hurt now was that Lucy was bringing him this news straight from Beatrice, meaning the rumor was true. Perhaps she felt something for Asher, after all. Charles couldn't face that possibility.

"He's going to ask her to marry him! Don't you understand? What do you propose to do about it?" Lucy demanded.

Charles schooled his features into a blasé mask. "I'm not going to do anything about it—I wish you and Mother would figure that out. If Beatrice wants to marry Randolph Asher, then that's her business."

"But she doesn't want to marry him."

"Then she won't. It's simple."

"No, Charles, you don't understand. She doesn't want to marry him. But she will."

Charles stood and began pacing, his affected disinterest gone. "If Beatrice has become so weak willed, then let him have her. *I* can't marry her."

"Can't, Charles? Or won't?"

He said nothing. He couldn't marry her. Lucy was right; he did care about Beatrice. He cared about her so much it hurt. But he couldn't attach himself to anyone else—it was tempting fate too much. What if something happened to him? Illogically, Charles still feared his own death. Perhaps Richard Milbanks *was* dead, perhaps he wasn't—Charles occasionally still had nightmares about that dark night nearly three years ago. He was certainly in no position to marry anyone.

Besides, if he married her, if he made her his, then he'd risk losing her, as well. And in losing her, he'd lose himself.

Who was he trying to fool? Beatrice *was* gone, and she'd already taken a piece of him with her. "I can't, Lucy."

"I couldn't disagree with you more, but the question isn't whether you can marry her, but whether you can live with her marrying someone else."

"I'll survive."

"Oh? Then you wouldn't mind if she married Asher? Or how about if Jack decided to seduce her? He seemed taken with her at Mother's party, if you didn't notice."

Charles's jaw tightened. "I noticed."

"I know you did," Lucy said as she rose, and with that angry parting shot, she turned and left. The door slammed behind her.

Charles closed his eyes, and after a moment returned to his seat at the desk. With a sigh, he put his head in his hands, feeling his temples pound. When he finally raised his head, five minutes had passed, and he felt worse than before. Damn Lucy for not being able to leave well enough alone! He couldn't change anything now.

His gaze wandered across his desk, taking in the neat piles of bills and correspondence. At least *that* part of his life was in order. His eyes narrowed as they lit on the corner of a gilt-edged card, peeking out from beneath one of the orderly piles.

Remembering what it was, he looked away. He'd received the invitation to the Sinclairs' party several weeks ago. Frankly, he'd been shocked to receive it, although he was certain Beatrice had nothing to do with it. She might not even know he'd been invited, or she may have invited him out of politeness, since the rest of his family had been asked to attend. She would have assumed that she had nothing to worry about. Naturally he would refuse.

Charles had spent a lot of time looking at that invitation. He didn't even know why he still had the blasted thing. He'd already determined not to go. He looked at his calendar. It was Thursday, and he had nothing planned for the weekend.

Perhaps it wasn't too late to change his mind.

Chapter Sixteen

On Friday morning, Beatrice was a wreck. She still had not dressed for company, and as she gazed at her reflection in her dressing table mirror, she cringed. Faint circles smudged the corners of her eyes, and her hair fell about her face in disarray. She had sent Meg downstairs to retrieve her riding habit, which was being pressed for the hunt that afternoon. Beatrice sighed. She would require a lot more help than that.

Her father knocked on her door and entered. "Bea, are you ready?"

She smiled slightly as she looked up at her father. David Sinclair, Viscount Carlisle, was a tall, handsome man of fifty-three, and Beatrice had always been particularly close to him—even when he did futile things like make her *try* to get married.

She shook her head. "Not even close to ready. How about you?"

"In body, but not in spirit." He entered her room. "But you could fool me about being ready."

Beatrice turned, giving him a sardonic look. "I'm wearing my dressing gown, Father."

"Well, you look beautiful, anyway. Just like your mother."

Beatrice smiled. Although she, Ben and Helen had all inherited their mother's coloring, Beatrice took after her the most, even to the odd amber hue of her eyes and the line of freckles on her nose. "I miss her."

Her father smiled back sadly. "I do, too. Having a party this weekend brings up a lot of memories. But Louisa insisted. I can never say no to her…she'll just give me one of her looks, and it'll bring me right back to being seven years old and in short pants."

"I wish you'd said no."

He shrugged noncommittally. "She's doing it for you…we've all been worried that you seem unhappy lately. We thought maybe a party would cheer you up."

"I suppose." Beatrice turned around, facing the mirror once more while she pinned up her hair. Still looking into the mirror, she said, "You know, Father, in a way I'm glad that I finally decided not to marry. I'm not sure I could survive the kind of loss you experienced with Mother's death."

He met her gaze in the mirror, very serious. "Don't be silly, Beatrice. Marrying your mother was the best thing I ever did, and I wouldn't have changed it even if I'd known that I would lose her before I was ready."

She immediately felt guilty for bringing the subject up. "I know. I'm sorry for mentioning it. I just wish that I could please you by making such a happy match."

"Never think that you displease me, Beatrice. Don't think for a second that the chance of losing someone is greater than the happiness you can have with them. If you love someone enough, they'll be with you forever."

Beatrice felt tears prick her eyes. She knew what her father was suggesting. He had accepted it when she'd said she didn't plan to marry, but she realized he still harbored some hope that she eventually would.

When he left, Beatrice began getting ready in earnest. Her talk with him, as always, had set her mind to rights. Resolved, she finished quickly and headed down to the stables, telling herself that marriage wasn't the worst thing in the world. She might even grow to enjoy it.

Beatrice's good mood didn't last much beyond the hunt, and by the supper hour her nerves had returned full force. She'd waited until the last possible moment to enter the dining room, not eager to engage in the requisite banalities and flirtation. Unfortunately, her lateness also meant that she was greeted with an intimidating mass of people, and she had to fight the urge to return to her bedroom. An extra table had been dragged in to accommodate all of their guests, and at this point every seat but the one reserved for her was full. Her tardy entrance prompted several heads to pivot in her direction, and she focused her eyes on the wall as she slid lamely into her seat.

She really wished she could enjoy the evening. The dining room looked splendid, the food was superb and for once she felt confident that she looked her best, her pale blue ball gown and sapphire jewels contrasting beautifully with her amber eyes. Indeed, if everything *hadn't* been going so well, Beatrice wouldn't have felt half so bad. But she was seated next to Randolph Asher, and every time he spoke to her, with love in his eyes and salmon on his fork, she wanted to cringe. He was enjoying himself immensely and assumed that she was, too, although in truth, all she wanted to do was hide—anything to prevent him from asking her to marry him. She'd resigned herself to accepting him if he proposed, but knew deep down in her heart that she'd be making the worst mistake of her life.

Beatrice shifted, trying to look across to the other table where both Eleanor and Lucy were seated. Her vision was obscured by an elaborate arrangement of flowers and a towering candelabrum.

She pursed her lips in annoyance and had to make a conscious effort soften them when Asher made her promise to dance with him later on that evening.

At the meal's end, the gentlemen and ladies separated. Beatrice hadn't had a chance to say hello to Lucy yet, and knew that she still needed to offer some sort of an explanation to Lady Summerson.

But before she could do so, Eleanor made her way over. Her eyes were alight with the pleasure of being included at a large social gathering for the first time.

"So, Ellie, did you enjoy yourself?" Beatrice asked fondly.

Eleanor beamed. "I did, Bea…even though Father made sure I was seated on the end next to a terribly boring Oxford scholar—perfectly harmless, you see?"

"I'm sorry if you didn't have much to talk about."

"Oh, no—we talked about Greek tragedy, off and on, anyway. He thought me quite astute. But mostly I was interested in observing everyone."

"Oh? Who did you watch?"

"You, a bit…you looked quite unhappy, by the way. And I watched your friend Lucy…she kept sending outraged glares down the table, and it took me all dinner to ascertain who she was glaring at."

Beatrice cocked an eyebrow, wishing that she'd been seated by her sister. It sounded as if she'd had an infinitely more interesting time. "Well? Who was it?"

"I believe it was that gentleman who lived next door to Louisa." Eleanor paused. "The gentleman of the indecent proposal, right?"

Beatrice was shaking her head vigorously. It couldn't be. "You must be mistaken, Eleanor."

Her sister nodded right back. "No. I'm quite certain. I wouldn't forget him. But I don't think you have anything to worry about…he must be sweet on your friend, what with the looks they kept exchanging."

"The looks?" Beatrice asked in alarm.

"Yes…looks of mutual aggravation, really. They didn't seem

to be particularly loving, but they did seem to know each other quite well."

Beatrice hoped Eleanor was wrong, but knew that Charles's was not a face anyone would forget. Slowly, she said, "Lucy is his sister."

"Oh!" Eleanor exclaimed. "That explains everything. How silly of me."

At that moment, Louisa announced that the gentlemen had finished their port and cigars, and that there would be music and dancing in the ballroom.

Eleanor groaned and put her hand on her sister's arm. "That's my signal to go, Bea. I was supposed to retire right after supper. See you in the morning." She then dashed off, before their father saw her downstairs beyond what was proper.

As the collected ladies migrated to the ballroom, Beatrice hesitated a moment. She wanted desperately to escape, but knew it was impossible. Asher was making his way over to her expectantly, and held out his hand, gallant as ever.

Beatrice smiled, determined to put on a pleasant face. She took hold of his arm and they hastened to take their place on the dance floor.

The first set, following tradition, was a country-dance. As the couples lined up in two rows, partners facing each other, Beatrice groaned inwardly. Personally, she preferred the waltz; these country-dances, at least at a large, formal gathering such as theirs, could prove interminable, and she would be doing a lot more standing around than actual dancing. From her position, she couldn't see everyone participating in the dance, but there were about twenty couples, and her lateness had put her and Asher at the end of their set. They would be standing there a long time waiting for their turn, watching couple after couple dance down the line and do their figures.

As she always did at times like this, Beatrice began to listen avidly to the conversations around her. In the line opposite her,

Georgina Emerson was leaning across a young man to gossip with Sissy Riggs. Although they whispered, Beatrice and everyone else nearby could hear them quite clearly.

"I cannot believe *he* showed up!" Georgina hissed loudly.

Sissy opened her eyes wide. "Do you think he came to see you, Georgie?"

Georgina scoffed, "Me? We were over last season. Besides, I've set my sights higher."

"But he *is* a marquess, Georgie. And he's rich. And quite attractive."

Georgina harrumphed. "He had his chance."

Beatrice had a horrible, stomach churning feeling that she knew exactly whom they were speaking about.

At that moment, the first couple made its way down the line, confirming her suspicions. It was Charles Summerson, with Priscilla Pendleton clinging daintily to him.

Beatrice lowered her eyes as he went past, and held her breath, too, as if that would make any difference. She hoped that he didn't see her, but she couldn't resist peeking to find out.

She soon wished she hadn't looked. She opened her eyes prematurely, and when he passed her, Charles gazed right at her, his expression cold and hard, before turning and heading back up the line to resume his place.

He hadn't looked very pleased.

Several more couples danced past, dizzying her with their movements. She swayed slightly.

"Are you all right, Miss Sinclair?" Asher asked. "You appear a bit pale."

Beatrice smiled weakly. "I'm fine, Lord Asher. I just hate these dances. One can be waiting forever."

He smiled back. "Never fear. Our turn is up." And with that, he stepped forward, and they began to move down the line. Beatrice never took her eyes from his face, but still she knew when they passed Charles. She could sense his gaze boring through her.

As Beatrice and Asher had been the last couple, the dance was declared complete. Asher offered to retrieve some lemonade, and Beatrice gratefully accepted. She searched the room, trying to see where Charles had gone; if she didn't know his whereabouts, she could hardly avoid him.

She noticed that Sissy and Georgina were standing along the wall behind her, their conversation still quite animated. She backed up, hoping to hear a few more choice phrases. Those two vultures would certainly know where he was…he and any unmarried man in the room with a title and a fortune.

"He's coming this way, Sis!" Georgina practically squealed.

Beatrice began looking around frantically, trying to locate Charles. It didn't take long—her eyes seemed naturally drawn to him. She hadn't had a good look at him yet that evening, and her breath caught in her throat. Against her will, her eyes wandered to his face, and down his frame. He was beautiful, his snug fitting, blue velvet coat accentuating his broad shoulders and trim hips. Beatrice had never really thought of a man as beautiful before, but so he was. Beautiful, like a Greek god, and…and something else. Something predatory. Charles began to cross the room, his eyes never once leaving hers.

Sissy began whispering frantically, "He's still coming, Georgie. Do you think he's going to ask you to dance?"

Georgina said nothing, but from the rustling sounds behind her, Beatrice assumed that she was busy tidying up her hair and yanking her bodice down an inch or two.

But when Charles arrived at their small group, he only had eyes for Beatrice. "Miss Sinclair," he said, picking up her hand and laying a kiss on the inside of her wrist—the inside of her wrist! "Would you honor me with this waltz?"

Beatrice was momentarily struck dumb. She merely nodded, knowing that every eye in the room was on her and that to do anything less would cause a sensation. She curtsied, he bowed, and they moved out to the dance floor to join the rest of the couples.

The orchestra had just struck up when Beatrice remembered Asher. She panicked. "Oh! I'm sorry, Lord Summerson—"

"I thought we agreed you'd call me Charles."

"But you just called me Miss—"

"We had an avid audience, Beatrice."

"Oh. I'm sorry. But Lord Asher had just gone off to get me some lemonade. When he returns and finds me gone he'll think I'm terribly ill-mannered."

Charles paused for a second. "One moment," he said, then guided her from the dance floor. Before she could ask what he was about, he left her. She felt foolish waiting for his return, but didn't know what else to do.

"What did you do?" she asked when he reappeared a minute later.

"I told him you'd changed your mind about the lemonade," he said, taking her back into his arms and leading her to the dance floor once more.

Beatrice's mouth opened in outrage, but before she could voice her protest, Charles leaned in to remind her, "You'd best try to smile, Beatrice. Everyone is watching us."

She smiled stiffly. Through her teeth, she said, "You had no right to do that."

He raised an eyebrow. "Excuse me, Beatrice? I couldn't understand you. Perhaps if you'd open your mouth—"

"I said," she snapped, still somehow managing to have a smile pinned to her face, "that you have no right to interfere like that with my life. What will he think of me?"

Charles shrugged. He bloody well did *not* care what Asher thought, and there had been no way that he was going to forgo dancing with Beatrice because of it. He'd had no idea that seeing her again, so beautiful, so perfect in her blue gown, would affect him so deeply.

He didn't know if he was glad that he'd decided to come; he'd spent all day debating whether to or not. He hadn't even driven there with his mother and Lucy, or told them that he was attending, for that matter. He still hadn't spoken to either of them, although his sister had given him speculative and irritated looks from across the table when she'd first noticed his presence.

Charles gazed into Beatrice's eyes. She was still waiting for an answer, and she looked furious. She'd probably have been furious with him even if he hadn't been so underhanded with Asher, but as he *had* been…

Blast it all. He hadn't come the whole way to Hampshire to have her peeved at him, but he bloody well deserved it and didn't know how to get around that fact.

"Asher will think nothing more than that you forgot. You did forget, didn't you?"

She blushed, knowing that she wasn't without fault. "I admit I shouldn't have agreed to dance with you, but having realized my mistake, you shouldn't have taken it upon yourself to tell Asher anything."

"I realize that now. Forgive me?" Charles asked, grinning boyishly. That grin, he knew, never failed.

There was a first for everything, though; his grin failed. "I do not," Beatrice answered haughtily. "However, I will admit that this predicament was partly my fault. I was almost as inconsiderate as you were."

Charles gave up trying to be charming. "Now you're being inconsiderate. And a brat."

Her jaw dropped. "I'm sorry?"

"You heard me. You're blaming me for your own mistakes."

"You're not a gentleman."

"I never said I was, but at least I'm honest."

"Are you implying that I am not?" Beatrice practically sputtered.

"No—I'm saying it quite clearly. You've a mind of your own—if you didn't want to dance with me, you wouldn't have. You said as much yourself."

She gritted her teeth. "*I did not.* All I said was that I *shouldn't* have agreed to dance with you—you merely took me off guard. But since we can't agree on that, perhaps we'd best not talk at all."

Charles wasn't about to drop the subject that easily. "*Anything* that has happened between us could have been prevented, Beatrice."

She wanted to protest. Her mind raced for any argument, but there wasn't one. He'd never forced her to do anything she didn't want to. He'd done his part to persuade her, certainly, but he hadn't forced her…. Beatrice hated to admit it, but she hadn't exactly just *allowed* his advances, either—she'd quite enjoyed them. Whether or not she now wished that she'd never kissed him didn't change the fact that, if she had put her mind to it in the first place, she wouldn't have. Charles was everything she'd always fantasized about, and she had allowed herself, briefly, to revel in his attentions.

But what to do about it? Admit it to him? Never. Change the subject?

Definitely. "What are you doing here, Charles?"

"I was invited."

Beatrice cursed Louisa once more. "You were invited out of politeness. It was assumed that you wouldn't attend."

"Then you were too polite." He paused. "Look, Beatrice, this is silly."

"What is?"

"This maidenly disapproval of yours. I kissed you, all right? If I'd known you'd get so bloody exercised about it, I wouldn't have bothered. So you can either accept my apology or not." Charles hoped to God she'd accept it. He hated himself for sounding so cavalier…it wasn't how he felt, really. But making her feel at least somewhat responsible for their situation was the only way he could think of to make her forgive him.

It worked. Beatrice blushed crimson. He had a point: he

shouldn't have kissed her, but she'd kissed him right back. Perhaps it didn't seem like *just* a kiss to her, but to him that sort of thing was probably routine. Whatever it was, she was overreacting, and she was equally guilty.

"You haven't actually said you're sorry," she murmured tentatively.

Charles wanted to shout for joy. "I'm sorry, Beatrice. Is it a truce then? All transgressions forgotten and forgiven?"

She thought for a moment. Even now she was thinking about the way he had kissed her before, so all things were certainly not forgotten. She supposed she could forgive him, however….

Beatrice sighed resignedly. "Forgiven. It is a truce."

His grin returned, unrepentant as ever. "I shall do my best to behave. As you pointed out, though, I am no gentleman—"

"Charles…" Beatrice warned.

His grin grew more wicked, and he spun her around in time to the music. "I'm only jesting, Beatrice. I know that you are looking to get married and I'm…well, looking for something else. How is your search going, by the way?"

"Search?" she asked, confused.

"Husband hunt, if you prefer."

She blushed profusely. "I don't prefer…and I think I've ended the search."

Charles arched an eyebrow in question, but she didn't seem to realize how enigmatic her words had been. Did she mean that she had decided against marriage entirely? He hoped so, although the prospect conjured up all the lecherous thoughts he was trying to suppress. But she could have meant that her search had ended because Randolph Asher was all but guaranteed to propose. What if he had done so already?

Charles didn't know if he could live with that possibility.

He didn't get a chance to ask her to clarify her statement, though. The waltz ended, and Beatrice pulled away. With a brief curtsy, she wisely hastened off into the crowd.

Chapter Seventeen

When Charles headed downstairs the following morning, he was greeted by a miniature image of Beatrice sitting on the landing, her ear pressed up against the bars of the railing. The sounds from breakfast wafted up the stairs and she was getting an earful.

"Ahem." He cleared his throat.

She spun around and quickly rose. "I dropped something," she said, lying baldly.

"You did not," Charles retorted. "Do you hear anything good that way?"

She grinned unabashedly. "Plenty. Who are you?"

He bowed. "Charles Summerson, marquess of Pelham, at your service. And might I inquire after your name?"

Her expression had changed. She now appeared to be quite curious. "It's Helen Sinclair. I'm thirteen and not allowed downstairs all bloody weekend. And by the way, I can inform you that I've heard plenty about you this morning."

Charles stared blankly, mainly because he'd never heard a thirteen-year-old young lady swear so comfortably in the presence of a complete stranger. "You know, half of what you hear is never true."

"Is that so?" Helen asked innocently. "That must mean that half *is* true, then."

Before he could respond—and he was about to forget that he was a gentleman—a stern voice came from behind them. "Helen! I cannot believe what I just heard come out of your mouth. That is no way to speak to guests."

"Sorry, Beazie," Helen responded, not looking at all contrite. She grinned mischievously at her sister. "Do you know Lord Summerson, Bea?"

Beatrice couldn't help but blush slightly as she looked at Charles. "We are acquainted, yes, Helen."

Helen smirked at Charles and whispered conspiratorially to Charles behind her hand, "As I said, half of what one hears *is* true."

He could contain himself no longer, and burst out into hearty laughter.

"What are you talking about, Helen?" asked Beatrice, annoyed.

"Just making conversation with Lord Summerson," Helen replied before changing the subject. "Do you suppose Father will let me take the dogcart into town, Bea?"

"I hope so," Beatrice retorted. "Perhaps you can stay away a very long time?"

"I'll do my best," said Helen, before spinning around and racing down the steps.

Beatrice called after her, "Stay out of trouble!"

"Does she drive the cart herself?" Charles asked.

Beatrice nodded, love for her sister shining in her eyes. "She does…heaven help anyone who happens to be on the road at the time. She drives into town to meet her friend George. He's the vicar's son, although I must say that the two of them together become perfect heathens. They'll probably be plotting some sort of prank today…. Eleanor and I have bets on whether they'll put eels in the lemonade or marbles on the ballroom floor."

Charles grinned. "I hope for marbles."

"I agree. Much more entertaining."

They were silent a moment. Beatrice began to edge uncomfortably toward the stairs, realizing that she had been prattling on again.

He didn't want to end their conversation. "I remember you telling me about Helen…the two of you look very much alike."

"I know," Beatrice said, relaxing once more. "Helen, Ben and I all take after our mother. Eleanor has dark hair and blue eyes, like our father."

"My brother, Mark, was like that," Charles said suddenly, wondering why on earth he'd thought to bring up that subject with her again. He didn't like to talk about it.

"Was he?" She'd sensed that his late father and brother were touchy subjects for him, even when he'd mentioned them for the first time during their walk in the park.

Charles nodded slowly. "Mark was fair like my mother."

Beatrice nodded back, noticing his discomfort. She tried—subtly—to change the subject. "I think Lucy is quite a bit like your mother, really. They don't look similar, but they each have a certain…"

He grinned, relieved to talk about something different. "A certain way about them? You could say that. And they're both determined to drive me mad. Are you on your way down to breakfast, by any chance?"

Beatrice nodded.

"May I accompany you?"

Beatrice nodded again, feeling suddenly shy. She accepted Charles's offered arm, and they walked downstairs together.

Although he neither said nor did the slightest improper thing the whole way, her heart still raced.

Beatrice secluded herself in the library for the rest of the day, having decided against riding with the rest of the guests. In her current state of mind, she needed to be alone to stew in her thoughts.

Mostly, she thought about her conversation with Charles. It hadn't been scary or overwhelming. Just nice.

Why did he have to make her life difficult again by being *nice?* Beatrice didn't want to like him. She wanted to *hate* him. Instead, he had to go and tell her about his family, and talk about his brother, and even look sad while he did it. Why?

He was supposed to be a cad. He wasn't supposed to have feelings, and she was *not* supposed to feel sympathy for him. It didn't make any sense.

She sighed and turned her attention back to her diary, which lay dejectedly in her lap. Beatrice stared blankly at the page for several minutes. She didn't notice that someone had entered the room.

"You look absorbed," Randolph Asher said as he approached her, taking a seat beside her on the settee.

She closed her journal and cast Asher a sideways glance…he was sitting a trifle too close. "I am, I suppose."

He moved closer and placed his hand on hers. "Can I ask what you're thinking about?"

Beatrice looked down her nose at his hand. *I'm definitely not thinking about you,* she thought to herself. To him, she said simply, "Chocolate meringues. Cook promised we'd have them for dessert."

Asher chuckled indulgently. "So you enjoy a good meringue?"

She nodded, still looking at his hand and wondering how she could tactfully ask him to remove it. "I do."

"Let me assure you that my chef makes an excellent meringue."

Beatrice chose to ignore the implications of that statement, and chose instead to concentrate on more immediate concerns. "Lord Asher? Would you remove your hand, please?"

"Oh! I beg your pardon, Miss Sinclair. I forgot myself for a moment."

"Do not explain. You were thinking about meringue. You were moved."

He nodded eagerly. "Yes…I mean, no, I was not. Miss Sinclair…Beatrice…there is something that I have been longing to say to you—"

"Please don't. Not here," she said, looking around the room desperately. The house was quite empty, as nearly all of the guests were out, enjoying the warm August sunshine. In vain, she wished that someone would come in and save her.

"No, Beatrice. I must. You know, I think, what I will ask you—"

Please don't ask me to marry you. Please don't ask me to marry you.

Suddenly, her prayers were answered…more or less.

The library door opened, and Charles entered. He was dressed casually and looked as if he planned to retrieve a book and head out of doors to enjoy the weather. When he saw them, he stopped, surprise passing suddenly over his face. Slowly, his expression hardened.

"Good afternoon, Miss Sinclair. Asher," he said, nodding a curt but polite greeting. "I see you've decided to remain indoors."

Asher flushed beet-red, and Beatrice could have clobbered him for it—he made it look as if something illicit had been going on. When she spoke, her words came out in embarrassed monosyllables. "No. I stayed in…to write, you see." She held up her journal to prove the veracity of her words.

Charles nodded dispassionately. "I see."

She didn't think he believed her, so she tried again. "Yes. That and I…I felt a bit too *ill* to be out of doors."

"Ill?" Asher asked in alarm. "You should have said something, Miss Sinclair."

"Why didn't you take to bed?" Charles asked. He knew she was lying.

"No, I—"

"No, of course not," he interrupted, his voice laced with disgust. "You could hardly entertain Lord Asher in bed, could you?"

"Summerson!" Asher sputtered, "I won't have you insinuating—"

"Don't bother. I'm leaving." He bowed mockingly at Beatrice, turned and left.

She was stunned. Fat tears began rolling down her cheeks, but she didn't notice.

"Oh, Miss Sinclair…please don't cry. I'll have words with him—never fear," Asher said, trying to be chivalrous and comfort her.

He failed completely. Beatrice only cried harder, and blinded by tears, she stood up and raced from the room. She didn't stop until she reached her bedroom.

Chapter Eighteen

Beatrice looked her worst. She didn't care. It was partly intentional. She didn't want Asher getting any more ideas, and if it took an orange ball gown to keep him at bay—such an unbecoming color on her—so be it. She had been crying all afternoon, and her dark, puffy eyes only added to her sallow complexion.

But it didn't work. Asher didn't even seem to notice. He'd cornered her the moment she'd stepped into the ballroom, and he had already danced with her twice. Finally, she had cried exhaustion, telling him that she intended to rest for a moment with some lady friends in the sitting room. She'd lied. She intended to escape.

Beatrice stealthily crept along the wall of the ballroom, her eye on Asher the whole time, willing him to keep his back to her until she could duck into the hallway. She reached the door just as he was beginning to turn, so she made it to safety in time.

She peered through the crack in the door, however, just in case. Asher was looking about the room, obviously growing impatient.

Beatrice leaned against the door, finally relaxing. *One danger averted,* she thought. *Now if I can just avoid the other one, I'll be all right.*

"What are you doing out here?"

Damn. Damn. Damn.

She spun around, every bone in her body protesting. She hadn't seen Charles since their encounter earlier that afternoon, but there he was, leaning against the wall and looking arrogantly at home. She tried for bravado, but took a small step back all the same. "This is my house. I should be asking you the same question."

Charles shrugged dismissively. He was out here because he'd caught a glimpse of Randolph Asher panting after her, and couldn't stand to watch it anymore. But he wouldn't tell her that. "I don't feel like dancing. Now answer my question."

Beatrice asked disdainfully. "What was it again?"

He repeated himself, moving a step closer. "Why are you out here, Beatrice?"

Her courage was quickly waning. "For some air. I'm ready to return to the ballroom now."

"You looked as if you were hiding," Charles said, moving nearer.

She shook her head and shrank back another step.

By this time, Charles had come abreast with the door, and he followed Beatrice's suit by glancing through the crack into the ballroom beyond. When he returned his attention to her, he looked cynically amused. "Your beau awaits, fair Beatrice. Aren't you going to dance with him?"

She didn't answer. Tears pricked her eyes and she didn't trust herself to speak.

"A little bird told me that you were getting engaged." Charles stepped even closer, his voice dropping to a husky whisper. "Are you?"

She shook her head. "Not yet. I mean, no, I'm not."

"Well, what would happen if you were found out here, alone with me?" By this time he stood directly in front of her, his intense green eyes practically piercing her very soul. He held out his hand to cup her face, and she gasped.

It was that gasp that caused Charles's control to snap; he saw her mouth open, the tip of her soft, pink tongue, and he knew that he had to possess her then and there. He leaned in and claimed her mouth, needing to taste her, to feel her, to own her.

This kiss was unlike the others they had shared. It was without gentleness, without preliminaries, without anything but mutual need and urgency born of desperation. Beatrice matched his hunger, forgetting the ball, forgetting Asher and the other guests, only one room away. Her hands reached up to run through his hair, pulling him closer. Her mouth opened wide to accept his kiss.

With a thud, she crashed into the wall behind her, Charles's body pressed intimately to hers. Neither of them even noticed, so wrapped up were they in the passion and intensity of the moment. Nothing mattered but their lips, their hands….

Charles lifted her up in his arms and started carrying her to the stairs. "Where is your room?" he whispered gruffly against her ear.

Beatrice felt as if there were cotton in her head. "Hmm?"

"Your room. I'm going to make love to you," he whispered back.

She began shaking her head. "Oh, no. Put me down, Charles. We—"

He cut her off with his mouth. There was a spindly-legged rosewood table nearby and he maneuvered to it; he shoved a vase of flowers out of the way, sending it crashing to the floor, and seated Beatrice on top of the table. Then he leaned in close, so close that she was forced to lean back as far as possible, and then grab on to him to keep from falling. His lips trailed down the exposed column of her throat and moved lower, blazing a path to the gentle swell of her breasts.

And Beatrice, groaning in pleasure too long suppressed, opened her eyes to watch his dark head move down her body.

What she saw instead were three horrified faces: Louisa's, Lady Summerson's and Lucy's, mouths agape and eyes wide.

Beatrice gasped in horror and began frantically pushing Charles away. Slowly, he raised his head in confusion, but the look on her face was answer enough. He turned around, straightening as he did so.

Beatrice scrambled from the table and raced up the stairs without a backward glance. She didn't care if it was the cowardly way out. She'd never been so mortified in her entire life, and she'd probably never be able to look at any of them again.

Downstairs the room remained oppressively silent. Louisa looked too angry to speak and Lady Summerson too embarrassed. Lucy knew that if she spoke she'd only get snapped at.

It happened anyway. "Lucy, would you leave us, please?" Louisa asked.

"But—"

"Now," Louisa practically barked.

Lucy turned to leave reluctantly, but not before shooting her brother a sympathetic look.

He didn't notice. His eyes were fixed on their mother, waiting for her to speak. When she finally looked up at his face, she seemed...disappointed. "Oh, Charles," was all she said, searching his face for answers.

Louisa had a bit more to say. "Summerson, I don't know what you think you were doing out here, but you won't get away with it."

Charles shrugged, but inside, his blood still throbbed in his veins. Kissing Beatrice in the bloody hallway of her father's house went beyond self-destructive. He hadn't had a care if they got caught, even knowing that discovery meant he'd have to marry her. And he didn't want to marry her, did he? Charles was no longer even sure.

So what *had* he been doing there? Just kissing the hell out of the most breathtaking girl he'd ever known, and he was afraid that whatever the consequences, it was worth it.

"Summerson?"

He looked up. "Yes?"

Louisa huffed loudly. "You're not even paying attention. Useless, good-for-nothing—"

Lady Summerson cut her off. "As Louisa said, Charles, was that you can't just pretend this didn't happen."

"I never said that was my plan, Mother—" he began angrily, but she interrupted.

"I didn't say you had. I just meant that you must take responsibility…." His mother paused, flustered. Taking a deep breath, she continued. "Louisa and I will talk to Beatrice's father. Would you meet us in the study in an hour?"

Charles nodded curtly and left.

An hour later, Lady Summerson, Louisa and Lord Sinclair were in the study. They'd been there for the full hour. Beatrice's father had remained remarkably calm, although both Lady Summerson and Louisa could tell that it was a facade. His tight jaw and fingers drumming on his desk revealed his true feelings.

"I don't know," he said slowly. "Beatrice has always refused to marry without love."

"Maybe she does love him?" Lady Summerson asked hopefully.

He looked doubtful. "She's never mentioned him…. I know that it's perfectly normal to keep that sort of feeling secret sometimes, especially from one's father, but I hardly think she'd consider marrying him if it weren't for this…situation."

Louisa snorted. "And it's not as if Summerson would have asked her, either."

Lady Summerson stood up, finally losing her temper. "Now, Louisa, I protest. Charles made a poor choice, but…but I do think he cares for her."

"I meant no offense, Emma. All I meant was that, care for her or not, Charles still didn't plan to ask her to marry him."

Lady Summerson sighed, deflated. "Charles is just set against marriage in general."

"Well," Lord Sinclair continued, "like it or not, he's getting married."

Before the discussion could go any further, there came a knock at the door. Charles entered, nodding briefly in greeting. Any emotion was deeply hidden. He appeared calm, dispassionate, relaxed.

Lord Sinclair cleared his throat. "Look, Summerson, I won't prolong this. You have compromised my daughter. You will have to marry her."

Charles said nothing.

Lord Sinclair continued, his voice taking on a more impatient edge. "Have you nothing to say for yourself?"

"I don't love her."

Beatrice's father dragged a hand through his hair, trying to maintain his composure. "Well, that might be a bit too much to ask in a situation like this. I wouldn't have her marry someone who would neglect or mistreat her, but I have discussed this with Louisa and she believes you to be of sound enough character. I can accept that you don't love her as long as you treat her respectfully. And perhaps with time—"

"I won't love her," Charles stated unequivocally.

Lord Sinclair crossed the room to stand right in front of him, shaking in fury. "Perhaps you've forgotten that *you're* at fault here, Summerson. You're in no position to be unreasonable."

Charles said nothing. His silence seemed cruel and indifferent, but in truth his tongue felt heavy and thick in his mouth. He couldn't speak; his feelings too powerful for him to cope with.

Lord Sinclair shook his head in disgust at his silence. "I knew your father…he was a friend of mine, in fact. You're the very image of him. I can't imagine what he'd have to say about your behavior right now."

Charles looked away, the mention of his father bringing back too many painful memories, reminding him of all the reasons that he didn't want to marry at all. He closed his eyes, willing himself the control to speak. "I didn't say I wouldn't marry Beatrice. I just said I wouldn't love her."

"Ah, the typical rake. I'll bet you don't believe in love, right?" Lord Sinclair asked scornfully.

Charles thought of his father and brother and knew that he believed in love completely. It didn't matter. "No. I don't."

The door opened just then, and Beatrice entered the room, looking stricken.

"Beatrice," her father said, "run upstairs and I'll speak to you later."

"Run upstairs?" Beatrice asked, her eyes wide in pain. "Why can't I be here? You're deciding *my* future, aren't you?"

"Beatrice, your future has already been decided, and that's not what I meant, anyway. I just don't want you to hear anything that might hurt you—"

She turned her gaze to Charles. "What—that he doesn't love me? I know that. I won't marry him. I—" She didn't finish. Instead, she turned and fled the room, slamming the door loudly behind her.

Charles flinched, the sound of the door reverberating inside him. The look on her face.... She despised him, and he deserved every bit of her contempt.

He crossed the room, hiding his pain beneath the motions of pouring himself a drink; it was almost a compulsive act, a need to occupy his hands to mask his feelings.

Lady Summerson watched her son sadly and sighed. "Perhaps I can talk to her."

Lord Sinclair rolled his eyes and sat down behind his desk. He looked tired. "You'd better hurry. Louisa and I can finish up in here."

She dashed out of the room to find Beatrice.

She was just in time to see her turn the corner at the end of the hall and head upstairs. "Beatrice!" she called. "Please let me talk to you."

Beatrice didn't want to talk to anyone. She wanted to cry. Charles had hurt her badly this time. She'd known he didn't care about her, but hearing it said so bluntly... She had some pride.

But she knew that Charles's callousness wasn't his mother's fault. "I'll talk to you, Emma, but I won't be convinced."

Lady Summerson caught up to her. "Where can we speak privately?"

Beatrice chewed her lower lip for a moment. "My room, I suppose."

Once behind the safety of Beatrice's closed door, Lady Summerson began. "Look, Beatrice, I shall be perfectly frank with you. I have never seen my son act as abominably as he has this evening, and I don't blame you if you don't want to marry him." She paused. "But you must."

Beatrice sat down on her bed. "I should. I know."

Lady Summerson huffed. "Not *should,* Beatrice. *Must.* You *have* to marry him."

Beatrice shook her head. "It doesn't occur to anyone, does it, that perhaps I don't want to marry Charles every bit as much as he doesn't want to marry me? Emma, I wasted four perfectly good summers in London, doing nothing but looking for a husband. When I left this year, I finally decided that I wouldn't marry at all. I don't have the temperament for it."

Lady Summerson nodded slowly, pretending to understand. "Temperament. I see. But why did you never marry in the past, Beatrice? You've never actually told me, and I know that it wasn't because no one asked you."

"Honestly, Emma? I think it's because I'm rather silly. I never could settle on anyone. I always had this romantic image in my mind of what my husband would be.... And then I came to London and discovered that marriage didn't necessarily have anything to do with love...it's more about just getting along with somebody, and being able to keep house with them, isn't it?" She shrugged. "Anyway, that's why I was never able to marry. I kept waiting for someone who doesn't exist."

Lady Summerson didn't believe her for one second. "I hate to point this out to you, Beatrice, but you are *not* a silly person. Just because you didn't marry the first man who could offer you a coach and four doesn't make you frivolous. I'm certain there's another reason."

Beatrice said nothing. Her eyes stung with the struggle of holding back tears, and she knew that trying to speak would make her lose the battle. Lady Summerson was right, of course. Beatrice knew that love was a real and powerful force—she was *confident* of that fact despite what she professed. Her parents were proof, and her father was no less devoted to her mother now, thirteen years after her death, than he had been during her life. Beatrice wanted that kind of love and that kind of marriage, but she didn't want the pain that could come with it.

"No, Emma, I know that love exists. My parents loved each other deeply. My father talks about my mother every day and the look in his eyes…it's as if she were still here with us. It's just…well, maybe it's just not wise to allow yourself to become that vulnerable—"

"Wise? What does wisdom have to do with anything?"

Beatrice had no answer to that question. She could only look down at her lap, at her tightly clenched hands.

Lady Summerson sat next to her on the bed and put her arm around her, sensing her distress. "I think you and my son have more in common than you realize, Beatrice."

Beatrice couldn't imagine what Lady Summerson was talking about.

Lady Summerson pressed on. "Look, Bea, my son's quite flawed, but I can also assure you that, although he may not realize it yet, he wants to marry you. Why else do you think he got himself, and you, into this mess? He's fully aware of the consequences of trifling with innocent, well-bred young ladies in public places, and he's avoided doing so in the past. That he made such a mistake now makes me think that he wanted to get caught."

Beatrice didn't let her finish. "He doesn't want to marry me, Emma. Please don't try to convince yourself that he does. But now…there seems to be no choice in the matter."

Lady Summerson wasn't going to argue with her, pleased that she had at least finally accepted the inevitability of this marriage. But to herself, she thought, *There's no choice in the matter at all, and that's exactly what Charles wanted.* "Well, you're right about that, Beatrice, neither of you has much option anymore. But I wouldn't worry…it might take Charles a while, but I think everything will work out in the end. It's clear as can be to everyone but you that he's already in love with you."

"It's not clear at all, Emma, but you don't have to try to cheer me up or persuade me. I'll marry him."

"Beatrice, I've been observing him very closely since he met you. You'll have to trust me on this one."

Beatrice withheld her opinion. She trusted Charles's mother just fine— She didn't trust Charles. He was charming, handsome, everything she had ever fantasized about. Even more, he was intelligent, he made her laugh and he obviously cared deeply for his family. He valued family so much that she could imagine—if she let herself—that he'd someday make an excellent father. Charles was also an unrepentant rake, and Beatrice knew she couldn't live happily with him. Infidelity was one thing she didn't think she could withstand.

Lady Summerson patted her hand. "Ready to head back downstairs and give your answer? Hopefully Charles is being more pleasant now."

They were never to find out. The study was empty. Charles had already left for London, and all that remained was a note, saying he'd acquire the appropriate license. They would marry in town in two weeks.

If he had waited downstairs only to hurl insults at her, Beatrice would have felt better. As it was, her eyes welled up with tears and she returned to her room to cry for the second time that evening.

Chapter Nineteen

⚬⚬⚬⚬⚬⚬⚬

The remainder of the house party, three more days of it, had been absolute torture for Beatrice. She had known that everyone was talking about her. No one had seemed to care that they were *her* guests in *her* house; the gossip was too sensational to ignore.

Charles, of course, had escaped all this censure by leaving that very night. Beatrice envied him the ability simply to get up and go, and she also despised him for it. She certainly hadn't wanted to remain at Sudley, with everyone staring at her and whispering her name; she simply had no choice. She'd actually begged her father to cancel the rest of the party, but Louisa had protested vehemently, maintaining that it was better to pretend that nothing had happened. No one aside from close relatives had actually witnessed the embarrassing scene, after all. The most anyone else could do was speculate on the cause for their hasty decision to wed.

Beatrice sighed. No sense in worrying about it now, she supposed. She was already back in London, safely ensconced in her family's cozy home. The marriage was less than a week away, and surely once she was married the gossip would diminish. She could survive until then.

No, Beatrice thought as she settled back into bed with a cup of tea, things weren't as bad as they *could* have been. She didn't even have to stay with Louisa this time. Her father and both her sisters had accompanied her, and Beatrice could go out of doors without anyone harping at her, and she could sleep until noon without guilt. Sleep was for the wicked—that's what Louisa always said. Of course, Beatrice didn't usually sleep the day away, but she definitely felt like doing it now.

That's what she was doing at the present moment, in fact. Actually, noon had come and gone. It was much closer to two.

"Beazie?" Helen called, knocking on the door.

"Yes?"

Her sister entered the room with uncharacteristic hesitation. "Are you well, Bea?"

Beatrice furrowed her brow in confusion. She was warm and well rested. What could possibly be wrong? "I'm fine, Helen. Why do you ask?"

Helen flopped down in bed next to her. "Well, we're all wondering, Bea. No one's seen you all morning, and you went to bed at seven o'clock last night…. Why, I don't think you've been out of bed for more than six hours a day since…well, you know. And that was over a week ago."

Beatrice sighed. "Yes, I know. I've been very tired lately…I think it's the change of season. Spores in the air, perhaps."

Helen wrinkled her nose. "Spores? You sound like Aunt Louisa." She curled up next to Beatrice. "Eleanor thinks you're suffering from…melancholia."

"Hogwash," Beatrice said, sipping her tea. "Eleanor always exaggerates. Perhaps you might say I'm feeling…*pensive.* But that is all, Helen. Do not worry."

"Oh. Then will you get out of bed now?"

Beatrice slowly shook her head. "No."

"You're still tired?" Helen asked doubtfully. "When will you finally be…rested?"

"Maybe tomorrow or the next day. I'm in no great rush."

Helen snorted. "Liar. I think you plan to walk down the aisle in your nightgown."

Beatrice smiled at the image, and Helen continued. "So, I guess you haven't seen Charles yet, have you? Funny he wouldn't come visit—he's in town, isn't he?"

He was. Beatrice knew that much. Louisa had *kindly* stopped by the day before to inform her that she had seen Charles entering his mother's house. Beatrice knew that her aunt had meant well by passing on this information, but she really wished Louisa had kept it to herself. Now she knew for sure that Charles was avoiding her, and that he was probably dreading their marriage even more than she was. "No, I haven't seen him."

Helen nodded. "Lucky for you Ben isn't back. He'll be livid when he finds out. Do you think he'll want to challenge Charles?"

Beatrice shrugged. Her brother was due back from the East Indies at any moment. He wouldn't be in the least amused by her situation. She wasn't sure if she and Charles would have any sort of honeymoon, but she hoped that they did, just to avoid her brother's inevitable reaction. Perhaps they could be in Scotland or France when he returned.

But Beatrice wasn't that lucky. At that very moment, in fact, her luck ran out.

Both she and Helen jumped when they heard the sound of the front door slamming, with such force that the windows rattled.

In the silence that followed, Helen asked, "Um…do you suppose it's—"

Before she could finish her question, Ben answered it, announcing his presence, more or less, with an angry shout. *"Beatrice! Where are you? What the bloody hell is this I hear about marriage?"*

"Do you reckon he knows, Beazie?" Helen asked this question with such cheerfully affected innocence that Beatrice couldn't help herself. She leapt from bed, swinging a pillow at her youngest and most mischievous sister.

Helen nimbly sidestepped her and dashed out the door, yelling over her laughter, "Father…Eleanor…I did it! Beatrice is out of bed!"

Beatrice *was* out of bed. To be precise, she was swearing a blue streak as she lay on the floor, having tripped on the hem of her nightgown in her haste to clobber her sister. She was only just sitting up when Ben barged in.

"Beatrice," he began, then stopped, looking perplexedly around the room. "Beatrice? Where are you?" He looked at the floor. "What the hell are you doing down there?"

She rose, rubbing her bruised posterior. "Oh, never mind. It's not important."

"Beatrice—*what* is going on?"

She walked back to sit on the edge of her bed. "It's a long story, Ben."

"Then you'd better start now," he said, making himself comfortable in her overstuffed armchair. He looked at her pointedly, waiting for her to begin.

It *was* a long story—made doubly so by her brother's frequent interjections. He was furious, and when Beatrice got to the embarrassing episode in the hall at Sudley, Ben practically flew out of his seat, vowing to call Charles out. When she pointed out that she would still be compromised, and that killing her fiancé would hardly help that fact, he had merely grumbled.

When she was finished, Ben sighed. "I don't like it, Bea. I've only met Summerson a few times, but his reputation precedes him."

She nodded, thinking that if her feelings weren't so wounded right then, she'd be able to say that she actually rather liked Charles. He just didn't want to marry her, that was all. "I don't have much choice, Ben…Charles's not *always* that bad—"

"Not that bad when he's trying to seduce you, Bea…but I suspect he'll be far less attentive when you're his wife."

She colored intensely at her brother's plain speaking. "Thank you, Ben. I'm aware of that. I was only trying to make the best of it."

He blushed, too, looking away in embarrassment. "Oh. Sorry. Look, I didn't mean…I just don't want you to get your hopes up about him falling in love with you. I know his type…hell, I *am* his type, Beatrice—"

She cut him off, not wanting to go over the subject of love anymore. "I know he won't love me, Ben. I overheard him telling Father that he wouldn't."

"He *told* our father?"

Beatrice nodded, trying to look very matter-of-fact and unaffected. She failed. Saying the words herself and seeing her brother's shocked reaction only made her realize what a fool she was for getting herself into this situation. Her lip began to quiver, and she crumpled back into bed, tears streaming silently down her face.

"Oh, damn" Ben cursed, rising from the chair to try to comfort his sister. He was bloody useless when it came to crying women.

Beatrice had been in London for over a week, and her wedding was a mere two days away, when Charles finally came to call. She was in the sitting room, tending to her long-neglected embroidery, when the butler announced Charles's presence. For a moment, Beatrice forgot everything that had passed between them and just looked. He filled the doorway with his frame, his lean body clad plainly but fashionably in buff breeches and a tailored coat. His hair was slightly disheveled from the wind, although she also noticed the faint trace of circles around his eyes. He looked rather as if he had just gotten out of bed. She swallowed, her throat suddenly tight.

"Hello," he said, walking into the room and closing the door behind him. He felt nervous, and he'd *never* felt nervous because of a woman before. He was trying hard not to show it, but his nerves had been what had kept him away from Beatrice even after he'd learned of her return to London. He'd acted completely abominably toward her, and their present situation was entirely his fault. It wouldn't be so bad if he thought she wanted to marry him, but she didn't. He was sure of it. She'd probably rather have married some dull, stable chap like Asher.

"Hello," Beatrice answered, blushing although she didn't quite know why. She'd been anxious about the possibility of this meeting, but she hadn't realized how distinctly uncomfortable it would make her feel.

He crossed the floor to the window and looked outside. "Thought perhaps you'd like to go for a walk in the park," he said without turning around.

She nodded slowly. "All right."

Charles turned then, his eyes wandering over her face. He wished he knew what she was thinking, but her expression was completely inscrutable. He walked over to the settee and held out a hand to help her rise. With downcast eyes, she accepted his assistance. He swallowed hard, wishing that he could pull her close. Not to kiss her, though; she looked vulnerable, and he wanted to hold her, to feel her, to assure her that everything would be all right. He didn't do it, of course. He merely let go of her hand and held the door for her as they left the room silently.

Charles had never felt so bloody divided in his whole life. He couldn't figure it out. There was nothing in the world he wanted less than marriage, and nothing that he wanted more than Beatrice. He felt things for her that he'd never felt before, but that didn't change the fact that he wanted to keep those feelings under control. If he let them get out of hand, if he let himself grow too attached to her, or she to him…it didn't bear thinking.

No, he had thought long and hard about how he was to prevent that eventuality. He didn't like the solution he had come up with, and he wasn't sure how Beatrice would feel about it, either. But there wasn't much choice. He had to protect himself, to protect her, as well.

Once in the park, they strolled for a while without speaking. It was the sort of clear day that only occurs in early fall, but despite the blue sky, it was deceptively chilly. Few people had ventured out, and they had the path to themselves.

He put his hands in his coat pockets. It was a nervous habit, but it had the effect of making him appear nonchalant. He was the first to break the silence, his internal debate still raging in his head. "Look, Beatrice, this can't go on."

A million questions flashed through her head, chief among them was what *this* referred to. Marriage? Did he plan to jilt her? "I'm sorry?" she asked.

Charles stopped walking and looked at her. "We're getting married in two days, whether we like it or not. Can we try to make the best of this situation?"

"What do you mean?"

"I know you're probably furious with me, Beatrice—I don't blame you. I'm furious with myself. I'm responsible for this muck we're in, after all."

"I see," she said, trying to keep the hurt out of her voice. She knew that their circumstances weren't ideal, but she hated to hear him refer to their situation as "this muck." She was furious with him, but it didn't mean she didn't harbor some ill-advised fantasies of a happy ending. "What, exactly, is your point?"

"My point is that we need to come to an agreement, Beatrice. We didn't plan on marrying each other, and I can't see us having a normal marriage. As you've pointed out yourself, neither one of us is exactly suited for it."

"Normal?"

"Yes—as in living happily ever after in our rural seat, producing offspring on a yearly basis. That kind of normal."

She flinched at his harsh tone, but Charles didn't notice. He barreled on. "Look, Beatrice, I think it is safe to say that we both enjoy each other's company, and I think we can agree that we…desire each other, as well. That's a lot more than most marriages begin with. I may not want to marry you, but I do want you, Beatrice—very much."

Her face was an impassive mask. "I see. What sort of agreement do you propose?"

He paused for just a fraction of a second before speaking. "If one of us should ever find ourselves in a position to…desire relations with someone else, then I certainly think we should discuss it. At that time, of course."

"You want me to have an affair?"

Charles grabbed her by the arm—not gently—forcing her to look at him. Realizing what he had done, he loosened his grip.

"No. I do not. But we are friends, Beatrice. We should approach this situation not so much as husband and wife, but as…equals."

"You mean *you* plan to have an affair?" she asked, her eyes flashing with anger.

He ran his hand through his hair in frustration. He bloody well did *not* want to have an affair. That wasn't it at all. He just wanted to establish some sort of barrier to prevent his feelings for her from ever getting too strong. Maybe it was an idiotic idea—maybe *he* was an idiot. But after a week of deliberating, it was the best thing he'd come up with.

"No, Beatrice. I don't *plan* to have an affair. You're the only woman I desire right now. But that may change, and I want you to be prepared for it and to be able to accept it. And, as we're friends, I think you should have the same freedom. Provided you are discreet, and you discuss it with me first."

She nodded slightly, feeling as if her body were disconnected from her mind, or as if she were in some sort of strange dream. She wasn't half as surprised that he was warning her that he might have an affair—she'd expected as much—as she was that he was encouraging her to do the same. Could she be understanding him correctly? Who would she have an affair with? Why would she want anyone other than him?

It was ridiculous, the whole situation, and for reasons that she didn't care to delve into, she would have preferred he hadn't just given her carte blanche. To do so only emphasized how little he really cared.

Charles could see that he had hurt her. He gently tipped up her chin with his finger, looking into her eyes. Softly, he said, "I'm not saying that I'll have an affair, Beatrice—maybe I never will. And you don't need to feel like you ought to, either. Hell, I don't *want* you to. I'm just trying to be fair."

She didn't recognize her voice as she asked, "I can have my affairs, too?"

He felt as if he'd been punched in the gut, but he nodded.

"All right," she said rather flatly. "As long as it's fair."

Charles had never in his entire life so disliked getting what he'd asked for. He wanted to shake Beatrice, to tell her that if she ever had an affair he'd…he'd…he didn't know what he'd do. He could never hurt her, but he would bloody well lose his mind.

"I'll walk you back now," he said curtly, needing to get away from her before he said something he'd regret.

Beatrice was somewhat surprised. They hadn't been out very long. Clearly his visit had been for business rather than pleasure. "Yes, I think that would be best," she said frigidly, turning to head back along the path.

They walked along in silence and soon reached the street. Beatrice rubbed her arms, trying to keep warm.

Charles noticed. He hadn't been looking at her, but he was aware of every tiny move she made. He put his arm around her shoulders reflexively and felt her stiffen. Perversely, he didn't remove his arm—she would be his wife, and he could bloody well walk down the street with his arm around her. After a moment, Beatrice relaxed slightly, at least enough that she no longer radiated tension.

Soon they were standing on the pavement outside her house. But before they turned up the path to the door, Charles stopped, forcing her to halt, as well. For a moment, they looked at each other in awkward silence.

He began rummaging in his coat pocket. "Here," he said rather gruffly, as he pulled out a small, black box. "This is for you."

Beatrice just stared at the object in his gloved hand, not knowing what to make of it.

"Are you going to open it?" He seemed almost annoyed.

She nodded and took the box from him. She opened it and drew a small, shocked breath. Nestled in black velvet was a pair of the most intricate, beautiful earrings she'd ever seen. Each one was made of a golden stud shaped to resemble a violet, and at the center of each flower was a tiny pearl. Dangling from each flower were three small strands of emeralds; a final, slightly larger emerald hung at the bottom of each strand.

"Try one on," Charles said.

She carefully lifted an earring from the box and slipped it into her ear. "They're beautiful, Charles. Thank you."

He lifted the second earring and handed it to her. His voice husky, he said, "I'd help you put it on, but I'm afraid I don't know how."

Beatrice blushed. "I can manage." She slipped the final earring in. "How do they look?"

Charles thought she'd never looked lovelier. He had bought the earrings just that morning, completely on impulse. He'd realized he'd never bought her a present before—it would have been improper. But now he could. "They look beautiful. You look beautiful. I thought the green…" He didn't finish his sentence. He just leaned forward, lightly cupping her face, and kissed her softly.

The kiss was over before Beatrice realized what had happened. She stood there, slightly dazed, still feeling his warm lips on hers even though he'd already stepped away.

"Shall we?" Charles asked.

She nodded, and placing her hand on his arm, turned up the path to the house.

"I'm not going to come in," he said as they stood in front of the door.

Beatrice nodded. She hadn't expected him to. She also hadn't expected him to kiss her again, but he did so. Not a hot, passionate kiss, but warm and soft and brief. Too brief.

As Charles pulled away, he nearly groaned at the look of reluctance on Beatrice's face. She wanted more, and he did, too. *Just two more days.*

Tipping his hat slightly, he turned and left.

As Beatrice watched him walk back down the path, she realized that she'd never been so confused in her life. One minute, he had treated her coldly, and the next…there were times when she thought he might care. She just wished he'd be consistent.

Chapter Twenty

Despite her nervousness, Beatrice yawned as she waited in her bedroom. Meg had just gone downstairs to see if everything was ready, and if it was…well, Beatrice had better be ready, as well. That meant that Charles had arrived, and that their few guests—family, mostly—were all seated and waiting. That meant it was time for Beatrice to make the long trip downstairs to be wed.

She began pacing about her room, the restlessness of her activity incongruous with her occasional, sleepy yawns. She'd spent nearly the entire night tossing in her bed, thinking about her conversation with Charles and about the resolution they—no, *he*—had come up with. She certainly didn't have any plans to have an affair—the very idea was ridiculous. But the fact that he had proposed such an absurd solution indicated, if not guaranteed, that *he* planned to have an affair. Maybe not immediately, but eventually.

Beatrice yawned again and walked over to her window. It was about ten o'clock. Despite her trepidation, she was relieved that the wedding would take place in the morning; that way, they could simply get it over with. Charles had sent word that they would travel on to his family seat in Kent immediately following the ceremony—probably, Beatrice thought wryly, to get as far away from *her* family as possible.

She was glad that they would be leaving town, not being eager to face family and friends herself. But she hadn't the faintest idea what to expect at Pelham House. Would they have a true wedding night? Beatrice wasn't even exactly sure what happened during a wedding night. That was the sort of thing a girl's mother discussed with her, and she was not going to ask her father about such particulars.

A soft knock came from the door, and Meg poked her head around it. "Are you ready, Miss Beatrice?"

Beatrice turned away from the window, going quite still. "I'm as ready as I'll ever be, Meg. Come on in."

"Everyone has arrived, Miss Beatrice, but take your time. They can all wait if you need another moment," she said while bustling about the room. "How are you feeling?"

Beatrice shrugged. "I'm nervous, Meg. *Really* nervous."

Meg nodded. "That's to be expected. Everyone is nervous on their wedding day."

"Yes, but this isn't a normal wedding, seeing as we're being forced. I don't even know if Charles will want to look at me, much less touch me, after he signs away his freedom in order to salvage my reputation. He'll probably hate me! And then—"

"Oh, dear," Meg clucked. "There's more?"

Beatrice sank dramatically onto her bed. "Yes, Meg. I don't even know what happens on a wedding night. Do you?"

Her question held a note of desperation that Meg couldn't ignore. Blushing, she answered, "Well…I've never been married myself, but…well, he's kissed you, right? I know he has, or you wouldn't be in this fix now."

Beatrice rolled her eyes. "Yes, Meg. He's kissed me."

The maid settled into the dressing-table chair. "I take it you…enjoyed it?"

Beatrice mumbled her answer.

Meg smiled. "I don't think you have anything to worry about, Miss Beatrice. At least as far as a wedding night is concerned. I suspect that your Charles will take care of all the explanations you need. Who knows, you might even enjoy it."

Beatrice buried her face in her pillow. "You've told me nothing."

"What—did you want actual mechanics?"

"I…I…oh, never mind. I just want to get it over with." She swung her legs over the side and climbed from bed. As she stood, Meg hurried over to tidy her hair and gown.

"Shall I walk down with you?"

Beatrice nodded forlornly. As they made their way down the wide front staircase, Beatrice felt as if she were walking toward her doom. She didn't want to go through with it, although she knew she had no choice. When she reached the bottom of the staircase, she could hear the quiet din of the guests' voices to her left, where everyone was assembled in the drawing room. But her eyes were drawn to the front door right in front of her, its gleaming brass doorknob, tempting her to escape.

If Meg hadn't been by her side, Beatrice might have continued right out the front door. Instead, she followed the sound of voices to the drawing room.

After all her anticipation, the wedding came and went in a confused flash. Charles was there, looking blasted uncomfortable with her whole family glaring at him and no one but Helen bothering to speak to him. Lady Summerson and Lucy appeared worried. As Beatrice walked down the aisle, her mind felt disjointed from her body, and her mind begged her feet to stop.

But she walked on, until she reached Charles's side. Lightly, he gripped her hand, and the vicar began the ceremony.

Words, words. I do. I do. A ring slipped onto her finger.

And then it was over. They were married.

After the ceremony, a light luncheon was served in the dining room. Charles and Beatrice sat next to one another at the end of the table, hardly speaking but each extremely aware of the other's presence. She ate nothing, but downed several glasses of champagne. Charles did little better, attempting stilted conversation with Eleanor, who sat uncomfortably on his other side. Louisa and Ben, the family pit bulls, had been intentionally seated as far away from Charles as possible and glared at him from the other end of the table.

After half an hour, Charles bent his head to Beatrice. "Beatrice, let's go," he whispered.

"Now?" She looked anxiously around the room. Her whole family was there, as was his…could they really just leave?

He seemed to think so; he had already begun to rise. "Yes, now. I can't take this bloody torture any longer."

His mother, seated a few chairs away, noticed him rise. "You're not leaving, are you? We've only just started."

Charles nodded curtly, holding out his hand to Beatrice.

She took it and rose, uncomfortable beneath the intense scrutiny. "Yes. I think we'd better. It'll be very late when we arrive as it is."

Her father nodded, wanting to smooth over the sudden awkwardness. "Of course. We'll walk you to the door."

The carriage was already waiting, their things having been packed earlier that morning; Meg would follow behind them in a separate carriage. Beatrice was eternally grateful that her long-time companion had chosen to accompany her. She didn't know a soul in Kent and would appreciate her presence. But as Meg following behind meant that she and Charles would be alone in the carriage for several hours.

Her palms began to sweat.

Beatrice turned around to bid her father goodbye.

"I have a feeling, Bea, that everything will work out," he said, squeezing her hand.

She just nodded absently, feeling quite ill.

After her family had made their goodbyes, Charles's mother and Lucy stepped forward. "We'll come for a visit soon," Lady

Summerson promised. "It's been ages since we've been to Pelham House. I'm glad someone will live there again."

Beatrice smiled politely, although she hadn't the faintest idea how long they'd remain in Kent. They hadn't had the time to discuss that sort of detail.

Charles put his arm over her shoulder, and they stepped out into the brisk autumn air. With a chorus of merry goodbyes behind them, they walked to the awaiting carriage.

For most of the first hour they sat—on opposite seats—in complete silence. Occasionally, Beatrice peeked over at Charles, trying to guess what he was thinking about. He appeared to be deep in thought.

"Um, Charles?" she said at last, unable to take the silence any longer.

He said nothing, but looked up.

"I'm not really sure what to expect."

He sat up slightly straighter. "What do you mean?"

"Well, I don't know anything about your house. What's it like?"

He thought for a moment. It had been years since he'd been at Pelham House himself. Being there always brought back too many painful memories. "Well," he began, "I haven't been there for a very long time. I prefer town."

"Oh," Beatrice said, trying to keep the disappointment from her voice. She, on the other hand, had always preferred the country. "But surely you remember it well enough to tell me something about it."

He remembered it only too well. "We live close to Dover…it's only a few miles to the coast, actually, and you can easily walk. On clear days, you can see all the way across the strait to France. In the spring—when I was a boy, that is—my family used to walk down to the cliffs to picnic."

"Oh?" she asked, trying to imagine him as a young boy and failing. "I've never been to Kent, but I hear it's beautiful."

Charles just shrugged. "The house itself was built in the late sixteenth century. I hate to inform you, Beatrice, but it probably will require a bit of work. It's not just me—no one has lived there in years."

"Not even your mother and Lucy?"

He shook his head. "No. It's a very large house...much too large for just two people."

"I see."

After a moment of uncomfortable silence, he asked, "Is that all that you were wondering about?"

Beatrice bit her lip and shook her head slightly.

"Come here," Charles said, indicating for her to sit next to him on the seat. She moved, not meeting his gaze, feeling suddenly shy. He put his arm around her and pulled her close. Soon, Beatrice relaxed enough to lay her head against his chest.

Charles sighed, relaxing into the seat, as well. He knew what she was really thinking about—the same thing he was. He kissed her softly on the top of her head and gently stroked her hair.

Beatrice looked up. "Charles?"

"Hmm?"

She wanted him to kiss her again, on the lips this time. She stared at him a moment, trying to work up the nerve to ask him. But she didn't have the nerve. Instead, she closed her eyes, leaned forward and kissed him herself. Briefly, but she did it.

When she pulled away, Charles was regarding her with curiosity. Beatrice's cheeks flamed and she looked away, mortified by her unseemly boldness.

"I'm sorry," she mumbled.

"Look at me, Beatrice."

Slowly, she turned back around.

He didn't seem angry. Didn't appear shocked, either. "You needn't apologize," he said, his eyes darkening wickedly. "Perhaps you'd like to do it again?"

When Beatrice didn't move right away, he asked, "Or did you want *me* to kiss *you* this time?"

Could her face get any redder? "No. I would like to try it, if that's all right."

He nodded, trying to look calm while his blood raged through his body.

She leaned forward somewhat awkwardly, then paused for a moment, wondering how best to approach this novel situation.

Charles cleared his throat. "Beatrice? May I offer a suggestion? Perhaps if you moved a bit closer…oh, here." In frustration, he picked her up in his arms and deposited her in his lap.

She blushed. "Sorry. I've never done this before."

"You've no idea how happy that makes me," Charles said, grinning wickedly. "You may practice on me all you like."

Beatrice sat up slowly once more. She was seated sideways on Charles's lap now—an excellent position if he were kissing her. But in order for her to kiss him…she turned around to face him, so that she was kneeling on the seat with her legs straddling his.

Charles sucked in his breath. She had no idea what she was doing to him, no idea how suggestive her position had become. He watched her get settled, thinking that the most experienced courtesan could never be more alluring than she was at that very moment. "Ready?" he asked, his voice dropping an octave.

Beatrice nodded. She felt nervous…she felt rather ridiculous, in fact. But she *wanted* to kiss him. She had so many questions, and kissing him seemed to be the only way to answer them. She leaned forward, her eyelids closing.

In that instant, Charles forgot about letting her have control. His hands snaked up behind her head, pulling it down to meet his ravenous lips. There was nothing gentle in this kiss, nothing soft or slow. He'd meant to let her explore kissing him at her own pace, and instead he was devouring her. But Beatrice met his kiss with equal desperation, her tongue dueling with his, creeping beyond his lips to taste him fully.

While he kissed her, Charles's hands moved down her back, his fingers tracing a path along her spine. He cupped her bottom, dragging her closer and fitting her tightly against his groin. Then, with the slightest of pressure, he rocked her forward against his hardness, only to release the pressure and rock her forward once more.

Beatrice cried out, her head falling back in ecstasy. Charles pulled his lips from hers only to blaze a trail down the column of her throat, not stopping until he had reached the swell of her breasts. One of his hands crept up to her bodice and tugged the fabric down gently.

He wanted to shout in male satisfaction at the sight of her pert nipples, begging for his touch. He let his fingers wander lightly over her breasts, watching them tighten and pucker, before he lowered his mouth to savor her taste and texture.

"Did I tell you that you're beautiful?" His voice was soft, hoarse, and his tongue still spiraled hungrily against the taut skin of her nipple.

Beatrice said nothing, too far gone with pleasure to respond with anything other than a groan. Instead, she pressed herself against his hardness, needing the firm, unyielding pressure of his body against hers.

With a groan of his own, Charles lifted her from his lap, laying her down on the seat and settling himself on top of her, fitting his hips between her legs. His lips returned to her mouth, and his hand moved to her nipple, his fingers circling, lightly pinching.

Beatrice mewled at this double onslaught, and Charles thought he'd never heard a more beautiful sound in his life. But when she tore her mouth from his, her lips wandering over to his ear with abandon, moaning his name and begging him for something she didn't yet understand, Charles knew he had to stop. He was moments from making love to her, and he would not take her virginity in a bloody carriage. He pulled away, swearing, rasping for breath.

Still absorbed in pure sensation, Beatrice blinked, her eyes clouded with passion. She was lying on her back on the seat, her pink nipples peeking over her bodice, her lips just as pink and swollen. Charles had to tear his gaze away, knowing that he'd quickly lose his resolve otherwise. "I'm sorry, Beatrice. We have to stop now—if we don't, I won't be able to."

She touched him gently on the shoulder. "I don't mind. Please."

He looked at her again, the regretful note in her voice almost making him change his mind. "I do," he groaned. "Not here, Beatrice. We have to wait until we get home." But he knew he couldn't just stop, couldn't just leave her with a taste of what was to come, wanting more so badly that it hurt. Charles leaned over her, his hand creeping beneath her skirt, sliding slowly up the inside of her leg.

Beatrice tensed. "What are you doing, Charles?"

"Shh," he said softly. "Just trust me."

He let his fingers brush ever so lightly against her skin, just the softest, teasing touch. He paused, his fingers tracing circles on the smooth spot behind her knee, before traveling on along the inside of her thigh.

Charles closed his eyes when his fingers grazed the soft mound at the juncture. She was damp and hot, mindless with pleasure…. Charles would have sold his soul to have been able to free himself from his breeches and plunge inside her, to feel her body grip him tightly, pull him closer, to feel her convulse and climax with him.

But he wouldn't do it. His fingers gently teased her soft flesh, stroking her and slipping inside, first one finger, and then two. He moved slowly at first, painstakingly slow, seeing the uncertainty in Beatrice's eyes, feeling the tenseness of her body. But after a moment, all her tension disappeared. Her eyes grew soft, and her flesh…if it were possible for her to become softer, warmer and more giving, she did. And suddenly, she was moving her body against his hand, meeting him stroke for stroke, moving faster, slower, faster again, without reserve, without anything but passion.

Charles pressed his thumb against the tiny nub within the folds of her womanhood, needing, for his own sanity, to give Beatrice her release. And the second he found her, she exploded, her hips rocking against his hand as she rode the waves of her climax. Her hands gripped the seat, her fingers digging into the supple leather, and her whole body tensed and shuddered as she cried out his name one final time.

Charles just watched, stunned. He'd never seen any woman find her release so quickly, and with such freedom and abandon. And he hadn't even taken her virginity yet.

After a moment of recovery, Beatrice stretched slightly, a satisfied smile creeping around the corners of her mouth. He'd been afraid she'd feel shy once she regained her senses, but instead she seemed to feel empowered. Catlike, she curled up against his side. "I didn't know what that would be like," she said.

Charles smiled, ignoring the twinge of pain in his groin, too inordinately pleased by the note of awe he heard in her voice. "Enjoyed yourself, did you?"

Beatrice craned her head to look up at him, a large grin on her face. She nodded. "Um…did you enjoy yourself?"

He had enjoyed himself so much that he was now in a great deal of pain. He didn't tell her that, though. He just nodded, dropping a kiss on the tip of her nose. "I did."

"Meg told me that I had nothing to worry about, that you would show me everything."

Charles smiled ruefully, thinking to himself that he was in for the longest carriage ride in history. "You haven't seen half of it."

Chapter Twenty-One

The sun had long since set when they finally arrived at Pelham House. In that light it appeared a forbidding black silhouette, stark against the clear night sky.

Charles stepped from the carriage first, and then turned to help Beatrice down. She held her hand out, but gasped in surprise when instead of taking it he grabbed her around the waist and lifted her into his arms.

"What are you doing?" she asked, blushing in alarm.

Charles began striding toward the front door. "I thought," he said deliberately, looking down into her eyes, "that I was supposed to carry you over the threshold."

"Oh," she said, somewhat confused. She hadn't been expecting that.

Charles mounted the steps and carried her through the door. His butler and housekeeper stood expectantly, waiting to greet them, both smiling.

"Beatrice, I'd like you to meet Wilson and Mrs. Hester. They're all that's kept this place from falling down."

She blushed from her husband's arms, embarrassed to be presented for the first time in such an undignified position. "How do you do?"

Mrs. Hester curtsied and Wilson bowed deeply, but Charles didn't pause for any further pleasantries. "You shall have more time to meet with them tomorrow. Wilson, Mrs. Hester, it's lovely to see you, but I don't think we'll need anything further this evening."

"Very good, my lord," Wilson said, smiling at Charles's receding back.

As Charles mounted the steps, Beatrice wondered what on earth she would talk to his servants about. She wasn't even sure if he meant for her to stay in this house, or if she would have any real authority over the servants. Theirs wasn't a true marriage, after all—did he expect her to behave as a true wife? All of these questions had been running through her head during the drive, but she hadn't had the nerve to ask them, especially not when she had more pressing concerns. Like their wedding night.

When they reached the top of the steps, Charles carried her down a long, tapestry-lined corridor before stopping in front of a door. Without asking, Beatrice knew that they'd reached their destination.

He slowly eased her to the floor, letting her slide down the length of his body, closing his eyes against the flood of sensation that threatened to overpower him. Once Beatrice was standing, he turned her to face him. Charles said nothing, nor did she. They just gazed at one another.

She looked so lovely that it made his heart hurt. No matter how much he had resisted their marriage, he suddenly felt oddly satisfied…good, for lack of a better word. That wasn't how he wanted to feel. He wanted to feel nothing. He certainly hadn't expected the warm comfort that had enveloped him as Beatrice lay nestled against his side during the drive.

"I don't love you," Charles whispered gruffly, his words sudden and harsh. He needed to distance himself from her, from the way she made him feel. And yet he was drawn to her like a magnet, taking a step closer, drinking in every inch of her skin with his eyes.

Beatrice gulped under his hot gaze, feeling her knees, her legs, her belly, everything go to liquid. "I know," she said, her eyes drawn to the hard line of his jaw, the intense green of his eyes. "I don't love you."

"Then we understand each other," he replied, before dipping his head and catching her lips in the most searing kiss of his experience. He had meant to go slowly, but the heady knowledge that she now belonged to him made that impossible.

His lips on hers, Charles reached for the doorknob, rattling it slightly before, with a frustrated groan, he gave the door a decisive push and opened it. He practically pulled her into the room, closing the door firmly behind them as he began shrugging from his coat, his mouth never leaving hers.

As his coat fell to the floor, Beatrice lifted her hands to his chest, reveling in the feel of his hard, warm body through the fine linen of his shirt. Emboldened, she tugged at his cravat, fumbling in her inexperience, but too impatient to wait. Growling, Charles tore his lips from hers long enough to help her loosen it. Then, his hands once again on her, he slipped her pelisse from her shoulders. It joined his coat on the floor.

Beatrice blushed and lowered her head when he stepped back to look at her more fully.

"Don't," he said, tipping her chin up with his finger. "You're beautiful."

Beatrice didn't know what to say to that, so she said nothing. Instead, she looked her fill, as well. Charles was always impeccably dressed in her presence. She'd certainly never seen him without a coat before, and with his cravat loosened, falling away from his bronze neck in snowy folds, he was so masculine. She drank in every detail—the soft, black hair that fell over his temple, the faint trace of growth on his cheeks…

Her brow furrowed slightly as she noticed the faint but jagged scar that ran the width of his throat. With a question in her eyes, Beatrice reached out her hand to touch it, wanting to soothe whatever long-ago pain had caused it.

But Charles caught her hand in his before she could touch him, bringing it up to his lips and placing a kiss on each finger. Then he moved close again, this time to sear a trail down her neck with his lips—and lower, to the crest of her breasts. He reached behind her, hastily popping buttons from their holes. Her gown fell to the floor and he slid her chemise over her shoulders to let it settle at her waist. Before Beatrice could become self-conscious about her exposed breasts, his mouth returned, his tongue spiraling over her nipples and making her gasp for air.

Somehow they made it over to the bed, Charles's mouth still at her breast, and her hands in his hair, pulling him closer. When they reached the bed, she gasped in shock as he lowered her onto it. He leaned forward, his body looming over hers, but there was nothing threatening in his manner. Lazily, he flicked her nipple with his tongue, sending shivers up and down her body. He tugged gently at her chemise but, wrapped as it was around her hips, it didn't move.

"I've had this problem before," she said as if reading his thoughts. "I manage to get stuck in my clothes whenever I try to undress without Meg's help."

"I'm contemplating tearing it off."

With an impish composure that was fading fast under the delicious torment of his mouth, Beatrice replied, "Meg has never tried that technique."

"I shouldn't think so," he said, giving in and tearing her chemise straight down the front.

Beatrice gasped in surprise, suddenly realizing that she was completely nude and that he was, except for his coat, still fully dressed. She began to sit up, but he gently pressed her back onto the bed.

"Don't, Beatrice," he said, his voice thick and his eyes so dark they almost appeared black. "I've been waiting for this moment since I first laid eyes on you. Let me look."

Beatrice said nothing, but when Charles moved away from her slightly, putting just enough space between them for him to regard her fully, she didn't try to cover herself. She blushed, for sure, but she let him look.

And Charles looked long and hard. It was just as he had imagined in his countless erotic dreams: her flaxen hair pooling on his pillow, her nipples swollen and pink from his tongue, her subtle curves golden in the warm light of the fire and the silky nest of curls at the junction of her thighs….

Charles nearly lost control. He wanted to unfasten his breeches and plunge into her, virginity and inexperience be damned. He wanted to own her, to feel every hot inch of her gripping him tightly, to spill his seed inside her. He throbbed for release, and he reached out to grasp Beatrice's hand to guide her toward him.

When Beatrice felt the size of him, she went still, suddenly unnerved. For a moment she did nothing but look up at him. He met her gaze, and his eyes held a fierce heat that she'd never seen before. Curiously, she moved her hand. The results were immediate. He groaned, closing his eyes.

Beatrice pulled her hand away in surprise. "Are you all right?" she asked.

Charles swallowed and opened his eyes, but nodded in response to her question. Maybe it wasn't such a good idea for her to be touching him this time—he didn't think he'd last long if she were to do so again.

He began to unbutton his shirt, never taking his eyes from her face, watching her pupils dilate as his chest was revealed. He shrugged off his shirt and then began on his breeches.

Suddenly, Beatrice looked terrified.

Charles stopped and leaned forward. "You seem frightened."

She nodded, covering herself with the sheet and sitting up.

"I am frightened. It…it felt so large, and I don't know exactly what will happen. I mean, I have a rough idea, but it doesn't seem possible."

Charles struggled for control. She didn't realize what she did to him with those words. He would soon regret what he said next, however. "Perhaps if you help me?"

Beatrice thought for a moment and nodded. "I think that would be a good idea."

His mouth went completely dry as she rose from the bed, leaving the sheet behind. She was directly in front of him, and as her hands moved shyly toward his trousers, she lowered her head to concentrate on her task. Charles inhaled deeply, filling his nostrils with the scent of her hair. Lilacs.

He thought about lilacs, about anything to keep himself from ravishing her. But when he felt her fingers gently tug at the front of his trousers, he drew his breath sharply.

Beatrice paused and looked up. "You're certain I'm not hurting you?"

By this point, Charles actually was in pain, and he knew that if he weren't inside her soon he'd go mad. He gently pushed her away and quickly finished the job on his own, laying her down on his bed and covering her with his body.

Charles's lips returned, trailing from Beatrice's ear down to her breasts and lower. She gasped when his tongue found its way to her navel, where it stopped for a moment before traveling on, lower still, to the insides of her thighs….

She tangled her hands in his hair, oblivious to all but the sensations he was giving her. When Charles moved back up her body and his finger gently entered her, she thought the world had ended, so intense was the pleasure that racked her, making her call out his name.

But before Charles's name had even fully formed on her lips, he eased himself inside her—not far enough to breach her maidenhead, but enough to accustom her to his size. Beatrice opened her eyes wide at the unfamiliar sensation, but when he pulled back, the heady friction of his movement made her moan. Her mouth found his, and she pleaded against his lips for more.

With one swift thrust, Charles entered her fully, groaning in pleasure so long denied. Beatrice met his groan with her own, mindless to anything but a pleasure so deep, so penetrating, that it obliterated the faint prick of pain as he tore through her maidenhead. For a moment, he didn't move, just held himself very still, suspended above her, letting her body adjust. Then slowly, very slowly, his hips began to rock back and forth, faster and harder with every stroke. Without thinking, acting on pure instinct alone, Beatrice joined him, meeting him thrust for thrust, a sweetness and heat growing inside her with every movement until, with a thrust so powerful that they cried out in unison, the feeling burst, raining wave after wave of pleasure upon them.

For many minutes, maybe an hour, they lay numbly in each other's arms, not speaking, not moving, and yet so moved. Occasionally, Charles stroked her hair, letting his fingers wander down her back.

They fell asleep just like that, damp with sweat. And as Beatrice passed into oblivion, she couldn't help but have the optimistic thought that, as her father said, everything might be all right after all.

Chapter Twenty-Two

When Beatrice finally awoke, it was nearly noon. The sun shone brightly into the room, casting a rather harsh light onto her surroundings. She felt warm and cozy wrapped in the blankets of Charles's bed, but when she rolled over she realized that his side was quite cold.

She sat up quickly, looking about the room for any sign of her husband, but he was gone. Beatrice then noticed a note on the bedside table. She picked it up and read.

> B—
> I had some business to attend to in town…it will last all of today, and probably tomorrow, as well. Sorry I didn't tell you earlier, but I didn't want to spoil the evening. I shall probably return by the end of the week.
> C.

Beatrice read the note twice, not quite sure what to make of it. After the night they had shared, it wasn't exactly what she was expecting. Oh, she wasn't expecting roses and professions of love, but she did at least think that she'd see him in the morning. She had thought that—perhaps—he'd felt something, too.

Apparently she was wrong. He hadn't even bothered to wake her up before he left.

Beatrice sighed and sank back into bed. She'd been a fool to expect anything more, to expect that he might care to spend their first day as husband and wife together. *I may not want to marry you, but I do want you.* That's what Charles had said, after all. She shouldn't be surprised by this. It wasn't as if she played any important role in his life, or he in hers. This was what they had discussed: they'd each maintain their previous lives—with discretion—and go on about their business. Beatrice had no right feeling hurt.

But that didn't change the fact that she did. Very hurt. And very angry.

She rose from bed, not bothering to ring for Meg. Her maid would just force her to answer all sorts of unpleasant questions that she wasn't ready to face. Instead, Beatrice chose her simplest gown—one that she could manage on her own—and tidied her hair. Then she headed downstairs, determined not to dwell on her wounded pride.

Mrs. Hester was the first person she saw. She was dusting the furniture in the front hall. "Good morning, Lady Summerson. May I show you to the breakfast room?"

Beatrice blinked, startled by the strange sound of her new name. "Oh, good morning, Mrs. Hester. Um, not quite yet."

"And where's Lord Summerson this fine day? I haven't seen him all morning."

Beatrice smiled tightly. "He had some business to attend to in town…I thought perhaps you could show me about the house today?"

"In town! Why, I'm surprised you two didn't just stay in town then. Will Lord Summerson be back later today? It seems a lot of traveling in a such a short time."

Beatrice shook her head, wanting to cry. "I'm afraid he won't be back today…something important came up and he won't return until the end of the week."

Beatrice was actually afraid that he wouldn't return at all. If he wanted to be with her, they would have simply stayed in London until his business was complete. What if he intended to abandon her in the country?

Mrs. Hester patted Beatrice on the hand, sensing her distress. "Well, I'd be pleased to show you around the house. It wouldn't be any problem at all. And Wilson can show you around the grounds later, if you like."

Beatrice nodded, pleased to have found a friend. "Yes. I should like that. I could see very little when we came in last night."

Mrs. Hester laid down the rag she had been dusting with. "To begin with, this is the front hall. Not very interesting, I suppose. It does need a bit of work."

Beatrice looked around the space. It was impeccably clean. Yet clean was about the only compliment she could pay it. The carpet was worn and decades of harsh sunlight had faded the curtains. Even the paint on the walls was beginning to peel in the corners. A bit of work? Hardly. It needed a lot.

But Beatrice was determined to put on a good face. "It's a bit threadbare, but *spotless*. A coat of paint might help."

Mrs. Hester was obviously pleased. "A coat of paint would be a start. Do you think that you will be living here primarily, then? If you don't mind my asking, that is."

Beatrice could only shrug. "I don't mind at all. I'm always asking too many questions myself. And to answer *your* question, I don't really know where we'll live. We haven't even had a chance to speak about it yet."

"Well, I for one hope that you settle here, at least for part of the year. It's a shame to let such a beautiful house go to waste, and it has been too long since this house has been lived in. *And*," she added meaningfully, "it's just the place for raising children."

"Oh?" Beatrice asked with interest. She wasn't at all eager to talk about children, but hoped that Mrs. Hester would reveal something—anything—about Beatrice's uncommunicative husband.

The woman nodded, enjoying the opportunity to reminisce. "Why, I can remember Lord Charles and his brother having a grand time growing up here…Lucy, too, although she came a bit later. Pelham House was full of life and activity then—not like now, with just a few old retainers puttering about. Those children got into enough scrapes, I can tell you that."

Beatrice's ears perked up at the mention of Charles's brother. "My husband and his brother were very close, I take it?"

Mrs. Hester nodded. "Indeed. I mean, they fought like brothers do, but they were extremely close." She paused. "Have you ever seen what your husband's father looked like?"

Beatrice shook her head, appreciating Mrs. Hester's voluble nature. Charles would never be so open about his past, but she sensed that it was very important to him.

"Then we'll go to the portrait gallery next. There's a picture of the late marquess in it. Used to be one of the marquess and the two boys, as a matter of fact," the housekeeper said, leading Beatrice down a long hallway. "But I haven't seen it in years. I think someone put it in storage, although, of course, I've never asked. There's still an empty spot on the wall for it." She stopped in front of a large painting. "Here you are. This is Lord Summerson—the elder, of course."

Beatrice blinked. She could have been looking at a portrait of Charles, so strong was the resemblance between father and son. Charles's father had the same black hair, the same brilliant green eyes. Indeed, if Mrs. Hester hadn't already told her who he was, Beatrice would have thought it *was* Charles.

She narrowed her eyes and took a small step back to get a better look. No…there *was* something different, some inexplicable disparity between father and son, even though they were physically so alike.

It took her a moment to place the difference. It was something in the eyes. Charles's father wasn't smiling in the portrait, yet Beatrice could almost hear his laughter, could just *sense* his happiness. His green eyes sparkled with joy, and with something else that was all but absent from her husband—peace.

Beatrice had never thought of Charles as being unhappy before—he was usually teasing and laughing—and yet as she looked at this portrait, she realized that he was never as happy as he seemed. He certainly wasn't at peace with himself.

Feeling suddenly very sad, Beatrice remarked, "Charles thinks very highly of his father. He's never really spoken about him, but it's apparent enough."

"I've never seen children adore their father so much," Mrs. Hestor replied proudly. "They were such a happy family, and such a pleasure to work for. 'Tis a tragedy what happened. But I'm glad that Lord Charles is finally wed…and soon enough there will be children here again."

Beatrice smiled weakly. She and Charles hadn't discussed children, although they were the natural conclusion of most marriages. She didn't know how he felt about babies, but she didn't think that he wanted them. He'd said plainly enough that he wanted to maintain his prior way of life, and that didn't include a family.

Although Beatrice was innocent, she knew that children were a possibility. What if she became pregnant? Would Charles change? She somehow didn't think so.

"Are you all right, Lady Summerson?" Mrs. Hester asked, concerned.

"Hmm? I'm sorry. I'm fine…just woolgathering."

"Ah, well, you've had a tiring couple of days, I'm sure. How about a nice cup of tea before we finish this tour?"

Beatrice nodded. To be perfectly frank, she could use a cup of something stronger.

Charles had no plans to meet Beatrice at Pelham House, later on in the week or ever. Nor did he have any pressing business in town. He already had a host of excuses for why he wouldn't be able to return, none of which were close to the real reason at all. Rather, he spent his first day as a married man getting drunk with Jack.

By early evening, which it currently was, he was foxed *and* had a splitting headache.

Jack saw nothing but humor in the situation. "I never thought I'd see the day that Charles Summerson, confirmed bachelor, was not only a married man but was banishing himself from his own home for fear of his wife. 'Tis a sad state of affairs."

Charles stared at the wall, knowing that if he looked at Jack he'd succumb to the urge to plant his fist in his friend's face. Instead, he slowly counted to ten. "I am not afraid of my wife, you ass. I would just prefer that we live separately. She tells me that she likes the country, so she can live there. I don't care for Pelham House, anyway."

"You don't plan to live with her at all?" Jack asked in surprise. "What's she think about that?"

Charles was close to losing his temper completely. He really didn't want to discuss this subject, but Jack was leaving him little choice. His voice came out clipped. "I haven't told her yet."

Jack raised an eyebrow. "You haven't told her?"

"Are you hard of hearing?"

Jack ignored that comment, still trying to get to the heart of the matter. "So if you didn't tell her, then you just up and left this morning? Without a by-your-leave?"

"No," Charles retorted tightly. "I left her a note. I told her that I had some business to attend to and that I would come up later in the week."

"But you don't actually plan to go up later in the week, do you?"

"No."

They sat in silence for several minutes, until Jack murmured, "Beatrice isn't so bad, you know. I don't think her teeth are at all crooked. You could do a lot worse for a wife."

Charles felt an irrational stab of anger hearing Jack compliment Beatrice, remembering how he had ogled her at his mother's party. "I *know* she's not so bad. You needn't tell me. I just didn't want a wife."

"I see." Jack nodded his head. "You should have thought of that before you dallied with her, hmm?"

Charles slid his chair back, ready to pounce on his friend. He took a deep, steadying breath. Through clenched teeth, he said, "I wasn't thinking."

Jack continued cheerfully. "I guess not, because it didn't seem to me that you were trying very hard to avoid her."

"Not hard enough."

"You were actively pursuing her, one might say."

"One might."

Jack was quiet for another minute, but Charles didn't bother to hope that it would last. His friend was battling, obviously, with some obnoxious witticism.

Finally, Jack could no longer resist. "Know what I think, Summerson?"

"Enlighten me."

Jack's eyes gleamed with mischief. "I think you *love* her." Then he promptly burst out laughing.

Charles sighed in disgust and rose. Jack stopped laughing, although only just barely. "You're not leaving, are you?"

"Yes."

"Because of that quip? I was only jesting. Besides, I wanted to stand you a drink. You're in no condition to be wandering around town by yourself."

Charles sighed. Jack was at least as foxed as he was, and probably more so. "All right…but no more ribbing about this marriage business. I don't want to think about it."

Jack rose and put his arm around Charles's shoulders. "Not a problem. I know the best way to put it out of your mind."

Charles arched an eyebrow as they ambled from the club. "What's that?"

"You mean 'who.' Her name's Simone…French, or pretends to be, anyway."

Charles groaned inwardly. He couldn't imagine anything he'd rather do less. "Not tonight, Jack. I have some business to attend to in the morning—"

"Business? You're giving me the same excuse you gave your wife?"

Charles groaned aloud, seeing that he wasn't going to get out of it. "All right, but just for a little while. I'm in a bloody rotten mood, and nothing will change that fact."

"Never say never," Jack replied, and they continued down the street.

Chapter Twenty-Three

Pelham House *could* have been beautiful. As Charles had mentioned, the main house dated from the late sixteenth century, but she learned from Wilson that the great hall went back to the thirteen hundreds. Much of the stone that had been used to build the house had been salvaged from a nearby monastery, dissolved under Henry VIII. As a result, the house seemed even older than its years, and its crumbling gray stone appeared soft and silver in the sun.

Yet Pelham House wasn't a home. Entire wings had been closed off, the curtains drawn and the furnishings covered in eerie white sheets. The majority of the house was clean and well cared for, but it felt empty. It looked as if it hadn't been lived in for over a decade—as was in fact the case.

Beatrice gazed forlornly around the library, where she sat surrounded by piles of books and clouds of dust. For lack of anything better to do, she had begun to reopen several of the rooms. She'd taken on the library three days earlier, and although she didn't sneeze *quite* as much from the dust anymore, she still had a lot of work to do. The walls were lined with bookshelves, but the books had been arranged without any seeming order, and many of them had been damaged by dust and damp. The wainscoting in the room suffered from the same ailment; at one time or another, it had surely gleamed, but now it was dark and cracked.

Beatrice sighed, preparing herself to return to the grimy task of sorting through books. But before she could motivate her body into action, she heard the unmistakable sound of Wilson, whistling as he passed below the window. She crossed the room to wave to him. "Good morning, Wilson," she called down.

A slim, wrinkled man of about sixty, he looked up, a shovel over his shoulder. At one time he'd been solely the Summersons' butler, but now, for lack of anything else to do, he spent most of his time digging in the dirt out in the rose garden. "Ah, good morning to you, Lady Summerson. Still hard at work in there?"

Beatrice nodded. "And you?"

He just grunted. "I'm trying, myself. But the ground's getting a bit hard, especially in the morning. It's all right, though. Happens every fall."

Beatrice wrinkled her brow. Wilson was getting on in years. He shouldn't be doing such a hard task all by himself. "Perhaps I should see about getting someone to help you?"

"Oh, that'd be very kind, Lady Summerson. I could sure use another set of hands, especially now that the house is being lived in again."

Beatrice nodded firmly. "I'll see to it tomorrow." She supposed she should notify Charles first, seeing as it'd be his money paying another salary, but she wasn't going to let that detail stop her. Wilson needed help, and since Charles wasn't there, she'd have to take charge.

Wilson looked up at her, chuckling. "Thank you, Lady Summerson. You know, I believe you'll banish all of our ghosts in no time."

Beatrice cocked her head. "Ghosts? What do you mean?"

"Oh, I don't mean real ghosts, Lady Summerson. Nothing to worry about," he said, scratching his head and gazing about the grounds. "I just meant that there are a lot of memories at Pelham House, and not much else."

"Bad memories?"

He shook his head. "No, no. Good memories…but old ones. Nothing has changed since the old marquess and Lord Mark died. That's why we're all so glad you've come. We're ready for some new memories."

"Oh. Thank you, Wilson," Beatrice said, genuinely touched by his compliment.

He tipped his cap and continued on his way.

Beatrice sighed, turning from the window and sinking into a faded armchair. She hadn't had the heart to tell Wilson, but she was contemplating leaving Pelham House. Why should she stay? It didn't seem as if her husband would be returning anytime soon.

Her suspicions had begun the day he left but now, after she'd been by herself for over two weeks, Beatrice *knew* he wouldn't come back.

She fisted her hands, as angry with herself for getting into this mess as she was at Charles for abandoning her. She'd almost let herself think that their marriage could work. He'd been so tender, and for a brief moment he'd even seemed happy. She'd certainly been happy when he'd held her in his arms…happier than she could remember.

She rose from her chair suddenly and began pacing. Of course she'd been happy. Charles had led her to believe that she could be. He didn't have to bring her all the way out to his family's country seat; to do so, naturally, made her think that he'd stay there with her for at least a little while. And why did he tell her that he'd return, when he'd had no intention of keeping his word? He could have been honest with her. Beatrice knew that theirs was no love match, and she wouldn't have been surprised if he'd said that he would stay in London indefinitely. Hurt, yes, but not surprised. It was what they'd discussed, wasn't it? That they'd never have a normal marriage? Charles had probably felt it would be too impolite to tell her simply that he didn't want to live with her.

But none of this changed the fact that he had probably been carousing around London while she was buried in his dark, empty house with virtually no one to talk to. If Charles had thought that he'd protect her feelings by not telling her that he didn't plan to live with her, he was in store for a shock: she was furious. *Furious.* If only she had some way of getting back at him.

Beatrice sighed and flopped into the depths of her armchair, thinking about revenge. Deep down, she knew that leaving wasn't really an option. Even after this whole fiasco, she still had some pride left. She couldn't return home. To do so would alarm her family, and they were concerned enough as it was. Beatrice couldn't let them know how miserable she was, and she had to conceal Charles's abandonment at all costs. She could only hope that rumors of his presence in town hadn't reached them already. Ben would surely want to call him out, and Beatrice couldn't allow that. One of them was certain to get very hurt—or worse— and she feared that her brother, a couple of years younger and rasher than Charles, would be the one. And she couldn't live with that….

She'd just have to keep a stiff upper lip and suffer her hurt and anger privately. But that didn't mean she'd have to accept it.

Beatrice cast her eyes around the room. Until she figured out how she could quietly seek her revenge, there was certainly plenty of work to keep her busy. She hated to make any sort of improvement on Charles's house; he definitely didn't deserve it. Yet it seemed that Pelham House would be more her house than his.

Her house. *Hers.*

Beatrice began to smile, the seed of a diabolical plan taking root in her mind. She could make it her house. And she could wreak havoc on his wallet while doing so. It was a petty plan, but satisfying.

With renewed vigor and a spring in her step, Beatrice headed into the hallway, searching for Mrs. Hester. As she went, she noted anything that looked in need of repair.

After she spoke to Mrs. Hester, she would see to the stables…the gardens…. She paused, putting her finger on the side of her chin in thought. Perhaps she could have someone install a grotto by the lake. She'd always fancied a grotto.

Laughter bubbled up inside of her, and for the first time in weeks Beatrice had something to look forward to.

Chapter Twenty-Four

After a month of hard drinking, Charles gave up. He'd tried his damnedest to erase Beatrice from his mind, but had failed. He'd gone out with Jack, had met every bloody Simone and Suzette that London had to offer. All that had proved was that he had absolutely no desire for another woman, and every one of these nights had ended with him returning home early, unsatisfied. And every night as Charles tried to sleep, he thought only of Beatrice.

He'd been miserable. His family all but refused to speak to him, and *her* family—that was another matter entirely. Ben and Louisa were in town, and they were the worst of the lot. For the most part, Charles had managed to avoid them, but he was certain that they were aware that he was in London and not with his wife. Charles had had one uncomfortable moment at White's, when he was leaving the club as Ben entered it. Charles, foxed, had bumped right into the younger man in the doorway. Ben had looked as if he wanted to call him out then and there, and had shown remarkable restraint by *not* doing so, particularly when Jack, who was a few steps behind Charles, had broken out into hilarity over the situation. Instead, Ben had angrily shoved passed both of them; Charles had just hiccuped. Sober, he could have held his own against Ben, but foxed as he was at the time, Beatrice's brother would have destroyed him.

Although Charles hadn't encountered Louisa, he suspected she was keeping tabs on him. On the few occasions that he'd been to his mother's house—few because all she did was glare at him—Charles had had the uncanny sensation of being watched as he stood on her doorstep. One time, he'd turned his head to look at Louisa's house, quickly enough to see a curtain flutter ominously closed.

Old dragon. He assumed that she was reporting everything that she saw and heard back to Beatrice's family, and he knew that his dissolute antics could hardly endear him to them. He didn't care. He was leaving, anyway.

Charles looked out his carriage window, watching the scenery creep by; it seemed to be moving painfully slow, so eager was he to arrive at Pelham House now that he'd finally made up his mind to return. He wasn't sure of the exact moment he'd made that decision, but the second the thought had occurred to him, he realized what sense it made. Charles would never admit it to her, but he missed Beatrice. He didn't have to stay with her long—he wouldn't want to, anyway. He had intentionally brought Beatrice to Pelham House knowing that his painful memories of the house would help keep him away from her. Spending too much time with her was still too risky to consider.

But he didn't see the harm in a short visit. He needed to make love to her at least once more, and besides, they'd discussed everything before getting married. They'd both agreed that they desired one another. So why shouldn't they enjoy each other's company? As long as they didn't do it too frequently…

He drummed his fingers impatiently on his leg. Of course, he was aware that Beatrice might not welcome him with open arms. She *might* be furious with him. But he would take his chances. She'd been angry with him before, and he'd seen his way around it.

When the carriage began to pull up the long drive to the house, Charles felt an unmistakable jolt of expectation course through his body. Whether or not Beatrice was angry with him—and he knew he was kidding himself if he thought she wouldn't be—he hoped that by the time they retired for the evening she'd have changed her mind. He certainly planned to try his hardest to convince her.

Imagine his surprise, then, as he stood at the front door of his house. It was nearly suppertime; he'd had visions of a bowl of soup, a hot bath and, after apologizing thoroughly, a warm body to sleep next to. Instead, the door abruptly swung open, almost hitting him in the face. And instead of Wilson, Charles was confronted by a burly man walking out the door backward.

"Oi, there—comin' out," the man barked, not bothering to stop as he did so.

Charles quickly stepped out of the way, and the man carried on about his business: emerging from the house holding on to one end of a long, dusty Persian carpet. Another man carried the other end, merely nodding as he passed. They carried the carpet outside and deposited it in a dusty heap on the drive. Then they turned and walked back in, closing the door soundly behind them.

For a moment, Charles stared at the closed door. *What was going on?*

He began pounding on the door, and then stopped. What the bloody hell was he doing, knocking? It was his house, wasn't it? He pulled open the door, strode inside and then halted dead in his tracks.

Chaos reigned. The front hall carpet was gone, and Charles quickly opened the door and looked back outside for confirmation: yes, there was the carpet—the one in the heap. His disbelieving eyes roamed about the hall, not knowing which part of the destruction to settle on first. Although the carpet had been removed, its area was still clearly delineated, the only part of the hall floor neither faded by the sun nor scratched. Boxes cluttered the center of the room, and all the hall furniture—several small tables and a few chairs, if Charles could recall correctly—had disappeared.

"Wilson!" he bellowed, making the windows rattle with the force of his voice.

Wilson hesitantly peeked his head out from the sitting room. "Um…yes, Lord Summerson…?"

"Yes?" Charles practically shouted. "What do you mean, 'um…yes'? What the bloody hell is going on here?"

"Well, my lord," Wilson began as he stepped timidly out into the hall. He paused as the two workmen entered the hall. They seated themselves on the steps, each taking out a sandwich and commencing to eat. They regarded Charles and his butler with curiosity. "Perhaps," Wilson continued quietly, "we should speak about this somewhere—"

"Now, Wilson!"

"What are you yelling about?" Beatrice demanded, walking briskly down the hall, wiping her hands on her skirt. Her hair was in disarray, her face smudged with grime.

The workmen perked up at once, watching her appreciatively as she moved.

Charles, for once, was completely unaffected by her beauty. *"What is going on?"*

"I heard you the first time…all the way upstairs. You needn't yell," Beatrice responded mildly.

"Then answer me."

"Certainly, my lord. Do you mind if we talk about this in the study, or would you prefer to keep this conversation…public?" She didn't wait for him to answer before turning around and heading for the study.

Charles was mad enough to spit, but followed Beatrice into the study, staring daggers into her back the whole way. He slammed the door behind him.

She was seated serenely at the desk, her hands folded primly in front of her.

It took every last ounce of Charles's good breeding to keep him from picking her up and tossing her out the nearest window. With a deep, steadying breath, he said evenly, "I have not given you leave to make any changes to this house."

Beatrice furrowed her brow in delicate—and deliberate, Charles was sure—confusion. "You said that the house would need a lot of work. Do you not recall?"

He wracked his mind, trying to remember what he had said. "Obviously, I meant that it needed a lot of work *but* that you would have to run any changes by me."

"Obviously," Beatrice ground out, her illusion of calm vanishing, "you weren't here for me to ask you."

Seeing Beatrice lose her composure helped Charles get a grip on his own; it made him feel much better, in fact. He nonchalantly crossed the room to pour himself a brandy, and then swirled the amber liquid around in his glass, torturing her with his silence. After a minute, he asked quietly, "How much have you done?"

She reached into her pocket and pulled out a list. A long list. "Well, so far very little. The front hall is being worked on, obviously, and I've had the sitting room floor repaired. Basic maintenance, pretty much."

"There was nothing wrong with the floor."

"Yes, there was," Beatrice retorted. "I've had a few rooms painted or papered, as well."

"Papered? I didn't want the walls papered."

"Hmm." Beatrice hoped her disinterested reply would infuriate him. When he didn't show any marked reaction, she added, "Well, the workers will begin on this room tomorrow, and I shall endeavor to remember to tell them that."

"You won't change a bloody thing in here. Do you understand?" Charles's voice was low, sending shivers up Beatrice's spine. He sounded far angrier than he did when he yelled, and she feared that she might have finally pushed him over the edge.

She nodded curtly. "If you insist."

"What else?" he asked, walking over to where she sat at the desk. When he stood so close, he towered over her, and Beatrice had to crane her neck to look at him.

She thought for a moment, finally deciding that honesty was the safest route to take at this point. "Well, I've ordered new curtains for many of the rooms…the sun had faded most of them, and a few were becoming quite tattered."

Charles didn't wait for her to finish. "Where?" he said, walking to the door and throwing it open. "Show me what you've done."

She didn't budge, her own fury overwhelming her again. "How *dare* you speak to me like that?"

He strode back across the room, stopping in front of her once more. "This is my house and you are my wife. *That* is how I dare."

For a moment Beatrice truly thought she would humiliate herself. She felt her lip quiver ever so slightly, felt her eyes sting with the need to cry. But she didn't. Somehow, she didn't. She rose slowly from her seat and walked over to the study door. "Find them yourself. I'm leaving."

Charles followed her and put his hand on her arm. "Leaving? Where to?"

Beatrice took a deep breath. *Nowhere,* she thought. Where could she go? Her father's house? To stay with Louisa? Even if she had wanted to go to any of those places, she couldn't. Charles was right; she was his wife. His property. She couldn't leave.

Beatrice pasted a bitter smile onto her face. "Silly me. I can't go anywhere, can I? Then I shall be waiting in my bedroom for *you* to decide to leave. I was rather enjoying myself while you were gone." She pulled away and left.

Charles could have stopped her, but didn't. He was too angry. Damn it…he hadn't left London and driven all the way out there to fight with her. All he'd wanted to do was make love to her once or twice to tide himself over….

My bedroom? That's what she'd said.

Since when did she have *her* bedroom? She was supposed to be in *his* bedroom.

Charles sank down into a battered leather chair, absentmindedly rubbing his hand on the cracked arms. He'd made a bloody mess of everything, and he didn't know why. He'd known she'd be miffed with him, but he had planned to cajole her out of her pique. Instead he'd stormed in and behaved like a barbarian....

But all this change! Charles closed his eyes. It was too much change.... He didn't even know what she'd done yet, but he knew that it would all have to be undone. Pelham House had always been a certain way. He had memories of it like that....

He rose, striding to the door. If Beatrice wouldn't show him what disasters she'd endorsed in his absence, he bloody well *would* find them on his own.

When he stepped into the hall, Wilson was conspicuously absent. The two workmen were still there, though; they had finished their sandwiches and were moving on to the whiskey course.

Charles paused long enough to stare at them disdainfully. "Get out."

Neither man rose. Slowly, the large man's head swiveled around to face the smaller man, a question in his eyes. Then, just as slowly, his head swiveled back toward Charles. "Ye 'ave to pay us first, m'lord. 'Tis customary."

He rolled his eyes heavenward. "It's highway robbery, is what it is." But he took his billfold from his pocket and paid them, probably far more than they deserved.

"Mighty gen'rous of ye, m'lord. We was worried that we wouldn't get paid, wi' the state this 'ouse was in."

Charles narrowed his eyes. "What do you mean?"

"'Twas a bit run-down, m'lord, and we thought ye might no' be able to pay us."

His temper rose to the boiling point once more. They thought *he* was destitute? "There was nothing wrong with the house."

Both men shrugged, but finally left.

Charles glared at a crust of bread, left negligently on the steps, before setting off to examine the rest of his home. With every step he took, the angrier he became…angrier, and something else. Disconcerted. Ill at ease. Everything seemed different, the walls the wrong colors, the furniture arranged incorrectly. New rugs…

When he passed the dining room, he turned right, heading for the portrait gallery. But before he walked down the long, portrait-lined hall, he paused. He hadn't been there in years. Even on the rare occasions that he'd returned to Pelham House, he'd avoided it.

If Beatrice had changed anything down there…

He turned away and began climbing the stairs to the second floor. He didn't want to know if she had made any changes in the gallery. He wouldn't even ask her if she had, not until his temper cooled, anyway. He didn't trust his reaction.

When Charles reached the top of the stairs, he paused again, looking at the door to the master bedroom. The last time he'd stood in front of that door, it had been his wedding night, and his wife had been clinging to him seductively.

He looked down the long hall, wondering which of the many bedrooms Beatrice claimed as "hers." *Her* room. He'd see about that.

With a sigh, he opened the door to the master bedroom, thinking he'd at least find solace there. It had never actually been his bedroom; the few times that Charles had been at Pelham House since the death of his father and brother, he'd stayed in his childhood room. His wedding night was the one exception.

He fumbled around for a lamp, finding it vaguely irritating that no one had bothered to light a fire for him. He couldn't see a blasted thing in the dark.

He located a lamp and lit it, expecting to be soothed by sedate blue walls. Blue had been his father's favorite color. But as light suffused the room, Charles had a vision of hell so ghastly and vivid that he dropped the lamp. Disbelieving his eyes, he reached down and picked it up. He lit it again.

She hadn't.

But she had. Beatrice had papered his room—his father's room—and she had papered it with...Cupids. Lots of them, dancing across the walls in the most grotesque excuse for a wall-covering that Charles had ever seen. A whole militia of Cupids firing arrows haphazardly at hundreds of galloping satyrs and nymphs.

And in that moment, he knew she had done it on purpose.

And that meant war.

Chapter Twenty-Five

Beatrice had remained in her room for the rest of the night. She had expected Charles to come barging in, especially after he got a glimpse of the paper she'd maliciously hung in the master bedroom. She'd almost talked herself out of that final touch, thinking it *just* a bit egregious. But now that Charles had returned—blustering and obnoxious—she was pleased that she hadn't lost her nerve. He deserved that wallcovering and worse.

When she rose from bed early the next morning, she wore a smug smile at the corners of her mouth; even though she hadn't slept well during the night, Beatrice still felt refreshed, as if she had won some sort of minor victory. And when she stepped into her favorite pair of worn slippers and covered her flimsy nightgown with a bulky cotton robe, she felt as if she were donning armor.

But as she shuffled across the room to ring for Meg, she noticed something on the floor by her door. It was a note, and her husband's bold handwriting stared up at her, taunting her. She picked it up. He'd written on the reverse side of a piece of the wallcovering. Charles had trimmed the paper into a neat square, and Beatrice briefly wondered where it had come from; she didn't think that there had been any remnants left about the house. The note was written on one of the nymph sections, depicting a fair Grecian maiden swathed all in white.

Actually, Beatrice corrected herself before she began reading, it *would* have been a nymph section, if it weren't for the fact that Charles had cut the paper just above the nymph's shoulders, effectively beheading her. Beatrice briefly mused on whether that was a coincidence or not. Glowering, she decided it was not.

She turned the paper over and read:

B—
I applaud your taste. You must have searched far and wide to find a wallcovering as glorious as this. Unfortunately, I must have walked in my sleep last night, for when I awoke I realized that massive strips of it had, regrettably, been torn from the walls. Pity.

I have sent for workers to come repair the damage— they will be repainting the walls blue, and will be making a few other changes, as well. Please do not interfere.

Here is a piece of the paper for you to keep as a memento.
C.

Beatrice narrowed her eyes, crumpled the paper up and tossed it into a drawer. Slamming it shut loudly—and then again for good measure—she took a seat at her dressing table.

She looked at her reflection in the mirror and stuck out her tongue. She shouldn't be annoyed—how else had she expected him to react? It wasn't as if she'd actually believed that the paper would stay on the walls for more than one day, anyway.

And, Beatrice admitted grudgingly, if Charles hadn't just spoiled her victorious mood, she might have even admired his ingenuity.

She continued to frown into the mirror, retaliation on her mind. When Meg entered the room bearing a large basket of clothes, Beatrice didn't even notice her until she spoke.

"Goodness, Miss Beatrice. You look like a storm cloud."

Beatrice turned her frown on her maid. "Thank you, Meg," she replied, her words laced with sarcasm.

Meg ignored her tone and went about her business of putting away clothes. After a minute of silence, she remarked nonchalantly, "So Lord Summerson is back, I hear."

Beatrice sighed and turned to look up at her. "Unfortunately."

"Do you think that he'll be staying this time?"

"For a bit," a deep voice said from the doorway. Both women turned around with a start.

Charles stood leaning against the door frame. "Would you excuse us, Meg?"

She nodded without a word and left. Charles closed the door behind her and turned to Beatrice. He didn't know what he was going to say to her. He'd mulled over their situation all night, and he still didn't have any words to express his feelings. He'd been angry that she'd made changes to his house, and he'd reacted badly. But after a bit of reflection, Charles realized that she'd had no way of knowing that, for personal reasons, he would object to any change at Pelham House. He'd certainly never told her. All of the alterations could be easily reversed, and most of them even seemed to be sincere attempts at improvement, the paper in his room notwithstanding. Charles recognized that touch for the expression of feminine pique that it was, but once his anger had cooled, he could *almost* admire her ingenuity for it.

He definitely didn't care to fight with her. Even now, knowing that Beatrice was furious with him, he still wanted to take her in his arms and kiss her senseless. It didn't matter that she was wearing a horrible, high-necked white robe that covered her from the tips of her toes to her chin. The robe was so concealing that it would have made any rational man laugh. Instead, Charles began to contemplate the fastest way to remove it.

"Did you want something?" Beatrice asked coldly.

"You got my note, I take it?"

She had the nerve to roll her eyes.

Charles straightened his backbone. "There are to be no more changes, Beatrice. Do you understand?"

"Of course I understand. And I don't want to live in this cold, drafty house without any changes, do *you* understand?"

Charles closed his eyes, seeking patience. He'd started off on the wrong foot again by bringing up the house first. He hadn't intended on pursuing that topic again, or at least not for a while. She'd be defensive enough anyway, and he hadn't even spoken to her rationally since arriving.

He began to run his hand through his hair in frustration, but stopped himself, shoving his hands into his coat pockets instead. He took a deep breath. "Look, Beatrice, I don't plan to discuss this any further. There are to be no changes made to this house, and that is all there is to say on the subject."

"If you would be reasonable, you would realize that all the changes I made were necessary improvements—"

"All of them? You can't be serious."

"The wallcovering, Charles," Beatrice said through gritted teeth, "was an impulse. I hadn't meant for you to like it."

"Really?" he asked with mock disbelief.

She ignored his snide tone, but did rise from her chair to stand behind it, needing to put it between them for safety's sake. "I was angry—am angry still. What was I supposed to do out here? Sit around and wait for you?"

Charles merely raised an eyebrow.

"Can *you* be serious? I waited here for weeks for you. You didn't even bother to say goodbye before you left—"

"We have an understanding, Beatrice—"

"Yes, I *understand* that. But then why did you lie to me? Why did you tell me you would return? Clearly you had no intention of showing up."

Charles didn't bother to defend himself. He knew that he was in the wrong and that she had every right to be angry. But he still couldn't explain his motivations to her. "I changed my mind."

Beatrice was outraged. "You *changed* your mind! And you expect me just to sit here and wait upon your whim?"

Charles took a step forward and caught her by the wrist. "Not *here* exactly, Beatrice. You will no longer be staying in this room."

"You can't make me move."

He took another step closer. "Well, *wife,*" he said, "as your husband I can do just about any bloody thing to you I want."

"Get away from me," Beatrice declared stiffly.

Charles ignored her wishes. He pushed the chair out of the way and pulled her close, wanting to kiss away her angry words. Besides, why argue when she looked so beautiful, her amber eyes flashing?

The second their lips met, she pulled back as if she'd been slapped. "Why did you have to come back? Why?"

His expression became masked. "Because I want you."

"Well, I don't want you. Not anymore."

"Is that so?" Charles challenged, his eyes never straying from her mouth. "What if I don't believe you? How can you prove it?"

Beatrice didn't have time to answer. The second her lips parted to speak, he bent his head, his lips slanting across hers. She didn't have a chance to pull away this time. His hands tangled in her hair, his lips insistent.

Despite herself, she didn't want to stop. Her mind wanted to protest, but her body reveled in the contact, her mouth in the warm, rough texture of his tongue. Suddenly, she was kissing him back with all her heart.

The second Beatrice gave in, the second her lips softened, Charles pulled her closer, moaning her name. He ran his hand along her shoulder and downward, slipping it underneath the thick fabric of her robe to cup her breast.

"Beatrice? I don't want to fight."

But then he stopped. He wanted to keep kissing her, but he knew that they needed to resolve things. "Look, Beatrice, I'm sorry. I was a bastard for leaving you here, and I wish I could offer you some kind of an excuse. I came back hoping to make up with you. I was just surprised with all these changes—"

"But—"

He held up his hand. "No, please. Let's not talk about that anymore. I just wanted to say that...well, this marriage business is new to me—"

"It's new to me, too," Beatrice pointed out reasonably.

"Yes, well, you have reacted far better than me, Beatrice. I asked that we keep our relationship as friends, and I haven't done that, have I?"

She didn't know what to do other than shake her head. She didn't know how they could ever just be friends.

"Our situation isn't ideal, but it needn't be terrible. Can you forgive me?"

Beatrice didn't know what to do. She wanted him to hold her, to kiss her, to show her again what he had shown her on their wedding night. She *wanted* to forgive him. But could she?

"Beatrice?" Charles asked, gently reaching out to tip up her chin.

She said nothing, momentarily lost in his green eyes.

"Forgive me," he repeated, and Beatrice did. She hated herself for it, but she forgave him. She had no choice. His lips were on hers again, and even if she had found the words to reject his apology, her body rejoiced once more. Her hands crept into his hair, and her eyelids dropped shut. He slid her robe off her shoulders and she never thought to protest.

Charles stepped back to look at her more fully, and drew a breath. He didn't know what he had expected beneath that chaste robe, but certainly not this. Her high-necked, white robe had concealed a thin, silk gown that clung to her body like a second skin. The silk was a pale peach, the neck so low that it revealed a great deal of cleavage. And her nipples...Charles could make out the faint dark circles beneath the fabric.

He mentally kicked himself once more for leaving her so soon. He stepped in closer again, his eyes devouring every inch of her, watching the color rush to her cheeks, watching her nipples tighten. Charles reached out, dragging his hands over her bosom, letting his palms rub circles over the hard peaks of her breasts.

"I've been thinking about this every day," he whispered gruffly, nibbling on her ear.

"Every day?" Beatrice asked breathlessly, her lips doing some tentative nibbling of their own.

"Every hour." With a small tug, Charles pulled the thin fabric over her breasts and fastened his mouth to her nipple—first one, and then the other. Beatrice held his head, bringing him closer.

Without knowing how she got there, she was suddenly on the bed, with Charles leaning over her, his lips trailing down her belly, over the silk fabric. At the same time, his hands moved up her legs, taking the hem of her gown with them.

His lips moved down even farther, passing over the fabric across the most intimate part of her body.

Beatrice jerked, her body reacting to the shock and the intense pleasure of him being so close to her very core. "Charles—" she protested.

"Shh—don't say anything. I've been waiting for this too long."

His lips moved down farther, replacing his hands at her inner thighs. And then his lips began to move back up. Beatrice tried to relax, but her hips tightened in expectation. What was he doing?

Her question was answered when his lips and tongue found the soft folds of her womanhood. Sensation overtook her, reducing any nervousness, any reservations, to nothing. All she could do was feel.

Then her gown was being pulled over her head, and her own hands were at Charles's shirt, popping buttons from their holes with frantic need. With a groan, he worked at his breeches, freeing himself, and then he was inside of her, buried deeply in her hot center. Beatrice met him thrust for thrust, whispering his name in his ear, pleading for more.

Hearing her say his name, hearing her voice so heavy with passion and knowing that she needed him as much as he needed her, did something to Charles. He owned her. She was his. Coming home to her, finally giving in to the feelings he had fought against for months, knowing that she wanted him almost despite herself…all of these things combined brought out an almost animal possessiveness in him. He rose from her slightly, grabbing her by the knees as he did so. With a guttural cry, he lifted her legs up over his shoulders, burying himself inside of her to the hilt.

Beatrice cried out at the new sensation, at feeling him so deeply embedded inside her, at feeling him possess her so fiercely. Her body exploded, her mind, her whole entire world. In that instant, he *was* her world, and all that mattered was the way he made her feel.

Charles felt her tighten, and waited—he didn't know how— until every last wave of pleasure had crashed over her before he gave in to his own release.

For several moments afterward they lay very still, recovering from the intensity of their lovemaking. Yet even as they recovered, neither spoke nor moved. They lay in silence, stunned by what had just happened.

Beatrice wondered what she had just gotten herself into. She was uneasy about forgiving him, but what else could she do? She knew that it wouldn't last.

And Charles knew that it couldn't.

But for the moment, both of them gave in to the temptation to relax in one another's arms, to enjoy the simple pleasure of being together.

Charles and Beatrice moved into the master bedroom that afternoon and stayed there for the rest of the day. They stayed the next day, as well, taking all meals within. It was like a honeymoon, except it came over a month after their wedding day.

Despite Charles's initial demand, most of the changes to the house remained in place. They couldn't exactly crack the paint again, or chip the new sitting room floor to make it resemble the old one. Yet all of the work that had been in progress upon Charles's arrival came to a complete halt. Although the old curtains had not been rehung, the new ones remained in their boxes. The front hall remained eccentrically half-painted. The Cupid wallcovering, however, was gone by the end of the week. Much of the time in the master bedroom was spent laughingly stripping it from the walls. Beatrice hadn't protested at all. She was just as happy to see it go as Charles was.

Still, though, they didn't discuss the state of the house. It was too touchy a subject, and neither of them wanted to bring it up and disturb the delicate peace that now existed between them.

Chapter Twenty-Six

❧❧❧

A month later, Charles knew he had to leave again. He didn't want to, but he needed to. He wouldn't stay away as long this time, and he would tell Beatrice that he was leaving, but he definitely had to go. She was becoming too important in his life.

No, thought Charles. It wasn't that she was becoming too important—she'd been important, to some extent, since the first moment he'd seen her. No, it wasn't that at all. Beatrice was habit-forming, and his life at Pelham House revolved around her; his life in town had pretty much revolved around her, too, but at least there he couldn't act on his impulses. Now, he woke up in the morning to make love to her. They ate breakfast together. Even if he secluded himself at some point during the day to attend to paperwork, all he really did was think of her. And by supper, making love was on his mind again. As they sat at the table, he thought about removing her clothes, about hearing her call out his name. And then they were in bed again.

It couldn't go on. Much as he enjoyed it, it just couldn't.

After supper that evening, Charles and Beatrice retired to the study. They curled up on the settee, Beatrice in Charles's lap. For a while, they didn't say much, each lost in thought, enjoying the warm glow of the fire.

Charles didn't know how to bring up the subject of leaving. He didn't want to hurt her, and he didn't want to mar their last few days together, but it had to be done.

"I have to leave again, Beatrice."

She sat up slowly, turning to face him. "Oh?"

He nodded, wishing he could take his words back. "I have to meet with my solicitor in town, as well as review expenses and such things at my mother's house."

"When are you leaving?" Beatrice asked, trying to keep the hurt and confusion out of her voice. She'd known this was coming, but that didn't change the fact that it had caught her off guard. She'd begun to feel so contented and free around Charles that she'd temporarily forgotten about the constraints on their marriage.

"The day after tomorrow."

She frowned slightly. "That's very soon. How long will you be gone?"

He raked his hand through his hair. "I'm not sure, really…a couple of weeks, perhaps. A month at most. It will all depend on how everything goes."

"I see."

He turned her around in his lap so she was facing him. "I will write and let you know this time, all right, Beatrice? I promise I won't keep you waiting."

She nodded. It wasn't all right at all, but she couldn't do much about it. They'd talked about this happening before they even married, and she had agreed that it was for the best. She couldn't expect to have him around all the time. Besides, Beatrice told herself, if he stayed any longer she'd fall completely in love with him.

As if she wasn't already.

Very early the next morning, Beatrice lay in bed listening to her husband's even breathing as he slept; she'd spent a great portion of the night doing the same thing. Sleep had eluded her for a long time, and when she finally had fallen asleep it had been only for a few fitful hours. Too many thoughts troubled her mind.

Her monthly flow was two weeks late. She had acknowledged, at first, that she might be with child, but she hadn't been too alarmed; she'd never been terribly regular to begin with. But then, about a week ago, she'd woken up in the morning and gotten sick. All at once, she had known. It was terrible news.

She had always wanted children. It was impossible for her not to, having grown up in such a large, rambunctious family. But Charles didn't; Beatrice was certain, even though they still hadn't discussed it.

And he would be leaving in one day. Beatrice knew that she should tell him before he left, but she couldn't bring herself to do so. She felt too vulnerable still. She could write to him in London. Maybe that would bring him home sooner….

Beatrice wrapped the blanket more tightly about her body, immediately dismissing the idea. She couldn't start to think like that. Making Charles stay wouldn't make him love her.

She bit her lip, feeling the chills and dizziness of morning sickness coming on; if she couldn't get her nausea under control, he might figure out her secret. It was only about five o'clock in the morning, and her stomach was already beginning to roil. She closed her eyes, trying to will away her upset. Since the first day she'd been sick, the same thing had happened every morning. Luckily, she'd been able to conceal it from Charles so far. If only she could do the same thing today.

Beatrice slowly swung her legs over the side of the bed, knowing that sickness was inevitable. She grabbed her robe as she dashed into their dressing room.

When Charles quietly entered the room two minutes later, she was lying limply on the floor, the basin from the washstand at her side.

"Beatrice?" he asked in alarm. "Are you all right?" Before she had a chance to answer, he had crossed the room and was sitting beside her on the floor.

Beatrice sent silent thanks to God that she hadn't actually thrown up. That would have been too embarrassing. She did feel terrible, but she knew it wouldn't last much longer. Slowly, so as not to upset her stomach further, she rose to a sitting position. "I'm all right, Charles. I felt a bit ill when I awoke, but that's all. I think I'm fine now."

He wrinkled his brow. "Then why are you still on the floor?"

Beatrice shrugged. "I was just about to rise when you came in." To demonstrate, she unfolded her legs and carefully rose. The second she was standing, the room seemed to spin and, for just a moment, everything went black. She swayed.

Charles rose quickly to steady her, putting his arm around her shoulders to prevent her from falling. "I don't think so. Back into bed with you."

Beatrice allowed him to help her back into their bedroom. Inwardly, she was quite grateful. She would have been lying on the floor for quite a while longer if he hadn't helped her. As she sank into bed, she sighed with relief.

Charles's brow was furrowed in concern. "Perhaps I shouldn't leave tomorrow…no reason why my business couldn't wait another day or two."

Beatrice shook her head. "No, really, Charles. I'll be fine."

He pulled back the covers and carefully climbed into bed beside her, propping himself up on an elbow.

Beatrice looked up at him. His firm chest was just inches from her, his bronze-toned skin pulled tightly across it. He was so handsome, and he looked so warm and safe that she wanted nothing more than to burrow in his arms. She looked up at his face.

"What are you looking at?" Charles asked, regarding her quizzically.

"You," she said softly. "What are *you* looking at?"

"You," he said with a grin, before inclining his head to place a kiss on the tip of her nose. Then he wrapped her in his arms, enveloping her in warmth and comfort. She lay her head on his chest and fell asleep listening to his heartbeat.

When they awoke several hours later, she felt well again. She rose from bed, ate breakfast and went for a walk around the garden with him. When they returned, she ate her entire dinner and they spent the rest of the evening in each other's arms, making love until late into the night.

Beatrice was glad that Charles left early the next morning, for if he'd stayed another hour, he would have seen her get sick once more.

Chapter Twenty-Seven

Beatrice stared hard at the portrait of Charles's father, struck once more by the uncanny resemblance between father and son. In the three weeks that had passed since Charles left Pelham House, she had found herself in front of that portrait several times. It was the closest she could get to her husband, although looking at it usually made her feel even worse.

Nearly every morning of these three weeks she'd awoken feeling ill, and she had been unable to leave her bed until the early afternoon. There was no doubt about what ailed her now. Pretty soon, the whole house knew.

This morning was one of the few exceptions, however. Beatrice felt slightly queasy, but not queasy enough to force her to stay in bed. On the other hand, she hadn't felt well enough to manage more than a few bites of her breakfast. She left the breakfast room to wander around her big, empty house.

As had happened before, she ended up in front of this portrait, wishing she could understand her husband, and wondering what she could do.

Since Charles had left, he'd written twice: the first time to tell her that he had arrived in town, and the second to tell her that he would be gone a month at least. The note he had written on the back of the wallcovering when he was furious with her had been more interesting than these letters. He said nothing of his family other than that they were well, and he said even less about himself.

And for some reason, when Beatrice responded to his letters, she wrote with the same bland solicitude that he had, asking how he was, telling him she was fine and the weather was mild. She made no mention of her condition. She wanted to tell him, but she just couldn't do it. She was too unsure of how he would react, although she was fairly certain that he'd be devastated, if he cared at all. Charles hadn't wanted a wife; he definitely wouldn't want a wife *and* a child.

Of course, he'd know soon enough. He'd come back eventually, of that she was sure. It might not be for a while, and he probably wouldn't stay for long, but this wasn't the sort of secret she could keep forever.

Beatrice sighed deeply. She didn't want to keep it a secret. She was thrilled about having Charles's baby, whether he'd share her feelings or not. She'd always known she wanted children, and she could already imagine what their child would look like. With tufts of black hair, blue eyes that would eventually turn green, it'd be beautiful.

And yet Beatrice feared that she would gain a child but lose Charles forever. She could live with that—she wanted their child no matter how he felt—but she'd rather have both.

She looked away from the portrait, biting her lip so it wouldn't tremble. She couldn't have both, and she'd better get used to it.

She turned to leave, but the sudden motion brought on the familiar dizziness that she'd been staving off all morning. Fearful of fainting, she quickly sat down on the floor, trying to focus her eyes on the wall beneath the painting.

The spell passed, and Beatrice let out a slow sigh of relief. She had never fainted in her life, and didn't want to start now.

Of course, she'd hardly ever been sick, either. Pregnancy was doing strange things to her body.

Beatrice began to rise, but paused as the dull glint of brass, nearly hidden in the wood paneling of the wall, caught her eye. She leaned in closer. It was a small latch, and as she let her eyes roam she soon detected small hinges, as well: a door.

Forgetting her upset stomach and swimming head, she reached out and carefully lifted the latch. The door popped open, revealing a cramped, dark passageway, just over three feet tall. Beatrice wanted to see where the tunnel led. So, on hands and knees, she entered—although not without a backward glance, hoping that no one witnessed her in this undignified position.

Once she was through the door, the space became tall enough for her to stand, although not without hunching over. She did so, and edged along in the darkness with her hands held out in front of her, trying not to think about the mice that were surely scurrying around underfoot.

Beatrice had gone about fifteen feet when she felt something large and solid obstructing her path. Frowning, she tested its surface with her hands, unable to identify it in the blackness: sharp corners, smoother face. She tried lifting it and found that it wasn't too heavy; with an effort, she'd be able to drag it into the gallery, where she could look at it more clearly.

When she was back in the relative light of the gallery, she propped the object against the wall to get a better view. And suddenly a wave of revelation washed over her, and she understood. She immediately wished she'd left it where she'd found it—these were the ghosts that Wilson had spoken about. She'd known that Charles would never be a real husband, a true father, but for the first time she thought she knew why. He wouldn't let it happen. He had been hurt too much before and he wouldn't let it happen again.

And Beatrice immediately knew that she had to leave.

She carefully replaced the object back in the passage, exactly as it had been. She decided to depart on the morrow. She couldn't stay here anymore. Pride be damned, she was going home. She hadn't seen her family since her wedding, and she could no longer bear to be alone.

As Beatrice left the portrait gallery, she smiled ruefully to herself at the irony. Here she was, finally married, and still she would be living at home with her father.

Jack Davenport, lounging in his favorite chair at White's, glanced at his best friend of nearly twenty years and sighed. They'd been there for over an hour, and Charles had hardly uttered a word. Instead, he sat slouched in his chair, his faraway eyes watching the amber brandy swirl about his glass. They'd sat in a similar position at least four times a week since Charles had returned to London a month ago.

Jack had never seen his friend like this. Charles had been in sorry shape the last time he'd been in town, but this went beyond even that. He was clearly miserable. Whatever business it was that had brought him to town had been completed in all of two days, and he'd spent the remainder of his time rising late in the morning, dining at his club and getting splendidly drunk. Then the whole cycle would start over again the next morning.

Jack propped his fingers in a steeple, wondering how best to broach this subject. "So, any plans to head back home yet?"

Charles looked up. He had been brooding, and had all but forgotten that his friend sat across from him. "Why would I do that? I've only been gone a month."

"Right...." Jack said slowly. "Why are you here again?"

"Business."

"Oh, right. Business again. And what business is that?"

"Shut up, Jack. You bloody well know why I'm here."

"I beg to differ. I haven't the faintest idea why you're here when you have a beautiful wife at home. It's obvious that you'd rather be there, so why not just go?"

Charles didn't answer him right away. Jack was right. He would rather be with Beatrice. But how to explain that he wanted to be with his wife so badly it was necessary to avoid her? "I can't go back, all right? It's too difficult to explain…I just don't want to be in a position where I feel too dependent on a woman. On anyone, really. Don't want her getting too attached to me, either."

"Summerson." Jack looked perplexed. "I will never figure out the way your mind works."

"Well, don't bother trying. I am going back to Pelham House soon, anyway…I have been away for weeks, and it's time for a visit."

Jack snorted. "You sound like my bloody father. He came out to visit us once a year. His duty, he liked to call it."

Charles didn't view Beatrice as duty at all. Perhaps he was *trying* to view their relationship that way, but it wasn't working very well. Hell, who was he kidding? He thought about her constantly; he wondered if she was thinking about him.

But Jack didn't know Charles's real motivation for staying away from her. Charles had never felt comfortable telling anybody how terrified he was of losing someone else, and he especially didn't want to discuss it with Jack. Although they'd been best friends for years, Jack had family problems of his own; in many ways his problems surpassed Charles's.

Charles certainly couldn't see complaining to Jack because his father had died. Other people's fathers died. Their brothers, too. Charles didn't know why it had always been so hard for him, why their deaths had changed his entire life. He had always felt that it was some sort of a lack in him, some sort of a weakness.

It was that feeling, really, that had led him to the War Office in the first place. Oh, he had been twenty-four at the time, and the danger and adventure appealed for other reasons, as well. But really, all he'd wanted to prove, at least to himself, was that he wasn't afraid of death, his own or anyone else's. Instead, he'd learned he was terrified.

"I don't think of it as a duty, Jack. I have my reasons, though."

"Such as?" Jack asked blandly as he studied a loose thread on his jacket.

The question was simple enough, but Charles didn't want to examine the answer. He knew that Jack was aware of this, too. "I'd rather not discuss it."

"Milbanks is probably dead, you know."

Charles met his friend's gaze, irritated that he had to bring this subject up yet again. "Probably, yes. You've told me this already."

"*Probably* only because no one ever found a body, Charles. The ship sank a hundred miles from land. There's no body anymore to be found. Dead, *definitely.*"

"I know, Jack. We've been through this."

"I had a response to that letter I wrote." Jack began searching through his pocket, frowning slightly. As he did so, he kept talking. "That letter I wrote to the War Department—about Milbanks. Don't know what sort of answer it gives, of course, but I figured you might be interested." After another moment, he fished the letter from his pocket and placed it on the table before Charles.

For just a fraction of a second, Charles did nothing but stare at the sealed envelope. Then, slowly, he slid it across the table and into his own pocket. He did this only to placate Jack; he had no intention of ever reading the bloody thing. "Thank you. I'll have a look at it once I get home."

His friend didn't believe him, but let the subject drop. "You said you were leaving soon…when will that be?"

"End of the week. Friday." Charles made that decision on the spot. He hadn't planned on leaving quite so soon, but the second the words were out of his mouth he began to feel better.

"So I can expect to see you in…what—another few weeks? A month?"

Charles pushed his chair back and rose. He'd suddenly lost

all interest in being there. "Unless I invite you for a visit sooner than that."

Jack raised a brow, amused. "Oh? Do you plan to invite me for a visit?"

"No, Davenport, I do not."

Charles left, already mentally in his carriage, heading home to see his wife.

Chapter Twenty-Eight

Charles thought about Beatrice the entire ride to Pelham House. They'd parted on good terms this time, and he'd written to her to tell her roughly when he'd return, so he wasn't worried about how she'd receive him…or he almost wasn't worried, anyway. He *had* been gone a long time.

Charles grew more and more eager the closer he got, already starting to wonder what Beatrice was doing, and what he would do to her once he arrived—once he'd dragged her off to their bedroom, that was. It'd be around suppertime when he got there. She'd probably be sitting at the dining room table, or perhaps she would have finished her supper already and would be sitting in the study reading. Perhaps she'd be reading in their bedroom. Charles hoped so—that way he wouldn't have to drag her anywhere at all.

As the carriage pulled up the drive, he noticed that few lights shone from the windows. He dismissed the uneasy feeling that came over him. He was just used to town, where there were lights burning every hour of the day. Out here, with just Beatrice and a few servants to keep her company, it was no wonder the house looked so dark and still.

The carriage's wheels had barely stopped rolling before

Charles alighted from it and walked up to the door. He didn't bother knocking this time. No, this visit there would be no workers, no strange decor. Everything would be just as he'd left it, just as he liked it. And Beatrice would be waiting.

"Wilson!" Charles called as he stepped through the door and into the dark hallway.

There was no immediate answer, so he kept walking until he reached the dining room. He'd hoped to find Beatrice, but instead found Wilson, along with Mrs. Hester. They were sitting at the table, each clutching a hand of cards guiltily. Slowly, they rose.

"I finished my business earlier than I had planned." Charles glanced about the dining room. It didn't look as if it had been used for eating recently. "Do you know where I can locate my wife?"

Mrs. Hester's flushed face went quite pale. "My lord? Your wife?"

"Yes," Charles said, trying to keep the frustration out of his voice. "Lady Summerson. Where is she?"

Mrs. Hester and Wilson looked at each other in puzzlement before Wilson began, speaking slowly, "Lady Summerson is in Hampshire, my lord…she left about—"

"Two weeks ago," Mrs. Hester interjected. "Last Monday."

Charles stood very still for a moment. "Why…did she leave?" he asked, his voice not sounding like his own. It came out halting, gruff.

"She went to visit her family," Wilson explained.

Mrs. Hester began clucking maternally. "The letter must have gotten lost in the mail…."

"She wrote to inform me?"

The housekeeper knitted her brow. "Well, I would only assume…" She trailed off before turning to Wilson. "This all makes sense now, Wilson?"

Wilson nodded. Charles looked back and forth between them. "What?" he asked impatiently. "What makes sense?"

Mrs. Hester stepped forward. "Why, we were wondering what could have been so important for you to leave Lady Summerson in her condition. You must not have known."

Charles felt as if he'd been punched. Beatrice had left him. He'd told her when he'd be back…roughly, anyway. And what was Mrs. Hester talking about? What condition? Was his wife still ill? Was that why she'd left?

"Is Beatrice still unwell? Why did no one tell me? She seemed to be all right when I left."

Mrs. Hester nodded and placed a comforting hand on Charles's arm. "Lady Summerson *was* all right when you left—these things come and go, my lord. But she has been ill…every morning, in fact. No, it's not been easy for her."

Charles must have paled, because Wilson began steering him toward a chair. "There now, my lord, why don't you have a seat. There's nothing to worry about, you know. 'Tis perfectly natural. Why, when my Jane was first expecting—"

"Expecting what?" Charles practically snapped, ignoring the chair. How could they tell him not to worry if Beatrice had been ill every day for the past month? Perfectly natural? Had anyone called the doctor?

But as both Mrs. Hester and Wilson looked at him in blank surprise, suddenly Charles knew precisely what they were talking about. *Oh, God.*

He walked dazedly past the two, ignoring their alarmed expressions. He walked straight up the stairs to his room—their room. He closed the door behind him and sank to the floor, burying his head in his hands.

Expecting. His child.

He raised his head from his hands, feeling bleak. He would be a father. It didn't seem possible, and he didn't know how to react. He should be happy. If he were normal, he *would* be happy. He had a beautiful wife and he would be a father.

He'd never considered that he'd have a child. Oh, the thought had occurred to him that Beatrice might become pregnant—Charles wasn't an idiot. He bloody well knew how babies were made, and they'd made love enough times in the month that he'd been home to ensure that it was a possibility. And there hadn't been a chance in hell that he would have forgone making love to Beatrice to avoid that risk. But Charles had put the possibility of children far from his mind, thinking only of the immediate pleasures of making love to his wife.

Children were one of the main reasons he had avoided marriage. Not because he didn't like them—he was actually quite fond of children. He'd sort of been hoping that Lucy would get married and make him an uncle. But a child of his own…?

Charles knew how difficult it had been for him after his father had died. He didn't want to put anyone else in that position, and the thought that he might be putting *himself* into that position again… He closed his eyes and leaned his head against the wall. It wasn't a matter of might—he *was* in the position where he could lose yet another person. Children died all the time. They were susceptible to every class of disease and illness, to every kind of accident and injury. Sometimes they died before they were even born, sometimes during birth itself. Women died giving birth sometimes, too. Hadn't Beatrice said that her own mother had died giving birth to Helen?

Charles groaned, sitting up straighter. Bloody hell. What was his wife doing, traipsing across the country when she should be in bed? She had no right to leave him, putting herself at risk, putting their child at risk.

He rose, feeling anger, concern and fear battling for prominence inside him. But anger took over as yet another realization set in. Beatrice had known she was pregnant before he'd even left. Her illness that morning…for some reason, he hadn't put two and two together until this moment, but he suddenly knew that she'd been trying to conceal it from him. Beatrice had let him leave, and then she'd left herself. He couldn't believe she would deny him knowledge of his child…why had she done it? Why had she lied? He knew that no letter had been lost in the mail.

Charles began pacing the floor of his room in agitation. He would *not* go bring her back. He didn't care. Or he did care, but…

But what? He wanted to remain detached, didn't he? He wanted to keep more distance between them, and she was making it easier. She was helping the bloody cause.

Let her have the child without him. See if he cared.

It was still nighttime, but the full moon shone brightly through the window. Charles pulled his pillow over his head, trying to block out all light. He couldn't sleep.

He *had* slept for a brief while—the decanter of brandy he'd nearly finished off after supper had seen to that—but he'd awoken in the middle of the night, his throat dry, his head aching and the sheets bunched about his knees.

He knew what had wakened him: he'd had a dream. Charles had only the faintest recollection of it, but he knew he'd dreamed it nonetheless. It was one he'd had many times before, and he didn't need to remember having it to know what happened. It was as if he were looking down from above his body, watching himself sleep. As he watched, a dark shadow—undefined, not human—slipped into his room through a panel in his wall, watching him sleep, as well. Just as suddenly, Charles's perspective switched once more; he was back in his body, looking up, immobile. The shadow, now Richard Milbanks, looked down on him. Just stood there and looked, his features slightly blurry. Then, slowly, he reached into his pocket, and Charles, feeling pinned to his bed, could do nothing but watch, knowing what would happen next. This was when he always woke up.

His scar throbbed dully.

He restlessly changed position several times before giving up.

He rose from bed and pulled on trousers and a shirt. It was quite cool, and as he headed downstairs he grabbed his jacket from the back of a chair, putting that on, as well. He knew that lying in bed and looking at the ceiling any longer would drive him mad, although he didn't know what sort of distraction he hoped to find downstairs, either. At the very least he could find a drink or some dull book in his study—that alone might help him fall back asleep until a more reasonable hour.

His study was located at the end of the front hall, and as Charles wandered along, the thick carpet muffled his footsteps. Once inside the room, he didn't bother lighting a lamp, the moon providing ample light for him to pour himself a sherry and select a suitably soporific book—a Latin grammar he hadn't looked at in years.

Prepared to give sleep one more attempt, Charles silently left the study to return to his room. But at the end of the hall, he paused. The portrait gallery branched off to his right. In the entire month he'd been home with Beatrice, he still hadn't gone there. He'd contemplated it on several occasions, but had talked himself out of his curiosity. Suddenly, he changed his mind.

Compelled as if by some strange force, Charles slowly entered the long, portrait-lined hall. There were no rugs here, and his footsteps echoed softly against the hard wooden floor. He didn't pause, nor did he look to the left or right, until he reached the portrait of his father. There, he stopped and stared.

He hadn't seen that painting in years, but he remembered it vividly. Until that very moment, he had never realized how much he resembled his sire. Everybody always told him that he did, but the last time he had seen his father, Charles had been fifteen. He didn't look as he did today. But in this portrait, his father was nearly the same age that he was at that moment, perhaps only a year or two older.

It could have been a portrait of Charles, except he never felt that happy.

With a stab of pain, he wished that the resemblance weren't merely superficial, but he knew he would never be the man that his father had been. Oh, Charles knew he was honorable, an excellent son, brother, friend. But he could never have the capacity to love and be loved that his father had possessed. And that quality was what Charles missed most.

He cast his eyes down the wall beneath the painting, unable to look at the moonlit image of his father any longer. The pain was too great. As he did so, he noticed a small latch tucked into the paneling. Yet another memory came flooding back. The passageway.

Story had it that the first marquess of Pelham had installed the secret passages because he was having an affair with his children's governess. Charles didn't know how true that was—as a boy, he and his brother hadn't particularly cared for that romantic explanation. They had decided that the first marquess was an agent for the queen, and had used the passages to spy on guests he invited to the house.

Without pausing to think about it, Charles climbed in, finding it a bit more difficult now that he was well over six feet tall. He took a few steps forward and stopped, his path blocked by a large, solid object. He reached out his hand, feeling the smooth canvas and carved frame of a painting. Remembrance pricked at the back of his neck, and he backed out of the passage, pulling the painting with him.

Charles propped the canvas against the wall. The only light in the portrait gallery was from the full moon, yet Charles could quite clearly make out the subject of the painting—with his eyes closed he would have known every last detail.

The painting showed his father, Mark and himself. Mark, only three years old at the time, sat on the marquess's lap; Charles, the older brother at five, stood next to them. He hadn't seen that painting in years, but now that he looked at it again, he could remember the very day it was painted.

He wrinkled his brow, wondering how the portrait had ended up in the passageway. No one had ever mentioned the fact that it was missing. He'd have to have a word with Mrs. Hester about it. Surely the dust in the passage couldn't be good for it….

But even as these thoughts began to percolate through his mind, the memory came rushing back. Charles had put it there himself, and he could suddenly remember hiding it as if it had happened the day before. After the funeral…the guests had been gathered in the sitting room, and Charles had left, not wanting to speak to anybody, wanting to be alone. He'd put it there. He'd taken one look at the painting, seen the three of them together like they would never be again, and he hadn't been able to bear it. He'd hidden it, wanting to suppress the memory, wanting to cut out that part of his life forever.

And for years, all that had remained in its place was a hole.

It had been too painful for Charles to look at before, but now that so much had changed, now that so many things had become more important, had weighed on his mind…

Charles wasn't a boy anymore. He was a man, and now he'd be having a child of his own. A child who would never know its father like Charles had known his. Charles wouldn't let anyone get so close again—the pain of loss that came of such love was too much to bear.

Only he wasn't sure that he could keep that sort of distance. He wasn't sure if he could be cold and aloof. Hell, Charles had been trying that for months now, and failing miserably.

He loved his wife. He knew it in that instant, and he knew that he had *always* loved her. Nothing would ever change that fact. And he wanted her child—his child, their child—desperately. It wouldn't be possible not to love that child; he loved it already, with all of his heart. It terrified him, but it wouldn't go away.

He only hoped that he hadn't lost Beatrice already.

Charles bent over and carefully lifted the painting. It was dusty from being hidden for so long, and a streak of grime spread across his coat as he lifted it back onto its hook. He brushed the dust off with his hands and frowned as he did so, feeling something in his coat pocket, something rectangular, sharp-cornered: Jack's letter. He knew what it was without even looking.

Still without looking, without even contemplating his actions, Charles pulled it from his pocket, tossed it into the passageway and latched the door. He didn't need Jack's bloody confirmation; he needed his wife, her love. He recognized that now.

He stepped back, surveying his handiwork. The portrait now hung across from that of his father. In fifteen years, no one had thought to hang anything else in its spot.

Then Charles turned on his heel and left the portrait gallery. The day was beginning to break, and he had to go find Beatrice. That was all there was to it.

She might not love him—he didn't think she did, and he certainly didn't deserve it—but she would love their child. Charles knew that instinctively.

And she bloody well would not raise their child without him.

Chapter Twenty-Nine

It took Charles more than a day to reach Sudley, and he had to spend one restless night at an inn. By the time he finally arrived at his destination, just before the luncheon hour, his patience had been stretched exceedingly thin.

He didn't think he was being unreasonable. He could understand why Beatrice would be angry. Charles had hardly behaved as an ideal husband. But that didn't change the fact that she had concealed her pregnancy from him and that she had left him. Sure, he'd left her first, but they'd parted on good terms. And if he had known she was expecting their child, he wouldn't have left at all.

Nor did Charles plan to leave her again; he'd reconciled his conflicting feelings, and he'd admitted—to himself—that he loved her. He wanted to bring her home, to bring her back into his life forever; he wanted to start over completely if they had to.

As his carriage pulled up Sudley's long drive, Charles noticed Helen marching purposefully up the lane, a boy about her age in tow. He asked his driver to slow down. Helen was the only member of Beatrice's family who had deigned to speak to him at their wedding. She liked him a little bit, or at least he thought she might.

"I say, Helen," he called out the window, "do you and your friend need a ride?"

The girl stopped and gazed at him suspiciously. Her friend began to nod eagerly. They both looked as if they had been walking for some time.

Helen sent her elbow into her friend's ribs. "We do *not* want a ride, thank you."

The boy snorted. "I do," he muttered under his breath.

Helen just glared at him before asking Charles, "What are you doing here?"

He sighed. This wasn't going to be easy. This surly response, coming from Helen...the baby of the family and the one who *might* like him. He could only imagine what awaited him up at the house.

"I've come to collect my wife, Helen. Now do you want a ride or not?"

She narrowed her eyes suspiciously, but shrugged sullenly and climbed into the carriage. Her friend followed.

Charles realized he'd have to tread carefully with this prickly youngest member of the Sinclair family. "Introduce me to your friend, Helen."

"Oh. Sorry," she grumbled. "This is my friend George."

George smiled, and Charles sensed a possible ally. As a male, albeit a thirteen-year-old one, George would understand. Charles smiled back. "Are the two of you coming from town? You look as if you've been walking a while."

"Are you trying to change the subject, Charles?" Helen demanded.

He gave up on being pleasant. "Have you ever had your ears boxed, Helen?"

She gave him the evil eye. "No. I have not. Have you?"

"Yes. It hurts."

George looked out the window fixedly, the corners of his mouth twitching in his effort not to laugh. Helen continued to glare.

Charles broached the subject once more, trying to explain his motives with unarguable logic. "Look, Beatrice is my wife. As such she is meant to stay at my house—"

"*Your* house?"

"Our house, Helen," he amended, losing his patience. "Perhaps George here is getting bored listening to our dirty laundry. Perhaps we *ought* to change the subject."

George had been listening enthusiastically. His face, potentially quite angelic, assumed a wicked grin. "Don't mind me," he protested innocently.

"Why do you want my sister to come with you?"

Charles didn't have an answer for that question. He wanted Beatrice to come home because she was carrying their child, because he wanted to make love with her repeatedly throughout the night and in the morning, too. He wanted her to come home because for the first time in his life he realized that he didn't want to be by himself. But he could hardly tell all this to her sister. "Look, Helen, I really don't want to discuss this with you. But like it or not, Beatrice is my wife. If I ask her to stay at my— our—house, she's supposed to stay there."

Helen snorted. "I don't like it. That's why I'm never getting married."

Charles sighed, letting her have the last word. He sensed that she would keep arguing until she did, anyway. When they reached the house, he asked, "D'you have any idea where your sister is?"

Helen thought for a moment, as if debating whether to tell him or not.

"Helen…" he warned sternly.

"All right. She's probably in the stable. She usually goes there before lunch." Helen leapt from the carriage and bolted.

Charles stepped out more slowly, wondering if she were running off to spread a warning. He supposed it was too much to ask that she tell him where the stable was before she left; when he'd been to Sudley before, he hadn't had the time to visit it.

George climbed down after him. "Are you wondering where the stable is?"

Charles turned around, having forgotten about the third member of their party. And here was George, trying to help him. He smiled and nodded at him, man-to-man. "Just point me in the correct direction, George."

The boy pointed west. "Just follow along that way…it's about a mile or two."

"Two miles to the stable?" Charles asked, surprised.

He nodded. "Yes—if you come to the lake, then you've gone too far."

And then he, too, turned and darted off.

Charles shrugged and began to walk.

An hour later, he found the stable…situated in precisely the *opposite* direction from which George had sent him. Charles was hot and frustrated, but he took a deep breath, trying to remind himself what was most important. He hadn't gone all that way to yell at his wife about leaving him, about deceiving him. What he really wanted was to convince her to return to Pelham House, and he was willing to save the unpleasant discussion for when they got there.

Charles entered the stable, its massive size only vaguely registering as he began to wander down the aisle. He didn't know if Beatrice would still be there, it had taken him so long to find his way. For that matter, Helen might have been lying in the first place.

But then he heard the quiet rustle of paper. Charles followed the sound, ending up by the back entrance of the stable. And there was Beatrice, seated atop a bale of hay. Her head was bent, and she was hastily scribbling something into a notebook.

Charles frowned. She seemed to go *everywhere* with that book.

Suddenly, Beatrice sat up a little straighter, grinning at her work. "Oh, this is good," she muttered with satisfaction before hunkering down to resume scribbling.

Charles wondered what else she would say to herself if he just waited. He was tempted to eavesdrop on her, but didn't. Instead, he cleared his throat.

Chapter Thirty

Beatrice had reverted to form. Happy endings only happened in fiction, and if she wanted to be happy…well, she'd never find any joy in her own marriage. Was there really any harm in indulging herself with a bit of fantasy?

"Ahem."

Beatrice blinked, staring at her page. Her imagination was running away with her again—*really* running away with her this time if she thought her characters were actually speaking. She shook her head and poised her pen to write once more.

"Beatrice."

Her head jerked up in surprise. She would never mistake that voice. Her mouth dropped open, then closed again suddenly.

Charles leaned casually against the wall, waiting for her to regain speech. "I take it Helen didn't stop by to tell you that I was here?" he asked nonchalantly.

Beatrice's speech returned as she jumped up from the bale of hay. *"Get out!"*

He continued to stand there, unaffected. "But I've only just got here, Beatrice."

"Get out!" she repeated, louder this time.

"No," he said simply. "I've gone to great trouble to find you."

The stable door cracked open. Eleanor peeked her head in. "Bea? Are you all right in there? I was just coming to get you for lunch when I heard you—" Eleanor faltered as her gaze landed on Charles "—yelling."

"No, I am *not* all right."

"She's fine, Eleanor," Charles assured her smoothly.

Slowly, Eleanor looked back and forth between them, trying to decide how all right or not all right her sister really was.

With forced patience, Charles said, "If you'll please excuse us, Eleanor—"

"She will *not* excuse us," Beatrice interrupted, before turning to ask her sister accusingly, "You won't, will you?"

Eleanor stared, wide-eyed and not quite sure what to do. "Um…"

"Eleanor," Charles warned sternly, "please remove yourself, or I will toss your sister over my shoulder and remove *her.* I need to speak to Beatrice privately."

With an apologetic look, Eleanor mouthed, "Sorry, Bea," before dashing from the stable.

The second the door shut behind her, Beatrice fixed Charles with the most poisonous glare she possessed. "How dare you come to my house and tell me what to do? And tell my family what to do?"

"I can dare a lot of things with you, wife. Why weren't you where I left you?"

She matched his nonchalance. "I got tired of waiting. I hadn't seen my family in months. Perhaps you don't realize it, Charles, but when you hie yourself off to London to carouse with your friends or visit your bloody mistress or *whatever* it is that you do there, I'm sitting around bored with no one to talk to. What about the fairness we discussed? Does *that* seem fair?"

He didn't respond to her question. "What do you mean, 'mistress'? Is that what you think I'm doing?"

"How am I to know what you're doing? You don't bother to tell me!"

He took a step closer, his eyes narrowing. "You're the only woman I've made love to since I first laid eyes on you. Do not accuse me of something I haven't done."

Beatrice rolled her eyes. "I'm sorry if I don't believe you, but I've known all along that you wouldn't be faithful—that's what you promised, right?"

Charles ran his hand through his hair, not knowing how to counter her argument. She was right. If he could have been unfaithful, he would have. Only he couldn't imagine making love to another woman. Instead, he got right to the heart of his anger, asking, "When were you going to tell me, Beatrice?"

"Tell you what?"

"I know, Beatrice. I'm the last to know, it would seem, but I know."

She blanched slightly, but maintained her bravado…somehow. "Oh—you mean about being with child? I would have told you, except you weren't around."

"You *could* have written me."

Beatrice gulped. She knew she could have written him; even worse, she knew she should have. But she hadn't and she couldn't change that fact now. "I planned to write…I still wasn't sure of it until recently."

"You're lying," Charles said, moving closer.

Beatrice lost her patience once again. "How was I to know you'd care? Besides, you said you'd come back eventually. I thought I'd just wait."

"But you didn't wait."

"You're right, Charles—I didn't wait. I will *never* wait for you. Not again. How can you be so selfish to think that I should sit around your run-down, ghost-ridden house, just twiddling my thumbs until you return?"

He went still, saying nothing for several moments. "Ghost-ridden, Beatrice?"

"Yes, Charles. There are *lots* of ghosts there. I assumed that was why you didn't visit very often."

He crossed the floor in two quick strides, stopping in front of her and grasping her by the wrist. His voice deliberately even, he asked, "What, exactly, do you mean by that, wife?"

Beatrice blinked up at him, looming above her. She had never been frightened of him before. He was large enough to snap her in two, but she knew he would never harm her. Even now, she still knew…but he looked furious enough to do so. Although his tone was level, she sensed that he was deadly serious and very angry. She was scared. She'd pushed him too far, and he'd only be angrier if she told him the truth. She took a step back. "I'm not sure what I meant."

He didn't let go of her wrist. "This is my child, too, Beatrice. Don't forget it. You had no right to try to conceal it from me. You will return with me tomorrow." Every word was harsh and deliberate.

She tried to pull away. "I will *not* go back with you."

He brought her close against his chest. "You don't have a choice."

Beatrice struggled, her eyes flashing. "I hate you."

"I'll have to convince you otherwise," he said ruthlessly, before slanting his lips possessively over hers. His kiss was without tenderness, but with pure need; his mouth was fierce, devouring, searching, urging her to give him more. Charles focused every bit of experience, every bit of finesse, into that kiss. He was concentrating on it as if his life depended on it. He meant what he'd said: he *had* to convince her. He needed to make her mindless with passion, to prove that she needed him, too.

Charles could sense the strength of Beatrice's resolve in the very texture of her lips, and his mouth didn't leave hers for several moments, not until he felt her lips grow pliant, till he felt her respond. When her arms crept up behind his neck, his lips left hers to trail across the line of her jaw; he nibbled on her earlobe, and down her throat.

A sudden, sharp pain brought him to his knees.

Beatrice stared down at her husband, not quite believing that she had really done what she just did. She'd kicked him…. Oh dear. Beatrice turned quickly to escape.

She didn't get very far. Charles, grimacing, rose behind her and swooped her up into his arms.

"Do not do that again, Beatrice."

She began to struggle, already regretting her hasty action. "Let go of me, Charles."

"I. Will. Not. Let. Go." Charles gritted his teeth, willing his temper to stay in check.

Beatrice looked up at him, her mouth open in shock. Before she could close it, before she could utter a word, his lips fastened to hers once more.

She wanted to hate him, but at the moment she actually hated herself. Her mind and her will still wanted to fight, but her traitorous body and heart surrendered. She *couldn't* fight anymore, and her resistance vanished. Beatrice craved his touch, had always craved it, even when he infuriated her, even when he left her. She wanted to deny the power of his touch, but she couldn't. Instead, she opened her mouth wide, accepting his kiss, kissing him back and melting into his arms.

Charles slowly lowered her to the ground, and her fingers wandered to the front of his coat, popping buttons from their holes. She pushed it from his shoulders, her hands running along his chest, feeling the hardness beneath his fine linen shirt.

Charles groaned, feeling her succumb without a fight this time, without any resistance at all. He shrugged off his coat and pulled her tight, his hand running down her back, cupping her bottom, pressing her against his groin. One hand crept up to trace circles around her nipples through the fabric of her gown. Her breasts felt fuller than normal, and their firm weight aroused him, satisfied him, like nothing else. Charles lowered his head, needing to taste the salty, smooth texture of her skin.

He hadn't planned on any of this. When he'd first kissed her, he'd intended to stop and leave her bothered, to remind her of how much she needed him. But the second he'd begun, he knew that he wouldn't be able to stop. Everything about Beatrice felt so right. She fit so perfectly against his body, and when she whispered his name…he could have made love to her then and there.

"Beatrice? Everything all right in there?"

Beatrice pulled away immediately, rasping for breath. "Oh, God, it's my father. Charles, stop please. He can't see this—"

Lord Sinclair quietly cleared his throat behind them.

Beatrice spun around, her face filling with mortified color.

Her father was looking at the wall. "Eleanor told me that I ought to check on you two in case you were trying to kill each other, but clearly that's not the case."

Beatrice had never been so ashamed. This was worse than when Louisa and Charles's entire family had come upon them kissing in the hallway. This was her father!

"He's leaving, Father. Now," she said, challenging Charles to disagree.

"I will leave when you leave," he replied quietly, his tone brooking no arguments.

Lord Sinclair looked at them quizzically. Beatrice and Charles glared at each other.

Her father uncomfortably cleared his throat. "Perhaps you'd stay for dinner, Charles?"

He nodded slightly. Beatrice shook her head. They glared at each other again.

Lord Sinclair just watched the whole exchange with curiosity. "I'll ask Henri to prepare for one more."

Charles and Beatrice maintained their stony silence.

"So, then," Lord Sinclair said slowly, waiting to see if either of them would move or speak, "I guess I'll just leave you two alone now." He paused for a moment, waiting for Beatrice to protest, but she didn't. Nodding, he left.

The second the door closed, Charles turned to her. "Look, Beatrice, I want you to come back with me."

She set her jaw stubbornly. "I can't, Charles. Not if you're just going to leave again. I don't want to be alone now."

"I'll stay with you."

She huffed in frustration. "For how long? I'd rather be alone than have you reappear every month or two."

His eyes became suddenly intense. "Why do you care?"

"What do you mean, *why?*"

"Do you love me?"

"What?" Beatrice asked, blanching. His guess hit too close to the mark and it hurt. "Why would you ask me that?"

He looked away briefly, feeling silly for asking her that question. It had just slipped out. But now he felt absolutely compelled to know the answer.

"Do you love me?" he repeated.

Beatrice's face infused with color. "Of course not, Charles."

His expression hardened. "Then why should you care so much where I am?"

Beatrice couldn't tell him the real answer. "Because it doesn't seem fair for me to have to stay there while you get to do whatever you please."

"I told you I would stay with you," Charles said impatiently, beginning to feel desperate. "Damn it, Beatrice, you're carrying our child. *Our* child, not just yours."

Tears welled up in her eyes, but she fought them. He was right, but she wouldn't forgive him again. She'd forgiven him before, and each time she'd regretted it in the end, feeling weak and foolish. Since she'd first met Charles she'd consciously tried not to love him, and now more than ever it was important to keep that resolve. This time, she wouldn't be the only one he was leaving; he'd be leaving their child, too. She'd grown up in a large, loving family and that's what she wanted for their son or daughter. If Charles couldn't give her that, then she would stay with her own family.

"I won't go, Charles."

His jaw tightened, but other than that he made no response. Wordlessly, he turned on his heel and left.

Beatrice sank back onto her bale of hay, telling herself she had just done the right thing. It didn't make her feel any better, but she kept telling herself anyway, hoping that eventually she'd believe it.

Later that evening, Beatrice's father knocked on her door. "Mind if I come in?"

"Oh, come on in." Beatrice sighed. She'd already sent Helen and Eleanor packing, but she could hardly do the same to her father.

"So…we're to have a guest, I see," he said, taking a seat in the chair by her desk.

Beatrice blushed. "I'm sorry, Father. I'm sure Charles will leave soon."

He shrugged noncommittally. "I don't mind…he's your husband, after all."

"I wish he weren't."

Her father said nothing, merely raised a skeptical eyebrow. Color stained Beatrice's cheeks; she really wished he hadn't seen Charles kissing her in the stable. Of course he wouldn't believe her.

"I just had a talk with him, in fact."

Beatrice looked up suspiciously. "You did?" she asked a little too sharply. "What did he have to say?"

"Nothing much…he wants you to return home with him."

Beatrice snorted. "He told me. I won't do it."

"He *is* your husband, Beatrice," he reminded her gently. "And not that long from now, you will be having his child."

"He hasn't acted like my husband."

Her father nodded slowly, weighing her words. "No…but I think he has acted a good sight better than many husbands."

"Except he abandoned me, Father. Don't forget that."

"People make mistakes, Bea."

"In this talk of yours, did he say that he'd made a mistake?"

He sighed patiently. "Well, not exactly…though I think he knows it. I must say, Bea, I *didn't* like him at first, but I'm beginning to change my mind. You seem like perhaps you're changing your mind, as well?"

Beatrice cringed. "I didn't ask him to kiss me, all right?"

"You didn't ask him to stop, and from what I hear, he's quite in love with you."

She felt a stab of pain, but repressed it. "I'm certain that *he* didn't tell you that, either."

"No…he didn't. But his mother mentioned that she thought as much before you were married. I'll admit I wasn't convinced at the time, but Louisa has been keeping tabs on him in town. She wrote me a letter just last week, in fact, telling me that all of London is talking about how in love the marquess of Pelham is with his wife. Apparently he's been acting rather…melancholy. It's rumored that you refused to live with him, and that's why he returned to town without you."

Beatrice snorted in outrage. "*I* refused to live with *him?* It's never the man's fault, is it? If you'll pardon me, Father." She looked down at her lap before grumbling, "Shows how accurate the gossips are. People will talk about the stupidest things."

"And people in love will do the stupidest things, dear."

Beatrice looked up, her mouth parted in disbelief. "Whose side are you on?"

"Yours…but I can understand your husband better than you would think. Did I ever tell you that I had a falling-out with your mother?"

"You did?"

He nodded. "Right after we got married, in fact. I was wild about her, but wasn't quite ready to marry…. The circumstances surrounding my marriage weren't so very different from yours."

"You compromised her?" Beatrice asked, her eyes wide.

He shifted uncomfortably in his seat. "We were caught kissing in a dark hallway at a house party, yes—and don't go blabbing about it to your brother and sisters."

She smiled. "I won't."

"Anyway, even though I really wanted to marry your mother, I was forced into marrying her before I was ready. And, as you can imagine, I protested for a while…. I loved her, but wasn't quite ready to admit it. My behavior for the first few months of our marriage wasn't such a far cry from your husband's."

"There's only one difference, Father. Charles doesn't love me."

"I wouldn't be too sure about that."

Beatrice shrugged, wanting to drop the subject.

Her father took the hint and rose from his seat. "Will you come down to dinner, Bea? I asked Henri to hold off on serving it until I knew if you would attend."

"Charles is there, I take it?"

Her father nodded. "He is. I actually pity him. Eleanor has him seated between Helen and George."

"George is here, too?"

"Yes, and he's already determined that your husband is fair game for their pranks. He and Helen are up to something, I'm sure."

The prospect of watching Charles squirm began to cheer Beatrice…a little, anyway. "I suppose I'll come then. As long as *I* don't have to sit next to him."

"God forbid," her father said wryly as he walked to the door. But before he left, he turned around to gaze at his eldest daughter one more time. "Look, Bea…I don't mean to exonerate him, and I'm not on his side. But I want you to be happy, and I don't think it's beyond your reach yet. For a young gentleman such as him, things like wives and children come as quite a shock. A period of adjustment is inevitable. Just remember that he came all the way out here for some reason. If he didn't care about you, he would have stayed in town."

Beatrice didn't believe a word of it. "That or I just wounded his pride because I didn't sit around waiting for him."

Her father shrugged. "Perhaps. Perhaps not. Only time will tell."

Chapter Thirty-One

Several days later, very little had changed. Charles and Beatrice still were not speaking, and their only communication was glowering at each other. They even ate dinner in complete silence, aside from the occasional "Pass the lamb," or "Pass the parsnips." The rest of her family said very little, as well, too busy simply observing.

In fact, all that had changed, Beatrice thought bitterly as she walked down the town road, was that her family was beginning to like Charles. It irritated her so much that she had pretty much stopped speaking to them, too. In fact, she'd been avoiding everyone. She awoke each morning at the crack of dawn and spent her days going for long walks and not returning home until suppertime. But she always brought her notebook wherever she went, her mind fueled by her mental distress.

Beatrice looked around, trying to find a comfortable spot. She had gone about two miles down the road, where, she hoped, she'd find some privacy. It was cold out, but she could cope with the discomfort. It was better than being at home; Charles was there, insinuating himself into her family. Recently, he'd begun teaching her sisters how to play whist and piquet. He'd also been bringing Eleanor up to date on the who's who of eligible gentlemen, although only because she kept pestering him about it. Beatrice could kill him for being so charming.

With a scowl on her face, she located a suitable tree and seated herself beneath it. She took out her book, and she began to write. Beatrice was in the middle of a sentence when the sound of a twig snapping just behind her made her pause. Instantly, she was standing.

"Hello?" she asked nervously, peering around the tree.

There was no answer. Instead, the bushes rustled slightly and a resounding baying rang out behind them. A gray hare sprang from the underbrush and darted past Beatrice. Her eyes widened; she knew what would be in its wake.

A sudden rush of foxhounds bounded from the bushes, yelping, panting, tongues lolling. Beatrice grabbed hold of the tree for support as they raced toward her. The flood of dogs parted at the last minute, surrounding the tree on either side, not stopping for anyone or anything. She held her breath as they charged past… then they were gone, barking their way down the road to town.

Beatrice swore as the sound faded into the distance. Her father's dogs had stayed out of trouble for several months now. She'd have to go get them, or there would be hell to pay. Hiking up her skirts, she ran off, hot on their trail.

So flustered was she, she didn't realize that she had left her notebook at the base of the tree.

In a rare moment of peace, Eleanor and Helen decided to go for a walk into town, enjoying the late-autumn weather and chatting the whole way. They were discussing The Standoff, as Eleanor had dubbed Bea's predicament. Of course, she certainly hadn't shared this name with Beatrice who'd been decidedly humorless since The Standoff had begun; for that matter, Beatrice wasn't speaking to her, anyway.

Unfortunately, temporary peace aside, after walking about two miles, Eleanor and Helen could still only agree on one thing:

they felt like traitors because they couldn't help but like Charles a little.

Helen sighed, swinging a stick in her hand. "Do you think it's love, Ellie?"

"I think so…but I hope I'm not such an idiot when *I* fall in love."

Helen thought that Eleanor was a big enough idiot as it was, but refrained from comment. She tossed the stick to the ground and began kicking a pebble. "I don't think I'll ever fall in love."

Eleanor thought that Helen needn't worry much about anyone ever falling in love with her, but didn't say so. The pebble rolled into her path, and she kicked it back to Helen. "Beatrice is too proud, that's all. She's stubborn."

Helen scoffed. "I wish she'd get over it. Charles said he's sorry, didn't he?"

Eleanor shook her head. "I don't think so."

"Well, he's said he loves her."

"Actually—"

Helen cut her sister off impatiently, saying, "Everyone knows he does."

"Beatrice doesn't."

"Idiots. Both of them," Helen muttered. She kept walking.

Eleanor didn't follow. Helen turned around impatiently. "Aren't you coming?"

Eleanor was staring at some object to the side of the road. "Helen…what's that over there? See that red thing in the grass?"

She squinted in the sunlight. "Looks like a book."

Eleanor nodded. "I thought so."

For a moment, both girls regarded the object from a distance. It lay forlornly in the dirt at the base of an ancient oak. Then, very slowly, they turned their heads to face each other once more.

"Do you think it's…" Helen began, grinning from ear to ear.

Eleanor nodded, her eyes positively gleaming. "It is, Helen. *It is.*"

With a sudden burst of motion, both girls dashed off toward the tree. They'd been curious for years, but finally their chance had come: they had stumbled upon Beatrice's Secret Forbidden Diary. Loving, kind and genteel sisters though they may have been, they fought, for a moment, tooth and nail over who could get to the book first.

Eleanor won, and she sat down at the base of the tree to read. Helen shot her a venomous look, then sat next to her to read over her shoulder. They felt mildly bad for snooping, but not bad enough to stop.

An hour later, Eleanor carefully closed the book with a sigh. "Do you think she dropped it? I can't believe she'd knowingly leave something like this about, where anybody could read it."

"I'll say," said Helen. "What absolute rubbish."

Eleanor cocked her head. "I rather liked it, actually…it's funny, don't you think? Not what I expected, though…I thought this was just an ordinary diary. It's practically an entire book."

"Could have fooled me," Helen scoffed. "Beatrice must be daft."

Eleanor shook her head. "No, no, Helen. I think this diary means more than it *seems* to mean."

"You mean you *really* think Beatrice is daft?"

"Helen…" Eleanor's look promised dire consequences if her sister didn't behave. "Don't you understand? This whole journal is about nothing but romance, the one thing Bea believes is patently false."

Helen's lower lip jutted out sullenly.

"Oh…here, Helen, listen to this: 'His penetrating green gaze and dark hair…' Get it, Helen? Doesn't Charles have penetrating green eyes and dark hair?"

"Well," she said, her nose wrinkling distastefully, "I suppose so. I'm not so sure about *penetrating,* but…"

Eleanor began flipping through the book, looking for something a few pages on. "Here, it gets better—you know, the part where the hero kidnaps the heroine? Listen."

Eleanor adopted a read-aloud voice.

"'For the first time Drake looked like the pirate that he was. His normally impeccable clothes were gone, replaced by snug-fitting black breeches and a loose, white shirt. He stood on the deck of a ship, his legs spread wide.'"

"Oh, you must stop," Helen said, her voice bored but her eyes sparkling with interest.

Eleanor shook her head and continued. "'Before she could even gasp, Drake had grabbed her by the arm and jerked her to her feet. "You belong with me," he said gruffly—'"

"Eleanor!"

"Can't stop, Helen. It's not over yet. 'Drake tossed her into a dinghy and was rowing her back to his—'"

"Oh, please stop," Helen begged. "Once was enough."

Eleanor hit her sister—playfully—atop the head with the book. "I will stop, but only because that's where Beatrice seems to have left off. What do you think will happen next?"

Helen yawned. "He'll kidnap her, of course, and bring her back to his boat, where he'll profess his love."

"I think you're right, Helen. That *is* what'll happen."

"Oh, how pre*dic*table. Why couldn't I have had more brothers instead of you two soft-headed—"

Eleanor stopped her with a disdainful shrug. "Maybe you're too young for this."

Helen scowled. "I am not."

"Well, listen up, then, because I have an idea." Eleanor dropped the book back onto the ground where they had found it and put a conspiratorial arm around her sister. Heads close in conversation, they walked quickly back to the house.

Chapter Thirty-Two

Charles was about at his wits' end after a week. He didn't know how he could convince Beatrice to return with him if she wouldn't speak to him. He knew that, ultimately, she didn't have a choice. But he would rather not force her. Charles didn't know if he could wait much longer, but he wanted her to come of her own volition.

Even so, he was getting close to carting her off. Her family wouldn't like that—and he had been making great strides with them recently. But Beatrice was hiding behind her family here, and what the two of them really needed was to shout it out and get it over with.

"Charles?"

He looked up from the paper he was pretending to read, and sighed. Helen and Eleanor were looking at him expectantly. He lay his paper down in his lap. "Yes?"

"We have to tell you something," Helen said.

She looked to Eleanor. The older girl shifted uncomfortably, all too aware that she was about to betray her sister. "Well, you probably know that Beatrice keeps a diary."

Charles was silent, then slowly, cautiously, said, "Yes?"

"Well…" Eleanor fumbled and paused.

Helen rescued her. "We read it, Charles. All about you."

Wrapped, as they were, in supple brown leather, Charles wasn't certain if even his toes blushed, but it felt that way. *What had they read?*

Eleanor diplomatically amended, "Helen exaggerates. It isn't really about you—it's a piece of fiction. But it reflects Beatrice's feelings. We think…well, that she must love you."

"Do you have it? May I see it?" Nothing in Charles's voice revealed his feelings.

Delicately, Eleanor said, "Well, Charles, out of loyalty to our sister we just can't show you…actually, we left it where we found it, so she'd never know."

"But we can describe in great detail," Helen added, less delicately.

"Helen—"

Helen ignored her sister and sat down on the sofa next to Charles, very much in the manner of one dear old friend to another. "You see, Charles, it's about a young lady and this dashing gentleman she's just wild about…only he's not really a gentleman."

"No?" Charles asked hoarsely, unable to manage anything more, so confused was he by the scenario unfolding around him. *Were they all mad?*

"No, Charles. He's a pirate. Black hair, green eyes and shoulders as broad as—"

"Not *too* many details, Helen," Eleanor beseeched her.

She conceded without a fuss. "Yes, well, she loves him and he loves her, too, but neither will admit it. What does one do?"

Charles repeated the question, dreading the answer. "What does one do, Helen?"

"Well, in this instance, the pirate kidnaps her. In a boat. It's the only way she'll listen when he says he loves her. What do you think about that?" Helen cocked her head and performed a bit of wide-eyed eyelash batting.

Eleanor kicked her.

Charles looked back and forth between the two sisters, utterly nonplussed. Somehow he maintained an urbane tone. "Are you two quite all right?"

"Yesss…" Helen said slowly, nodding and smiling.

"Helen, stop that," Eleanor ordered. "Look, Charles, I'll be perfectly frank with you. We like you. Beatrice likes you, too, although she won't admit it. She's too stubborn."

"What is your point?"

Helen threw up her hands in exasperation. "We're saying that you ought to truss her up, toss her over your shoulder and cart her home with you!"

"Helen!" Eleanor shouted in shock. "That is *not* what we're saying!"

She drew her head back in surprise. "Then what are we saying, Eleanor?"

"Yes, Eleanor," Charles asked slowly, "what exactly *are* you saying?"

Eleanor flushed. "We're not excusing your behavior, Charles, but we just think she ought to give you another chance. But Bea's always had these ideas, see?"

"What sort of ideas?" he asked with trepidation. Eleanor's hemming and hawing was frighteningly starting to make sense; this could only mean their madness was rubbing off on him.

Eleanor was talking. "Ideas about marriage. She didn't want to get married."

Charles contained a bitter laugh. "She's made that abundantly clear, thank you. And I never wanted to get married, either."

Eleanor nodded patiently. "True…although for different reasons, I presume. Beatrice always had high expectations about whom she would marry, and when no one met her criteria, she decided that person didn't exist. But then you came along."

"I'm sure she's eternally grateful that I came along," Charles said sarcastically.

"She could be, Charles," Eleanor said hopefully. "We want both of you to be happy. But perhaps Beatrice needs to be *made* to listen and, well…we'd like to help you."

Charles looked back and forth between the two girls for several long moments. He'd reached a point of great desperation with his wife, and in that state her sisters were not only mad, they were brilliant. "Eleanor. Helen. I think you've given me an idea."

Early the next afternoon, Charles was back in London; to be precise, he was sitting in the study of Jack's town house. Jack was not in a particularly pleasant mood, having been awakened from a deep sleep by his good friend—not to mention that said good friend had traveled all the way from Portsmouth to London to talk bloody nonsense to him.

At the moment, Jack wore a look of bewilderment. "A boat?"

"Yes, Jack, a boat. By tomorrow. Can you help me?"

"Why do you want a boat?"

Charles ignored his question. "What about John Stout? He sailed with me several years ago…and he's captain of his own ship now, isn't he?"

Jack thought for a moment. "Yes…he's located in Portsmouth, too. But why do you want a boat?"

"Can you find me his address? He even owes me a favor, now that I think of it."

Jack sighed and opened his desk drawer, rummaging about in an unhurried manner. After a moment he handed Charles an address book, full to brimming with loose scraps of paper.

Charles just snorted, flipping through the book. "For a spy, Jack, you're bloody disorganized. Maybe *you* need a wife."

"Or maybe not. By the way, why do you want a boat? Does it have something to do with your wife?"

"Why would you think that?"

"Because even though I'm disorganized, I'm observant. If there were any other reason, you would have told me instead of acting so bloody evasive about it. Not to mention that you've behaved pretty damn peculiarly since you met her."

Charles pulled a scrap of paper from the book and began transcribing it into his own, neat address book. "My reasons are vaguely related to Beatrice, yes."

"You're not moving to the States to get away from her, are you?"

Charles grunted disparagingly.

"No, how silly of me," Jack said, nodding. "Seeing that you followed her to her father's house, and that you even now wait for her to soften her stance, that doesn't seem too likely. By the by, I thought that *she* was supposed to be at *your* house. Did she leave you?"

"Look, Jack, I really don't want to speak to you about this right now. It's more complicated than you can appreciate."

"Not really, Summerson," Jack said, rising to pour himself a cup of tea. "Why don't you just drag the girl home? Isn't that one of the few benefits of marriage?"

"I plan to, Jack," he said tightly.

"Oh. Is that what the boat's for?"

Charles flushed—only slightly, but Jack's keen eyes didn't miss a thing. "That *is* what the boat's for!" he positively crowed. "Are you *mad,* Summerson? You're going to *kidnap* your wife?"

Charles rose angrily, mentally crossing Jack off his best friend list, as he'd had to do periodically since they were twelve. "I have the address. I'm leaving now."

Still grinning, Jack asked, "You will let me know how it turns out, won't you?"

Charles just rolled his eyes and left. Tomorrow would be a busy day.

Chapter Thirty-Three

"Bea?"

"Yes, Eleanor?" Beatrice asked, looking up from her book.

"Would you come into town with me? I have to visit the Mortons and look for Father's birthday present. I've missed you, too, you know. I feel like you've been avoiding me."

Beatrice closed her book and sighed quietly, feeling guilty. She *had* been avoiding her. "All right, Ellie. I suppose I need to do both of those things, as well."

Beatrice and Eleanor opted to walk to Portsmouth. Although it was cold, it was a beautiful, clear day. After buying their father a brass fishing reel and a silver whiskey flask, they walked briskly to the Mortons' home.

Two hours later, they emerged from the cottage, utterly exhausted. Beatrice turned left, ready to head for home.

Eleanor grabbed her arm, pulling her to a stop. "Wait, Bea. I forgot—I need to get a book at Johnston's."

"Now?" Beatrice asked. Johnston's Booksellers was situated right along the waterfront and the day was growing late. It wasn't the wisest idea for two young ladies to frequent that part of town at this hour by themselves. "Can't we stop at Locke's, Eleanor? Or perhaps you could come back tomorrow? It's getting rather late."

Eleanor was shaking her head before Beatrice had even finished. "I can't come back tomorrow. Besides, Locke's is in the wrong direction and we'd get home even later. I know what I'm looking for. I'll be quick."

"All right," Beatrice said dubiously, and they began to walk.

It was just after five o'clock—not so late, but late enough to empty the streets. Portsmouth was a bustling, busy town, home to His Majesty's Royal Navy, but like anywhere else, when the supper hour neared, everyone returned home or tucked themselves into a cozy pub. All of the ships appeared vacant, their cargo having been unloaded hours earlier and their crews now otherwise occupied in the nearby taverns.

"Are you certain the shop is still open?" Beatrice asked.

Eleanor nodded. "It's open until half five. We still have ten minutes."

They turned down a narrow alleyway, heading toward the water. Beatrice's skin prickled, but she knew that they were perfectly safe. It was just that it got dark so early in the late fall…as it was, it'd be completely dark by the time they arrived at Sudley.

"Here we are, Bea," Eleanor said. She was glancing up and down the street rather anxiously.

"Is something the matter, Ellie?" Beatrice asked.

"No. Yes. I mean, not really…I just remembered I promised to get Helen a sweet from Pratt's. You know—one of those marzipan things she likes."

Beatrice snorted. "She doesn't deserve it."

"I know. But I promised. Would you run there while I'm getting my book? It's just two doors down, and they'll probably be closed by the time I'm done."

Beatrice sighed. "All right, Eleanor. But please be quick."

Eleanor dashed into Johnston's, and Beatrice turned, heading down the street in pursuit of sweets. She'd gone about ten steps when she felt a large, firm hand close over her elbow.

"I beg your—?" Her exclamation died on her lips as she spun around and saw who it was. When she finally regained her voice, she asked breathlessly, "What are you doing here?"

Charles grinned wickedly and Beatrice swallowed. She hadn't seen that wicked grin in a long time, and it always affected her in strange ways.

"I thought I'd accompany you home," he said, beginning to steer her away from the shops and toward the water.

She pulled back on her elbow, but he wouldn't let go. Through gritted teeth, she said, "I don't mind you accompanying me home, Charles, but I'm not going home yet. I have an errand to run and I have to meet my sister."

Charles leaned in close, putting his arm around her. "I think your sister will understand. Now you either walk with me, or I can pick you up and carry you." He wouldn't have done that, actually. He didn't want to get into any situation in which Beatrice might feel compelled to struggle. If that happened, she might injure herself or their child. With his arm over her shoulder he began to walk, hoping she'd follow.

She did. What choice did she have? Beatrice wouldn't embarrass her family by making a scene in the middle of the street, and besides, what good would it do? Charles was her husband, and he had every right to insist she come home with him. But she did shoot several glances over her shoulder, hoping to see Eleanor.

"Eleanor's not coming," Charles whispered into her ear.

Beatrice stopped in her tracks. "How do you know I'm with Eleanor? I never told you which sister I was with."

"Lucky guess," he said. "Here we are."

They stood in front of a large, two-masted schooner. Beatrice shook her head, taking a step back. "You said you were taking me home, Charles."

He bent, scooped her gently up into his arms and began walking up the ramp to the boat. "I did say that, didn't I?"

"Put me down, Charles," Beatrice said nervously, beginning to struggle.

He squeezed her tightly, keeping her still in his arms. "Do *not* struggle, Beatrice. You don't have any choice in this matter."

She wrinkled her brow slightly, confused. He was being extremely uncommunicative. "What are you talking about? Take me home, Charles."

He looked down at her, his eyes suddenly intense. "We are going home."

Beatrice felt the color drain from her cheeks. "Your home?"

"Our home."

"But I don't want to," she nearly whimpered.

"I'm sorry to hear that."

They'd reached the top of the ramp, and Charles stepped onto the ship.

Beatrice tensed in his arms. "Put me down," she repeated tightly.

"Not quite yet, love. But presently."

She seethed. She raised her head, looking over the ship's railing and down at the street below them. She saw the door of Johnston's open and her sister step out. She'd been expecting Eleanor to pause, to crane her head left and right looking for her. To seem, at the very least, concerned because she had disappeared. Beatrice certainly had not expected Eleanor to look directly at the boat, tighten her cloak about her shoulders and head briskly up the street as if nothing were amiss.

And when Beatrice saw Helen, dressed like a highwayman, rein in the dogcart at the top of the street and beckon for Eleanor to hurry up, she knew she'd been betrayed.

Her mouth fell open in outrage. "Why, those little—"

"Now, now, Beatrice, don't say something that you might later regret."

"I won't regret anything. They knew about this!"

Charles just shrugged again. He didn't mention that Eleanor

and Helen not only knew about the plan, but that they had con-
cocted it. "They're only looking out for your best interests—"

"*My best interests!* When my father finds out what you've
done—"

"I don't think he'll blame me all that much," Charles said with
a sigh. "But now is not the time for that discussion, love. Someone will overhear you."

"I don't care if—" Charles cut her off with a squeeze as a man
approached them.

"Good evening, my lord," the man said, smiling broadly. His
smile faltered a little when he saw Beatrice glaring at him menacingly.

"Good evening," Charles replied. "We're ready to set sail
whenever you are."

The man nodded. Beatrice vehemently shook her head. "We
are *not* ready to do anything. Put me down, Charles."

He didn't respond. He'd run out of patience. Instead, he carried Beatrice across the deck, trying to keep her still in his arms.
They went down a flight of creaky steps. At the bottom, he held
her with one arm as he opened a door.

She bit him. Hard. Right on the arm.

Charles closed his eyes in pain, trying not to drop her. Taking a deep breath, he opened the door and closed it behind them,
only then letting Beatrice slide to the floor.

"If you'd like to scream at me, now is the time."

She opened her mouth, ready to let loose, but closed it quickly.
She wouldn't give him the satisfaction. Instead, she stepped away
from him, looking around the comfortably appointed room. She
had little experience of boats, even though Portsmouth was one
of the largest seaports in England. But judging from the richness
of the room, they were in what must be the captain's quarters.

Beatrice turned around to demand that Charles tell her what,
exactly, was going on. Her mouth closed before her angry question could escape, and her brow furrowed.

He was gone. She hadn't even heard him leave.

Beatrice stalked over to try the door, and pulled on the doorknob with every ounce of strength in her arm. It didn't turn. Locked. *Damn.*

With a growl of frustration, she kicked the door. All that resulted in was a stubbed toe.

Chapter Thirty-Four

Above, Charles paced back and forth across the deck, expecting to hear the sound of breaking furniture. But Beatrice was being remarkably quiet. He almost wished she were shouting, for silence made him a little nervous.

Yet despite his nerves being slightly on edge, despite the fact that he had just abducted his wife and that said wife was now angry enough to spit blood, Charles actually felt more at ease than he had in months. He felt great, in fact.

It was an odd thing, going your entire life feeling that you'd lost half of your family and half of yourself, only to discover new family members later in life. That was how Charles felt, though. He had a wife, he would have a child, and he loved them both more than he would have imagined was possible.

He'd even discovered two new sisters. Eleanor and Helen had proved themselves true and loyal. And he considered himself forever in their debt. The rest of Beatrice's family might take a little bit longer, but Charles was confident that, with time, their families would meld into one.

He felt, for the first time in many, many years, as if he were whole again.

He wanted to give Beatrice's temper enough time to cool.

She'd still be angry no matter how long he waited, but he truly didn't want to fight anymore. He was willing to forget everything that had happened in their past. All he cared about was that Beatrice would forgive him and that they could live the rest of their lives together, without anger, without bitterness. He just wanted her to love him back.

When the moon loomed on the horizon, Charles knew it was time to return below deck. He stopped first to get a tray of food, although he was too anxious to feel any hunger. As he stood in front of the cabin door, he steeled himself, expecting the worst. Holding his breath, he opened the door, staying alert for flying objects aimed at his head.

Nothing happened. The room was absolutely silent.

"Beatrice?" Charles called out, concerned. There was no answer. He stepped fully into the room, locking the door behind him. She couldn't have escaped anywhere…the door and windows were locked, and besides, where could she go?

He put the tray down on the desk and scanned the room with his eyes. She wasn't in there and he headed into the bedchamber.

He found her. Beatrice was sitting on a chair in the middle of the room, looking angry. Positively livid, in fact. So livid that she hadn't even bothered to remove her shoes or cloak. She had probably been sitting there glaring the whole time he'd been gone.

"I brought some food," Charles offered.

"I do not want to eat. I want to go home."

Charles sighed and sat down on the bed. He'd been hoping she'd make this easy, but she was *still* glaring at him. "We are going home. We've been through this, Beatrice."

She raised an eyebrow defiantly. "And you think that this is all right? That you can just force me to do whatever you want?"

"I believe I asked you to come back to Pelham House with me *before* resorting to these measures, Beatrice."

"You did not *ask* me. You *told* me."

Charles groaned in frustration. "Oh, for the love of…it doesn't matter anyway, since you wouldn't come. You wouldn't talk to me at your father's house and I couldn't force you to talk to me there. This is as much your fault as anybody else's."

"My fault!" Beatrice shouted, shooting up from her chair. "*My* fault? How can this be my fault? How dare you be angry with me for leaving you when you left me twice? And you're angry because I'm not *thrilled* to come back with you?"

"Look, Beatrice, I never said I was right. In fact, I have said several times that I was wrong. I'll say it again—I was wrong. I'm sorry. I can't do any better than that, and if you won't accept my apology I don't know what else to do."

Beatrice stilled. Charles was looking at her, his expression so bleak that she almost believed him. The only thing that kept her from believing him was that there *was* something else he could do, something that would make her forgive just about anything. But Charles didn't love her, and she had too much pride to ask him to say he did. "What, exactly, are you apologizing for?" she asked instead.

He rose from the bed, never taking his eyes off her. "I'm sorry for leaving you, Beatrice…for not telling you that I didn't plan to come back. I was just trying to…I just didn't want to be near you so much—"

Beatrice's mouth dropped open in shock. She couldn't believe what he had just said. "I *beg* your pardon?"

He was shaking his head, his eyes desperate. "No, you didn't let me finish, Beatrice. You don't understand."

"I understand just fine. I'm sure you had much more…freedom…to do as you pleased in town without me around," she said nastily, her cold tone at stark odds with the pain and heartbreak that she felt inside.

"Are you implying again that I keep a mistress?"

"My, you're perceptive."

"And you, Beatrice," Charles said, taking a step closer to her, "are treading on very thin ice. Do not accuse me of being unfaithful. You're the only woman I want."

She shrugged nonchalantly and walked across the room, wanting to put more space between them.

Charles slowly counted to ten. "Beatrice, I do not want to fight with you. I don't blame you for leaving. I just want you to come back. I am sorry. Please forgive me."

"I don't know if I can," she said, trying to keep the hurt out of her voice. "I don't know if I can trust you, Charles."

He stepped close behind her, his voice ragged with need. "I don't care if you trust me. Just love me."

Beatrice spun around, those words—those magic words—startling her.

He reached out both hands to cup her face, his green eyes searching. "Please, Beatrice. I need you."

She didn't know if she believed him, but it didn't matter. Those words melted away every last bit of her resistance, and she forgave him with all of her heart. She really loved him, and she had known it for months. Beatrice had tried her best to deny her feelings, but she couldn't anymore. He'd asked her to love him, and she did. It didn't mean that he loved her, but it did mean that he needed her love.

Charles lowered his mouth to claim hers and she met his lips hungrily. When his fingers, made awkward by his frantic need, reached out to undress her, she helped him. When he lowered her to the bed, she pulled him down on top of her body, whispering his name. And when he entered her, crying out with need, Beatrice matched his cry. As they moved together until the early hours of the morning, they were one.

Feeling drained and sated, they lay quietly in one another's arms. Beatrice traced small circles on Charles's back, listening to his heart beat by her ear. It still beat quickly, but his breathing was even. He seemed to be asleep.

She held him tightly. Beatrice knew that he had been hurt, and that his protective shell was so thick that she might never crack it. He might never let himself love her back, but she would try. She loved him, and she *had* to try.

Just before she, too, fell asleep, Beatrice whispered, very softly, "I love you."

Charles heard her. He'd been asleep, sort of, but he heard her. And as those words registered, the strangest feeling came over him, a feeling he could barely describe. Wonder, awe and his own love built up inside of him, so overwhelming that he thought he would burst.

He felt so much, but not a bit of it was fear.

When Beatrice awoke later that morning, she was alone in bed. Sunlight streamed into the cabin through its small windows, and as she sat up she noticed her clothes strewn about the floor. Self-consciously, she realized that she was nude. She leaned over to retrieve her chemise, but the sudden motion brought on her customary nausea. Beatrice forgot about her state of undress and sank back beneath the covers with a groan.

Several minutes later, the door clicked open and Charles entered. "Good morning, Beatrice…I brought some breakfast," he called cheerfully. She heard the sound of him putting a tray down atop the table. He must have noticed her pasty complexion then. "Beatrice? Are you all right?"

She shook her head limply, not even picking it up off her pillow. "I'm just a bit ill, but don't worry. It hasn't happened in a while, but the motion of the boat…"

"Here," Charles said, sitting next to her on the bed and brushing the hair back from her face. "Don't talk. I brought breakfast, but I don't think you'll want it."

She smiled weakly. "How about some toast and tea?"

He nodded, his eyes never leaving her face. "I think I can manage that. Do you want it right away?"

She shook her head. She didn't really want to eat. She did want to know what was going to happen, though. "When will we arrive?"

"In half an hour. Do you think you can get ready?"

She nodded. "I'll be all right. Whose boat is this?"

Charles smiled down at her. "It belongs to a friend by the name of John Stout. For a few years after university, I did some work for the War Office...mainly just sailed about the coast trying to curtail French smugglers. At any rate, John sailed with me for a time."

Beatrice cocked her head to the side. "Smugglers? I never knew that about you."

"You like that sort of gory thing, don't you?" Charles asked, his eyes teasing.

She grinned and sat up with effort. "So what if I do? Used to play pirates with my brother—even had a wooden sword, I'll have you know."

"I can hardly imagine," he said dryly.

Beatrice poked him in the ribs. "I'm sure you killed *masses* of Frenchmen."

"*Masses,* Beatrice. *Thousands.*"

"Must be how you got that scar." She reached out and touched him gently on the throat, her eyes still laughing.

The teasing expression left his face and he went very still. He nodded.

Beatrice drew back slightly in surprise. "It is? I was only jesting—figured you'd probably gotten it falling out of a tree as a child, or something."

"No. A friend of mine, a man I trusted, did it."

"Oh." Beatrice was pale. Hesitantly, she asked, "What...what happened to him?"

"He's dead." Charles tried to speak with conviction.

She nodded gravely. "Good...er, I suppose. Did you...?"

He didn't let her finish her question. "No, I didn't. His ship was sunk, and there were no survivors. I…I think, anyway. No one is really sure."

"No one at all?" Beatrice tried to keep the concern from her voice.

Charles shrugged uncomfortably. "I have a letter back home that might tell me something. I don't think I'll open it, though…I've worried about Milbanks for a long time and think it's better just to let it rest."

"Wouldn't you rather know for certain that he's dead?"

"I don't want to know that he's not."

Beatrice paled even more and Charles realized he'd upset her. "Look, there's really no chance he's still out there. He's dead. I'm sure."

A moment of silence followed his words. Beatrice didn't really know how to respond, but wanting to lighten the suddenly somber mood, she said, "Well, I'm glad he's gone. I won't be forced to protect you."

"I've no doubt you could," Charles replied, leaning over to kiss her on the top of the head. "You're feeling a bit better now, aren't you?"

She nodded. He had distracted her quite nicely, and she felt fine.

He rose to leave. "I'll let you get your things together, then. I have to go have a word with John, and I shall be back in about twenty minutes."

Chapter Thirty-Five

Twenty minutes later, Charles reappeared, right on schedule. He put his arm over her shoulders and walked with her up the stairs to the deck. The boat was already pulling into its berth when they emerged. Beatrice walked over to the railing, the stiff breeze playing havoc with her hair.

With surprise, she noticed that Charles's carriage waited near the dock. "How did the carriage get here?"

He grinned as he walked up behind her. Putting his arms around her to keep her warm, he answered, "You didn't think this was a spur of the moment plan, did you, Beatrice? Oh, no—this required a great deal of foresight."

She turned her head to eye him skeptically. "*How* far in advance did you plan this?" she asked warily, almost dreading the answer.

He looked slightly sheepish. "About two days ago. Any longer and I might have changed my mind." He cleared his throat. "Ready, my dear?"

She nodded, and they began their descent.

Before they reached the bottom, however, Beatrice stopped and turned to him. She still had so many unanswered questions. "Charles?"

He looked down at her and smiled. "No more questions, Beatrice. Not yet. Wait till we get home and I'll answer everything."

"But why?"

"I have something to show you. Now come on."

She narrowed her eyes, wondering what he was up to. She wasn't sure what to expect after this recent exploit.

Charles took her hand and led her down the ramp and over to the waiting carriage. He helped her in, and they started for home. They rode along in silence for the few miles to Pelham House. Whenever Beatrice tried to speak, Charles would hush her with his infuriating, crooked grin. Finally, she gave up with a sigh.

When they arrived, he stepped down first, and then turned around to help her.

She didn't budge. "Why are you being so secretive?"

"I'm not, Beatrice. Why are you being so impatient?" Truthfully, Charles just didn't want to put his foot in his mouth again. He meant to apologize properly this time, once and for all. "Come on."

She still didn't move to get out, so he reached in and pulled her from the carriage. With his wife in his arms, he started for their house.

"Charles," Beatrice said between gritted teeth. "What are you doing?"

"I'm carrying you over the threshold."

"We've already done this!"

He snorted. "That's not very romantic of you, Beatrice. I'm disappointed."

"Charles—"

He chuckled and kissed her quickly. "I think we need to do it again. We'll do it right, this time." He paused to look down at her.

She couldn't help herself. His words thrilled her to her toes and she smiled up at him beatifically. Charles smiled back. Grinning like fools, they reached the front door. Holding Beatrice with one arm, he opened it. A beaming Wilson and Mrs. Hester waited within. With a groan of dismay, Beatrice buried her head in her husband's arms, embarrassed despite her pleasure.

"Good afternoon, Lord Summerson," Wilson said. Mischievously, he added, "And might that be Lady Summerson with you, my lord?"

Peeking up, Bea retorted, "Very cheeky, Wilson. But good day to you both." She waved to them over Charles's shoulder, as he didn't seem inclined to stop.

He didn't even pause, in fact, until he reached the portrait gallery at the end of the hall. There, he carefully lowered her to the ground.

"Now will you tell me what you're up to?" she asked, looking up at him.

Charles grabbed her hand and began pulling her along the gallery. "I want to introduce you to some people."

She furrowed her brow in confusion, but picked up her pace to keep up with him. "What people?"

"Ghosts," he answered cryptically. He stopped and looked into her eyes. "I have a feeling you might know them, but I don't think you've been properly introduced."

Before Beatrice could respond, he was in motion once more. She went along with him, too curious to protest.

"I have many secrets," Charles said as they walked. "So does our house."

"What kind of secrets does the house have?"

"Secret passageways." Charles put his arm around her. "When we were boys—long before Lucy arrived and spoiled all our fun—Mark and I used to hide in the passageways. Especially when we were supposed to do our lessons."

"Wise of you."

"I agree. Well, just after my father and Mark died—"

Beatrice stopped and turned to him, concern on her face. "You don't have to talk about it, Charles. I know you don't like to."

He put his hand on her shoulder, forcing her to look up into his eyes. "No, Beatrice, I don't. If we'd had this conversation a month ago, I wouldn't have given you the same answer, but now…. I can't focus on the past anymore. I've been in mourning for years, and it hasn't brought them back. But life goes on."

"It does?" Beatrice asked doubtfully.

"Doesn't it?" he asked, his eyes on her. "I never used to think so, but you've made me realize that I was wrong." He bent his head and kissed her gently on the lips before beginning to walk again, this time more slowly.

"Anyway, after the funeral I wandered about the house, feeling how empty it had suddenly become, and not quite sure what to do with myself. I ended up in the portrait gallery. There used to be a portrait of the three of us hanging down here, and I…I guess I felt like it was one way to see my father and brother again."

"I've seen it, Charles," she admitted quietly.

"You have?"

"I didn't mean to," she said, feeling for some reason guilty, as if she had intruded upon his deepest feelings; she knew how carefully he guarded that part of himself. "I discovered the passageway…I went in, Charles. It's in there."

He nodded. "I put it there. Fifteen years ago, on the day of the funeral. I spotted the portrait and didn't know how else to react. I just knew I couldn't look at it."

They stopped in front of the painting.

"Who hung it up again?" Beatrice asked in surprise.

"I did. Truth be told, I had all but forgotten about it. I couldn't even remember hiding it there at first."

"Maybe you didn't want to remember it."

Charles nodded slowly. "I don't think I did…." He paused as

if searching for the right words. "It was odd, Beatrice, but when I saw it again, I suddenly realized that none of it mattered anymore. Not when I knew that I would be having a child of my own, not when I knew that I had you…. I was so afraid that I had lost you, that I had pushed you away too many times."

"No," Beatrice said, her eyes imploring him to believe her.

He put his hand on her shoulder, and she was comforted by its weight. His eyes grew intense, his voice thick. "But I tried to, Beatrice. I *tried* to push you away. I was afraid to feel the way that I do, only…only I realized that I just can't help it."

Suddenly, Beatrice had to know; she had to know if he loved her or not. She wasn't sure how he would respond to her question, but pride had gotten in her way too many times for her to worry about his response. Her love bubbled over and she wanted to share it with him. "I said something to you last night, Charles…just before falling asleep."

His mouth slowly curved into a wide, seductive grin. His hand slid off her shoulder and, with just one finger, very lightly, he began tracing the line of her collarbone. "What would that be?"

"Well…" she began, "I said—"

Charles didn't let her finish. He scooped her up into his arms and lowered her onto the floor; he followed her, settling her into his lap. "You said that you love me, perhaps?" he inquired with wicked innocence.

"You heard me?" Beatrice asked, sitting up and wiggling off his lap.

Grinning devilishly, Charles began to pull her back again. "I did."

"Do you love me, Charles?"

He stopped pulling for a moment and held himself very still, not even breathing. It was a silly question. He loved her with all his heart. Why would she need to ask?

He nodded.

"Can you say it?" Beatrice asked.

He looked at her, wishing he could just kiss her senseless and *show* her how much he loved her. "I don't think I'm very good at saying it."

She smiled patiently. "No? Well, I'd have to agree with you there. Perhaps you could practice, Charles. Practice makes perfect, you know."

"I will practice," he assured her before pulling her back into his lap. He turned her around so that she was facing away from him, and nibbled on the back of her neck.

Beatrice enjoyed his nibbling for a moment, but she wasn't ready to let the subject drop. "I meant," she began, turning around to face him, "that perhaps you could practice now."

Charles tried to picture himself forming the words in his mind, and couldn't do it. He didn't know why. He knew he loved her. Saying it wouldn't make it any truer. "You know how I feel, Beatrice. You needn't be such a girl about it."

"Such a—!" She pushed him backward onto the floor and sat on him. Charles grunted in mock pain. She stared down at him, enjoying the novelty of her position. "Perhaps if I kiss you you'll be able to say it?"

Charles nodded. "Reasonable suggestion. It's worth a try," he said, putting his arms behind his head and grinning up at her.

"Beast," she muttered as she leaned over him, her eyes focusing on his lips. She lowered her head to kiss him.

But just before their mouths connected, his parted slightly in a smile and he spoke. "I love you, Beatrice."

She sat up quickly. "There! That wasn't so bad, was it?"

Charles wiggled his eyebrows at her. "No…but perhaps you should still kiss me so I can practice some more."

She pretended to ponder his suggestion for a moment. "Well…I suppose…"

He didn't wait for her answer, but pulled her down to him and wrapped his arms around her. She gasped in surprise as he rolled over, taking her with him. When she looked up next, their positions had changed and now Charles was on top.

He settled his hips between her legs and bent his head to kiss her again. "I love you," he said, nibbling his way down her chin. His lips continued to roam, moving down to settle in the hollow at the base of her throat. "I love you," he repeated, gently licking. "Very, very much."

Beatrice sighed in pleasure. "You're getting very good at that, you know."

"I know," Charles said, his lips trailing down even farther, to stop just above her breasts. "I have to get good at it. I'll have to tell it to all of my sons."

"And daughters, Charles, don't forget daughters."

"I look forward to each and every one of them," he said huskily, lifting his head to look into her eyes. "I want to be a father ten times over."

Beatrice blushed. "Maybe we can manage that."

He pulled her close, nibbling on her lips. "Do you think, Beatrice?" he asked, his eyes darkening wickedly. "I certainly think we can try. It will be hard work, but I suppose that with determination and—"

She cut him off by hitting him playfully in the shoulder.

"—practice, we can do anything. Maybe we could practice right now?"

Beatrice's eyes widened. "Charles! Not here! What if someone comes along?"

He rose, pulling her up with him. "Come on," he said, practically dragging her over toward the wall.

"Come on where?"

Still holding on to her hand, Charles bent down beneath the portrait of his father and opened the small door. "When you found this passage, did you not go in it?"

"A bit…not the whole way. Where does it lead?"

"Our bedroom."

"Really?"

Charles grinned, happier than he'd ever been in his life. "Really. I certainly never appreciated the convenience of it as a boy. Oh, and Beatrice?"

"Yes?" she asked over her shoulder as she preceded him into the passageway.

Charles followed. "Speaking of our bedroom, I suppose you ought to finish redecorating."

"Really?" she asked from within. "You're sure?"

"I've never been so sure…just please don't paper the walls." He reached out and closed the door behind them.

It wasn't until the next morning that Beatrice, delighted by the convenience of this new route for getting from the bedroom to the ground floor, discovered an object in the passageway that she hadn't seen before. Curiously, she picked it up. It was addressed to her husband. She put it in her pocket and returned to their room, where Charles still lay abed, arm over his head, half-asleep.

"Charles?"

"Hmm?" he mumbled.

Beatrice sat down next to him and drew the letter from her pocket. "Charles, I found this in the passageway. It's addressed to you."

He held out a hand, took the letter from her and put it under his pillow. "Thank you," he said, then continued to sleep.

Beatrice couldn't allow it. The letter had sent off fresh warnings in her mind, horrible new possibilities, and she had to know what it was. "Charles, it's from the War Department…. I didn't see it when I was in the passage before. I'm sure it wasn't there. What is it?"

He was slightly more awake now, but still didn't want to address this subject. "It's nothing. Just something from Jack."

"Is it the letter, Charles? The one you were telling me about?"

He sat up in bed, supported by several fat pillows. "You want me to open it, Beatrice, but I just can't. If it's bad news, then…" He trailed off, unable to complete that thought. "Look, for the first time, I'm not worried about Milbanks. All I care about is you, our child. I don't want to reawaken these fears again."

"Charles, these fears won't go away unless you address them. Uncertainty is far worse than even knowing bad news—you must realize that. Read it. Please."

He knew she was right. He dreaded the letter's contents, but it was time to know that truth, to put all bad memories to rest. "Would you like to open it, Beatrice?"

She did want to, but she shook her head. "I think you should."

He nodded and slipped his thumb under the seal and opened the letter. Quietly, his face revealing nothing, he read.

After a minute, Beatrice lost her patience. "Charles? What does it say?"

He didn't answer her at first. He just looked at her face, his eyes going over ever inch, every angle, every plane. She was perfect.

"He's dead, Beatrice," he said slowly. "Washed to shore in Suffolk several weeks ago…I don't know why I ever doubted it. It would have been impossible for him to survive a shipwreck in those icy waters, so far from land…. Why did I have so much faith in impossibilities when the truth was so plain?"

Beatrice said nothing. She just leaned forward and kissed him.

Charles sighed, slid back down under the covers and pulled her with him. He had thought that his happiness had reached a state of perfection when Beatrice said she loved him two days earlier, but he'd revised that opinion, thinking happiness could not be more complete when, just the day before, he'd finally been able to say the same words. But every day seemed to get better.

Now, his happiness changed, deepened, broadened into something else; for the first time in many, many years, a great burden was lifted from his mind and his heart, and he felt, sublimely, at peace.

* * * * *

If you enjoyed what you just read,
then we've got an offer you can't resist!

Take 2 bestselling love stories FREE!
Plus get a FREE surprise gift!

A BRAND-NEW BOOK IN
THE DE WARENNE DYNASTY SERIES
BY *NEW YORK TIMES* BESTSELLING AUTHOR

BRENDA JOYCE

On the evening of her first masquerade, shy Elizabeth Anne
Fitzgerald is stunned by Tyrell de Warenne's whispered suggestion
of a midnight rendezvous in the gardens. Lizzie has secretly
worshiped the unattainable lord for years. When fortune
takes a maddening turn, she is prevented from meeting Tyrell.
But Lizzie has not seen the last of him....

Tyrell de Warenne is shocked when, two years later, Lizzie
arrives on his doorstep with a child she claims is his. He
remembers her well—and knows that he could not possibly
be the father. Is Elizabeth Anne Fitzgerald a woman of
experience, or the gentle innocent she seems?

The MASQUERADE

"A powerhouse of emotion and sensuality."—*Romantic Times*

*Available the first week of September 2005
wherever paperbacks are sold!*

SHOWCASE

The first book in the Roselynde Chronicles from...

Beloved author

ROBERTA GELLIS

With a foreword by bestselling historical romance author Margaret Moore

One passion that created a dynasty...

Lady Alinor Devaux, the mistress of Roselynde, had a fierce reputation for protecting what's hers. So when Sir Simon Lemagne is assigned as warden of Roselynde, Alinor is determined to make his life miserable. Only, the seasoned knight isn't quite what Alinor expects.

Plus, exclusive bonus features inside!